SNOW IS FALLING

SARAH BENNETT

First published in Great Britain in 2024 by Boldwood Books Ltd.

Copyright © Sarah Bennett, 2024

Cover Design by Alice Moore Design

Cover Photography: Shutterstock and iStock

The moral right of Sarah Bennett to be identified as the author of this work has been asserted in accordance with the Copyright, Designs and Patents Act 1988.

Every effort has been made to obtain the necessary permissions with reference to copyright material, both illustrative and quoted. We apologise for any omissions in this respect and will be pleased to make the appropriate acknowledgements in any future edition.

A CIP catalogue record for this book is available from the British Library.

Paperback ISBN 978-1-80483-339-1

Large Print ISBN 978-1-80483-340-7

Hardback ISBN 978-1-80483-342-1

Ebook ISBN 978-1-80483-338-4

Kindle ISBN 978-1-80483-337-7

Audio CD ISBN 978-1-80483-344-5

MP3 CD ISBN 978-1-80483-346-9

Digital audio download ISBN 978-1-80483-343-8

Boldwood Books Ltd
23 Bowerdean Street
London SW6 3TN
www.boldwoodbooks.com

For Charlie, I hope you enjoy your cameo x

CHARACTER LIST

The Travers Family

Montague 'Monty' Travers Patriarch of the Travers family and current Baron. More interested in travelling the world in his old camper van than accepting his responsibilities.

Alice Travers The matriarch of the Travers family. Married to Monty.

Ziggy Travers Twin brother of Zap. Manager of the Juniper Meadows estate. Current heir to the Barony by a matter of minutes. Recently reunited with his first love, Daisy Riley.

Zap Travers Married to Rowena. Father of Rhys. Twin brother of Ziggy and second in line to the Barony. Brew master at the Juniper Meadows distillery. Good with hugs.

Stevie Travers Mother to Hope and Ben. Sister to Ziggy, Zap and Dylan. Manages the hotel side of the Juniper Meadows Hotel and Spa.

Dylan Travers Youngest of the Travers siblings. Hero of *Snow is Falling*.

Rowena Travers Mother of Rhys, married to Zap. Runs the spa side of the Juniper Meadows Hotel and Spa and also an accomplished artist. Fond of a kaftan.

Rhys Travers Son of Zap and Rowena, cousin to Hope and Ben. Runs the farm at Juniper Meadows. Third in line to the Barony. Hero of *Come Rain or Shine*.

Hope Travers Daughter of Stevie, sister of Ben. Manages many of the day-to-day tasks on the Juniper Meadows estate. Girlfriend of Cameron Ferguson and heroine of *Where We Belong*.

Ben Lawson Stevie's eldest child, Hope's brother. Former accountant and now aspiring potter. Lives with Amelia Riley in a small cottage on the Juniper Meadows estate. Hero of *In From the Cold*.

Theo Travers Dylan's sixteen-year-old son.

Avery Travers Dylan's fourteen-year-old daughter.

Cameron Ferguson Archaeology lecturer at the local university. Boyfriend of Hope Travers and hero of *Where We Belong*.

Amelia Riley Local resident and aspiring artist. Hope's best friend. Lives with Ben Lawson in a little cottage on the Juniper Meadows estate. Heroine of *In From the Cold*.

Daisy Riley Amelia's mother. Separated from her husband, Keith, and living with Ziggy Travers.

Tasha Clarke Runs the camping and glamping business at Juniper Meadows. Girlfriend of Rhys Travers and heroine of *Come Rain or Shine*.

Hercule Brussels Griffon terrier, owned by Zap Travers. Top dog of the Travers pack.

Samson Working sheepdog owned by Rhys Travers. A very good boy.

Delilah Miniature dachshund belonging to Rhys Travers. A pampered princess.

Sooty Black Labrador puppy owned by Hope Travers. A sweet, but not always very-good boy.

Sweep Black Labrador puppy owned by Hope Travers. Also a sweet, but not always very-good boy.

Pepper A dalmatian puppy. Owned by Ben Travers.

The Bingham Family

Sadie Bingham Recently taken early retirement so she can go travelling with her husband. Heroine of *Snow is Falling*.

Pete Bingham Sadie's husband. Ready to retire and go biking down Route 66.

Jake Bingham Sadie and Pete's son. Married to Rachel, father to Robbie and Zac.

Katie Jenkins Sadie and Pete's daughter. Married to Liam, mother to Isla.

Rachel Bingham Married to Jake, mother to Robbie and Zac.

Liam Jenkins Married to Katie, father to Isla.

Robbie Bingham Jake and Rachel's elder son.

Zac Bingham Jake and Rachel's younger son.

Isla Jenkins Rachel and Liam's daughter.

Margaret Dunlop Sadie's mother.

Celia Walsh Margaret's sister.

Other Characters

Jennifer (Jen) Dylan's ex-wife, mother of Theo and Avery. Engaged to Eric.

Eric Jen's fiancé.

Frank Jen's father.

Nancy Jen's mother.

Oscar, Harry and Gemma All work for Pete Bingham.

Charlie, Anna and Jane Three friends on a pre-Christmas break at Juniper Meadows.

Tara and Jon Staying at Juniper Meadows and visiting family nearby.

Marcus A lonely widower staying at Juniper Meadows.

Barry A competitive game player and guest at Juniper Meadows.

Lydia Caster-Hardwicke Friend of the Travers family, runs events for high-profile clients.

Justin Porter at Juniper Meadows hotel.

Penny and Sandra Run the café at Juniper Meadows.

Carrie-Ann Runs a silversmith's workshop at The Old Stable Yard.

Denny and Jos Farm workers at Juniper Meadows.

Graham Estate maintenance manager at Juniper Meadows.

Iain Landlord of The Stourton Arms.

Joe and Martha Run the local village shop.

Debbie Holiday rep at HappyHols.

Jim and Grace Carol singers.

Murder-Mystery night players

Inspector Turtle Hot-shot young crime solver.

Sergeant Dove Luke-warm older crime solver.

Millicent 'Millie the minx' Former showgirl and girlfriend of the Duke.

The Duke of Nortington Very recently deceased.

Dickie, Lord Monckton Heir to the Duke.

PROLOGUE
SPRING

'Thank you for holding. Your call is important to us. We are experiencing higher than usual call volumes at the moment.'

'Aren't you always?' Sadie Bingham cast a baleful look at her phone resting on the desk beside her laptop. A fresh breeze carried the scent of early honeysuckle through the open window and she closed her eyes and let the sweet scent calm her irritation. It was one of those warm spring days that made you throw open all the windows to blow away the cobwebs.

The recorded message continued. 'To avoid the wait, did you know you can search for availability and make a booking online by visiting our website, w-w-w-dot-happyhols-dot-com? If you already have a booking, you will be able to access the most up-to-date information by logging into your account.'

'I can't bloody log in to my account though,' Sadie told her phone through gritted teeth as the message ended and was replaced by an instrumental version of Kylie's 'I Should Be So Lucky' that was so tinny it sounded as if it were coming from the depths of a metal dustbin. 'I should be so lucky if you ever answer the pho-o-o-one,' Sadie sang along to the tune as she tried logging into her husband Pete's account for the umpteenth time that morning.

Password not recognised

With a groan, Sadie sent an imploring glance at her phone. *How much longer, for goodness' sake?* She had so much she wanted to get sorted out today, not least tackling the ironing pile on the bed so she could start setting aside the things she wanted to pack for their holiday. She could message Pete and ask him if he'd changed the password but he was up to his eyes at work. After nearly twenty-five years at the same company they still seemed as determined to squeeze out every last hour from him. It was one of the many reasons he'd finally made the decision to take early retirement in the run-up to his sixtieth birthday. At fifty-five, Sadie wasn't sure she was quite as ready to give up work, but Pete had wanted to kick the next phase of their lives off with a bang. If she got fed up there was no reason she couldn't look for a part-time job in the future.

She just wished he'd left the organisation to her, especially when Sadie managed all of their other home admin. Everything was usually set up in her name, but this trip was Pete's dream and he'd done all the research so it had made sense for him to sort out the initial booking. Cruising down Route 66 on a massive touring motorbike wasn't Sadie's first choice when it came to modes of transport, but he had his heart set on it and there'd be plenty of time over the coming years for the luxury cruises and country house hotel breaks that were more her style. Pete had worked hard to give them a lovely life so Sadie was determined to embrace the adventure. She figured the motor-bike trip was like the BMW convertible he'd bought last year – an attempt to ward off the creeping feeling of age. Her own efforts might be less flashy and ostentatious but, as he'd pointed out, if you added up the years of expensive hair appointments and spa treatments then they probably came out about even. Sadie just wished the car seats were a little less low slung so she didn't feel like an ungainly lump as she hauled herself up out of them. Plus she looked less like Grace Kelly and more like Hilda Ogden when she used a headscarf to protect her hair from the wind.

The recorded message started again and Sadie let out a little scream. She was going to be stuck in this loop forever.

'Hello, Happy Hols! Debbie speaking, how may I help you? Hello?'

Sadie snatched her phone up, hoping desperately that the woman on the other end hadn't heard her. 'I'm here! Sorry, I... umm, I have a booking with you, well, my husband has a booking with you, and I'm trying to print off the itinerary and tickets but I can't seem to log in.'

'Let me see if I can help you. Do you have a booking reference?'

Sadie consulted her notebook. 'Yes, it's BL7448097A, in the name of Bingham.'

There was silence apart from the faint sound of a keyboard clicking and then Debbie spoke again. 'And are you one of the passengers travelling on the booking?'

'Yes. As I said, the booking was originally set up by my husband but he's really busy at work so I'm just trying to get things organised.'

'I'll need to check what details are on the booking. Can you give me your full name, please?'

'Oh, yes, sorry.' Sadie rolled her eyes. She hated the way she apologised all the time. It was a habit she'd been trying to break for a while, but she fell back into it whenever she got flustered.

'It's Sadie Elizabeth Bingham. Do you need my date of birth as well?'

The keyboard click-clacked and then Debbie cleared her throat. 'I'm sorry, but your name doesn't match either of the ones on the booking so I can't continue with your enquiry.'

Not on the booking? 'I think there must be some mistake – perhaps you're looking at the wrong one. The lead passenger should be Peter Albert Bingham and I'm Sadie S-A-D-I-E. The reference is BL7448—'

'—097A,' Debbie finished the reference before Sadie could. 'As I said, I'm afraid I don't have your details on the booking so I'm unable to discuss it further.'

Was that a slight hesitation in the way she'd said 'your'? Sadie shivered as if a ghost of premonition had trailed its fingers down her spine. 'But you have Pete's name on there?'

The warmth in Debbie's tone had chilled to something almost robotic. 'If you think there's a problem with this booking, may I suggest you get the person who gave you that reference to contact us? Under our data protection rules I'm afraid I can only speak to them. Is there anything else I can assist you with?'

Sadie shook her head, before catching herself. 'No, no, that's fine. I'll speak to Pete when he gets home. I'm sorry to have bothered you.'

'Thank you for calling Happy Hols, goodbye!'

The phone went dead. Sadie stared down at the reference number Pete had given her. She'd had to badger him for even that much, her requests for more information batted away with irritated comments that he had everything in hand and for Sadie to stop fussing.

Stop fussing.

His use of that phrase had stopped her in her tracks. She'd put it down to the stress of trying to get everything at work tied up before he retired, making an excuse for what had to be a slip of the tongue because she hadn't been able to believe he'd say those words to her otherwise. Not when he knew full well they were part of the arsenal her mother wielded against her.

Margaret Dunlop was a bully; there was no way of sugar-coating it. She had picked and poked and undermined her husband until he'd withdrawn from the battlefield of their marriage, retreating behind a beautiful brick wall of art and literature. With her main opponent refusing to engage, Margaret had switched her attention to Sadie. Too young to understand the ugly dynamics of her childhood, Sadie had taken those bitter snipes and criticisms very much to heart. It had taken Sadie a long time to work out that it didn't matter what or how she did something, in her mother's eyes she would always be in the wrong. Pete had been the one who'd helped her realise the truth, encouraging her to break away from her parents. But Sadie had loved her dad as much as she had feared her mum. Even understanding his failure to protect her, Sadie had wanted his quiet presence in her life until he'd passed away a few years ago. Losing him might have softened some people, but it had seemed only to embitter Margaret further. Pete had told Sadie to cut her loose and even their children had urged her to distance herself, but she couldn't bring herself to do it. The trip to America would be a welcome escape from the self-imposed obligation of hosting her mother for lunch every other Sunday. Not that she'd told her they were going away yet.

The thought of how Margaret would react to the news was enough to drive Sadie into action. She couldn't do anything about the strange call to Happy Hols until Pete got home, but there were plenty of other things she could be getting on with, starting with that ironing pile in the spare room.

Sadie set herself up in the lounge, placing the ironing board in front of the TV and scrolling through the planner to find the next episode of the boxset she'd been watching. It was the third series and she'd given up waiting to watch it with Pete. He was always too tired these days to want to do much more than watch whatever was on Sky Sports Main Event. Honestly, the sooner he retired, the better.

She was halfway through the first episode, the same shirt she'd started with still a wrinkled sleeve short of being finished, when her mobile phone beeped. With a pang of guilt, Sadie paused the TV and picked up her phone. It was a message from Pete:

> Usual bloody panic before tomorrow's board meeting so it's going to be a late one. Don't wait on me for dinner. P.

Sadie blew out a frustrated breath as she tossed her phone onto the sofa. She made it halfway back towards the ironing board before she changed her mind and returned to retrieve her phone. She called Pete's number, surprised when it went straight to voicemail. Even when he was busy he usually picked up long enough to say hello.

She waited for the beep, then spoke. 'Hi, only me. I haven't thought about dinner yet so just wondered if you meant I should make something for myself or if you want me to put a plate in the oven for whatever time you get back.' It was on the tip of her tongue to mention the odd call with Happy Hols, but she decided against it. He didn't need the distraction. 'Anyway, give me a call or text when you get this and don't work too hard. They'll have to learn to manage without you soon enough!'

She regretted the words as soon as she'd said them, but it was too late to take them back. Pete was under enough pressure without her adding to it by nagging him for being dedicated to the last. Maybe she should make something special for dinner. There was some red wine left over from Sunday lunch – she could make a nice beef bourguignon. It would be easy for Pete to heat up and he'd need something substantial after a long day. Yes, she'd do that, once she'd finished the ironing, of course.

By quarter to five, the ironing was all done and the house was filled with the rich scent of the casserole but there was still no word from Pete. She'd had a shower and changed into a not-quite-pyjamas combo of yoga pants and an old T-shirt. Heading into the kitchen, Sadie lifted the heavy cast-iron Le Creuset pot out of the oven using a tea towel to protect her hands, and gave the bourguignon a stir as she thought about what to serve with it. There were roast potatoes in the freezer. She could do enough for two in the air fryer, but Pete was on a no-carbs kick and had even skipped them with his roast dinner on Sunday. That meant rice was also off the menu. She pulled open the cupboard next to the oven and surveyed the contents before closing it with a huff. If it were up to her, she'd have the potatoes and a couple of slices of bread to mop up the gravy and do a couple of extra miles on the exercise bike as penance. Rather than fretting about it, why didn't she just ask him?

Sadie picked up her phone and dialled Pete's number. *Straight to voicemail.* On a whim, she called his office number and it was answered almost immediately. 'Pete's phone, Oscar speaking.'

An image of a smiley young man with blond hair that flopped into his eyes sprang to Sadie's mind. They'd met a few times over the years at company events and the summer barbeque Pete hosted for the team. 'Hi, Oscar, it's Sadie Bingham. Is Pete about?'

'He... umm, he's not here just now, Mrs Bingham. Can I... err, can I take a message?' The hesitancy in Oscar's voice surprised her as he'd always struck her as possessing the kind of brash confidence that occasionally shaded into cockiness.

'I know you're all busy with the board-meeting prep, but can you ask Pete to give me a very quick call when he's back at his desk, please?'

There was a long uncomfortable silence before Oscar spoke. 'I'm just heading home, so if it's urgent perhaps you could call him on his mobile?'

Why would he be heading home if they were all supposed to be working late? An uneasy feeling stirred in Sadie's gut. 'I already tried but it went to answerphone. Perhaps you could get one of the other team members to give him the message. Harry, maybe, or Gemma?'

'I really think you should give Pete's mobile another try, Mrs Bingham. Look, I have to go, sorry.'

Sadie found herself staring in consternation at her mobile for the second time that day. *What the hell was going on?* Another thought followed hard on the heels of the first. *Where the hell was Pete?* She scrolled through her apps and clicked on Find My Phone. She'd originally downloaded it when the children went off to university but hadn't looked at it in ages. Her finger hesitated over the devices button. How would she feel if Pete was snooping around after her? The answer came instantly: he'd never have to because he always knew where she was. She selected his device. *It would be fine. It would show the location of his office and she could get all this silly nonsense out of her head.* The map zoned in on a residential property about a mile away.

Oh.

The phone slipped from her fingers and clunked on the counter. Sadie stared down at the little indicator for a moment, then tapped the screen to zoom in. She recognised the area as a new estate that had gone up in the past couple of years on the derelict ground of a long-closed factory. It was all starter homes and maisonette flats. The sort of place a young person might choose when looking for somewhere to buy or rent. Her mind flashed back to the barbeque, at Gemma's excitement over the new house she'd found to rent at The Potteries.

Oh.

Not stopping to think about what she was doing, Sadie shoved her phone into the side pocket of her yoga pants, then plonked the lid back onto the casserole dish and picked it up with the still-rolled tea towel. She stopped by the front door only long enough to grab her car keys.

Sadie followed the map directions on autopilot until she pulled up by the kerb in a cul-de-sac. For the entirety of the short journey she'd told herself she was making a stupid mistake, jumping to conclusions. A black BMW convertible nestled on the narrow drive behind a little red Mini. The little red Mini Gemma had stood next to rolling her eyes as a slightly worse for wear Oscar and Harry had tumbled into the back seat after the barbeque.

Sadie's gaze shifted to the anonymous little box of a house, to the lit window of the kitchen. To Gemma standing at the sink, her attention fixed on someone out of sight. She was laughing, her head thrown back to show the soft, dewy skin of a neck that didn't need expensive creams to ward off the wrinkles, long blonde hair untouched by a hint of grey tumbling over her shoulders. A hot tear streaked down Sadie's cheek.

Oh, Pete, you absolute bastard.

Her attention flicked back to the shiny convertible with its soft-top tucked away to display the pristine white leather of the low-slung seats that she bet Gemma and her tight little abs, unravaged by time and the rigours of carrying two babies, had no difficulty getting out of.

I'm sorry, but your name doesn't match either of the ones on the booking so I can't continue with your enquiry.

If it's urgent perhaps you could call him on his mobile?

Sadie climbed out of her boring, sensible compact SUV with wide seats at just the right height and ample boot space for carting around shopping, and dry-cleaning, and all the other things a family needed to move from A to B. She marched to the front door, pausing only long enough to press the bell before returning to her car for the casserole dish.

She was halfway up the drive, thinking she'd dump the pot on the doorstep and leave with at least her dignity intact. That was until Pete answered the door. As casual as you liked, as if he had no concerns about being seen in the house of a woman young enough to be his daughter. 'Sadie? What are you doing here?'

'I brought your dinner, you lowlife cheating bastard.' Sadie upended the pot and tipped the still-steaming beef bourguignon all over the shiny leather seats of the BMW.

'Sadie! What the hell?' Pete took a couple of steps towards her then held out a hand when she raised the heavy pot like a weapon. 'Hey, come on, now, there's no need to make a scene. Come inside and we can talk about it.'

Sadie glanced around. Several people were standing at their open front doors, drawn by their raised voices. A man out walking his dog had stopped on the pavement, his wide grin saying he was clearly enjoying the show.

Dignity was overrated, she decided. Sadie turned and threw the cast-iron pot at the bonnet of Pete's car as hard as she could. It bounced, then ricocheted into the windscreen, sending a spider web of cracks across the glass. The indicators began to flash and the alarm blared. Ignoring Pete's apoplectic face, Sadie looked past him to a wide-eyed Gemma standing on the doorstep with a hand raised to her gaping mouth. 'He's all yours, dear.'

1

'You look beautiful,' Dylan Travers said to the woman dressed in a confection of pale gold lace and cream silk as she descended the stairs before him. The dress was an elegant frame-skimming number, the delicate lace covering her shoulders and arms sheer enough to allow Jennifer's all-year tan to glow through. 'Like a glass of the finest champagne.'

Jennifer paused on the lowest step, their eyes at the same height as she leaned over to brush a kiss on his cheek. 'Much better than the meringue I wore for our wedding, you mean?'

'Well, now you come to mention it...' Dylan ducked and laughed as Jen pretended to take a swipe at him with her bouquet of cream roses. 'Come on, you,' he said, offering her his arm to lead her across the highly polished marble floor of the hotel towards the ballroom where the wedding ceremony was to take place.

It might strike most people as strange that he had offered to step in and give Jen away after her father had suffered a stroke, which had left him having to use a walker, but Dylan hadn't thought twice about it. He cared deeply for Jen, but they hadn't been in love for a long time. Thankfully, they'd had the sense to recognise that before things had had the chance to degenerate into the toxic stew that was the sad end of too many marriages. Their divorce had been finalised more than ten years ago and Dylan was truly happy that Jen had finally given herself permission to think about her own happiness now that their kids were well into their teenage years.

As they reached the closed door to the ballroom, the hotel's events coordinator gave them both a broad smile. 'Everyone is ready when you are, so just say the word and I'll get the music started.' She tapped the arm of her headset microphone.

Feeling Jen's grip on his arm tighten, Dylan smiled at the coordinator and said, 'Give us a moment,' before turning to face Jen. 'Everything okay?'

'Do you think we should've waited until next year? It seems so selfish of Eric and I to be jetting off for Christmas and leaving you with the kids and Momma to take care of Daddy.'

Dylan placed his free hand over the one gripping his arm and patted it gently. 'I couldn't be happier about getting to spend the whole of the holidays with Theo and Avery, and your mom is grateful they won't be dealing with a houseful while your dad is still in recovery.'

'You spoke to her about it?' Jen smiled as she shook her head. 'I should've known.'

'I wanted to make sure they were okay with everything before I offered the kids the chance to go away somewhere.'

'And you're sure you're happy with the choice they've made?' Ah, now they were getting down to things.

'It was a bit of a shock at first, but it's past time they got to know both sides of their heritage. Besides, if Theo is as dead set on going to a British university as he seems to be then it makes sense for him to meet my family so we all know he has somewhere to turn to if he needs help.'

'And you think it'll be that easy, after thirty years with almost no contact?'

No, Dylan didn't think it would be easy, but, regardless of his own estrangement, he knew one truth deep down in his bones. 'My brothers and sister will welcome the children with open arms.' He patted Jen's hand again. 'Right, do you think you can stop worrying about everyone else for the next few hours and focus on what's important right now? If you leave Eric hanging on any longer, he might think you've changed your mind!'

Jen laughed. 'Well, we can't have that, now, can we?' She took a deep breath and Dylan watched as the tension eased from her shoulders and her chin lifted. 'I'm ready.'

'Then let's get you married.' Dylan nodded to the coordinator and a few seconds later they could hear the faint strains of a string quartet.

'Big smiles!' the coordinator urged as she reached for the door and swung it open.

Dylan didn't need the instruction and his grin only stretched wider as his gaze alighted on their gorgeous girl, Avery, waiting at the side of the aisle with a small basket of rose petals held in one hand. She was the perfect combination of both of them, with her mother's delicate features and athletic frame and his dark hair and blue eyes. At fourteen she was moving from that awkward gangling growth spurt when her arms and legs had seemed to take on a life of their own, and today she was all poise and elegance in a pretty dress with a golden bodice and a wide ballerina-style tulle skirt spilling down to her knees. Her face lit up with delight as she caught sight of her parents and she stood and stared at them. When she didn't move, Dylan gave a gentle nod towards the basket and he couldn't help but laugh when her eyes widened and she turned on her heel and all but scampered down the aisle, flinging handfuls of petals with more enthusiasm than grace. Dylan's heart squeezed in his chest, taken aback as he so often was at how there was always room to love his children more.

He and Jen followed at a more sedate pace over the carpet of petals, and Dylan smiled at the friends and family who caught his eye, though most – quite rightly – had their attention fixed on the woman at his side. Eric left his spot at the front before they were even halfway down the aisle, as though he couldn't wait to claim Jen, and Dylan was more than happy to yield to him. He waited until the pair had reached the front before slipping quickly into the empty seat on the second row behind where his children were sitting on either side of their grandparents.

Theo tipped his chair back enough to whisper, 'Nice job, Dad.' Dylan placed a brief hand on his son's shoulder and gave it a squeeze, wondering again how on earth he could've been so lucky.

After the service, they exited the ballroom via a pair of wide doors that led out onto a terrace overlooking a garden kept artificially green in an endless sprinkler war against the Florida sunshine. Accepting a couple of glasses of Buck's fizz from a passing waiter, Dylan settled himself beneath one of the broad sunshades on the terrace beside Frank, his ex-father-in-law, while the rest of the wedding party continued into the gardens. They watched in quiet amusement as an overly officious photographer herded guests this way and that. 'How long before Jen tells him to wind his neck in?' Dylan mused as the photographer adjusted her stance by a couple of inches.

'Oh, about two minutes, I reckon,' Frank replied, raising the glass Dylan had set down in front of him with only a small tremor in his hand.

'How's the physio going?'

'Slowly,' Frank grumbled. 'I made them change out my therapist because it was taking too long. They've sent me this tiny little thing with the face of an angel.' He grinned. 'She's meaner than my old staff sergeant.'

Dylan laughed. 'She'll have you whipped into shape in no time, then.'

'I sure hope so.' Frank's smile faded. 'Shoulda been me walking my baby girl down that aisle today, but I'm glad you were there to step in.'

'I was happy to do it.'

Frank set his glass back down. 'Will you step in for me one more time and dance with Nancy later?'

Dylan found himself swallowing around a sudden lump in his throat. 'It'll be my honour.'

Frank held his gaze for a long moment, then nodded. 'You're still our family, son. Don't you go forgetting that.'

'I won't.'

'It'll be tough for you going home again, huh?'

Dylan barked a laugh. 'You never were one to pussyfoot around a subject, were you, Frank?'

'Ain't got time for that kind of nonsense. It's been a long time for you.'

'Too long.' So long that it was impossible to recall the rage and hurt that had driven him away in the first place. Seeing his girlfriend in the arms of the brother he had hero-worshipped had broken something inside Dylan. He'd run away from everything – his home, his studies, his entire life – first backpacking around Europe for a few months before deciding to try his luck across the pond.

Getting a visa to work had been a lot easier back then and, after he'd spent a summer sweating on an orange farm, the owner had helped him with a sponsorship so he could go to college and pick up his studies. He'd met Jen there for the first time and they'd dated off and on. Neither had wanted anything serious, Dylan still too wary after what had happened with Rowena, and Jen focused on moving up to New York where she had a job offer with a prestigious legal firm.

They'd kept vaguely in touch after graduation, through early Internet chat forums set up by the computer boffins on campus and then through the miracle of AOL email and instant messaging. After ten years, the freezing winters of the East Coast had proven too much and Jen had headed back home to the Sunshine State. It had seemed only natural to take her out to dinner. One dinner had become two, and the old spark between them had soon reignited. They had married within a couple of years, had waited a while before starting their family. Dylan hadn't minded either way, but Jen's biological clock had been ticking. It was the best decision they'd ever made, and, even with the subsequent failure of their marriage, there wasn't a single thing he would change. Apart from one.

Any animosity Dylan had held towards his brother Zap had long since faded, but by then he'd been away for so long it had felt too late to bridge the gap beyond the odd postcard letting the family know he was alive and well. As communication methods had improved and his family had updated their estate's online systems, Dylan had been allocated an email address. Like clockwork, his other brother, Ziggy – oh, how their rebellious father must have delighted in irritating his parents by rejecting propriety and naming his four children after his favourite rock stars – had sent him regular updates, including a statement showing Dylan's share of the estate's earnings. Dylan had never touched the money. It wasn't his and he'd said as much in more than one terse response to Ziggy's emails. Ziggy hadn't responded, but the quarterly updates had kept on coming.

In the end Dylan had decided just to ignore the financial statements but he hadn't been able to stop himself from greedily devouring the snippets of family life Ziggy included in his emails. When the kids had come along, he'd sent photos, which had prompted birthday and Christmas cards and gift vouchers, but still something had held him back. As they'd grown, the kids had asked questions, of course, but Dylan had kept his responses vague and non-committal. He'd assumed they'd accepted the situation until they'd blindsided him completely when he'd asked them where they wanted to go for their special Christmas getaway. He'd pulled together a load of suggestions – skiing in the French Alps with a visit to Paris to see in the new year; sunbathing and sightseeing in Mexico; a beach-front haven in the Maldives where they could scuba dive off their own private dock; shopping and ice skating in New York City.

Theo and Avery had exchanged a look with each other before Theo had pulled a printout from his pocket and slid it across the dining room table. 'We want to go here.' Dylan had stared at the flyer advertising a twelve days of Christmas event at one of England's premiere country estates. *Juniper Meadows.*

Dylan reached for his Buck's fizz and drained it in a single long swallow. 'It's what the kids want, and that's all that matters.'

2

'You still haven't done anything about these awful curtains, I see,' Margaret Dunlop said with a sniff as Sadie closed the door behind her. The curtains in question had been purchased as part of a hasty sweep around the local discount furnishings ware-house just after Sadie had moved into the little two-up, two-down terrace a few months ago when all that had mattered was having something to cover the windows. It had been all she could afford and still retain some savings. The monthly maintenance Pete had agreed to didn't quite cover everything so she'd found some admin work close to her new home. It was only three days a week and she shared the role with a woman who hadn't wanted to come back full-time after maternity leave, but it gave Sadie just that extra bit of financial security while stopping her from going completely stir crazy. The people there were friendly enough, but Sadie had so far kept herself to herself and the mostly younger crowd hadn't pushed her to join in.

Pete had used his share to buy a villa in Spain, reasoning that he and Gemma could use Gemma's house on the few occasions they were back in the UK. Sadie hadn't been able to face bringing much from the old house after they'd sold up. There were simply too many memories, too many reminders of what she'd had and lost – or rather Pete had taken away from her.

'At least wait until you've got your coat off before you start moaning, Gran,' Katie chided, unzipping her own jacket and hooking it over the end of the stairs. 'Hello, Mum, something smells good.'

Avoiding eye contact with her mother, Sadie leaned forward to kiss Katie's cheek. 'Hello, love. Thanks for fetching your gran, I really appreciate it. How was the traffic?'

'Bloody awful. A couple of flakes of snow and everyone turns into an idiot.' Katie smoothed a hand over the pink polo-neck she was wearing with pale blue jeans and black Ugg boots. 'I hope it stops soon or we'll all be stranded here, which would be the last thing you want!'

Sadie rather thought she'd be delighted to have both Katie and her older brother, Jake, snowed in with her. Not for long, but a couple of hours just the three of them would be bliss. It wasn't something she ever gave voice to though as they had their own families now and it was enough that they continued to give up a few hours of their precious time every other weekend so she didn't have to face Sunday lunch with her mother alone.

That was something else Pete had left her to deal with – he'd been the one always keen on playing happy families and insisting everyone get together. At first it had been every Sunday and Sadie had come to loathe the smell of roasting meat as she sweated in the kitchen to turn out a huge meal while Pete played the good host and dished out a few bowls of nibbles and looked after the drinks. As the kids had grown up and begun to claim their independence it had reduced to once a fortnight. Once they'd moved out, the children's presence at the table had grown even scarcer because somehow they had managed to 'accidentally' double-book themselves more often than not. Sadie hadn't blamed them in the least for wanting to live their own lives, had even dreamed of making her own plans to avoid it though never had the courage to follow through. Even with Jake and Katie absent more often than not, Pete had failed to take the hint and continued to collect Margaret like clockwork.

Now he'd gone, but Margaret still expected to be hosted and Sadie hadn't found the wherewithal to stand up to her, not when she'd been barely holding herself together at the seams as she tried to get to grips with her new reality. It was too much to expect the children to continue trying to be a buffer between them so come the new year things were going to be different. Sadie was going to make some changes, even if the thought of it made the little girl deep inside her quail at the idea of standing up to her mother.

'What can I do?' Katie asked as she cast a glance towards the kitchen.

'Nothing, darling, thank you, Jake's got it all in hand. Go on through and make yourself comfortable and I'll sort out some drinks.' Because she'd put it off long enough, Sadie forced herself to turn and meet her mother's disapproving gaze. 'Sherry, Mum?'

'As long as it's not that cheap supermarket muck you tried to fob me off with last time.' Margaret held out her coat and scarf. 'On a hanger, please.'

'Of course. Go on through to the sitting room.'

'Sitting room? There's barely room to swing a cat in there. I still don't understand why you had to give up the house in Bayden Drive for this pokey little hovel.'

Katie stuck her head back round the sitting room door. 'I know you're getting on a bit, Gran, but did you forget the bit about Pete the Perv shagging off with another woman?'

Sadie bit her lip to hold in a laugh at the mention of the awful nickname the children had coined for their father, while her mother sputtered in disgust. 'Of course I haven't forgotten. I'm just disappointed that your mother showed her usual lack of backbone and let him walk all over her.'

'I'll get that sherry,' Sadie said, turning on her heel before her mother could settle into a full tirade of all her faults. Jake met her coming the other way, his overlong fringe flopping into his eyes, a large dark stain on the front of the blue and white striped butcher's apron he was wearing to protect his red and white checked flannel shirt.

'How's the dragon?' he murmured with a wicked grin.

'Don't call her that,' Sadie said automatically, before pulling a face. 'Fire-breathing as usual.'

'Chin up, only two hours to go.' Jake took the coat from her and tossed it along with the scarf in the understairs cupboard, shutting the door as Sadie squawked in protest. 'Leave it, she won't even notice. Come on, I've got a bottle open.' He took Sadie's hand and pulled her into the kitchen before she could retrieve the coat and hang it properly.

The smell of rich tomato sauce and garlic filled the tiny kitchen with the familiar warming scent of Jake's favourite spaghetti bolognese. That was one change Sadie had implemented after Pete left – no more roast bloody dinners, although she'd have to make an exception for Christmas lunch, she supposed.

A bottle of red wine stood open on the counter, a half-drunk glass next to it. Jake topped it up then poured a second generous measure into a glass that he thrust into Sadie's hand. 'Cheers!'

Sadie clinked their glasses together. 'Cheers, my lovely, lovely boy. You and Katie shouldn't have to give up your precious Sundays, you know.' She would still make an effort to see her mother, but they could go out for lunch instead. Margaret was all about appearances and tended to hold her tongue more in public so that in itself would be a relief. And if her mother didn't like the change of plans? Well, then Sadie would take herself out for lunch instead. Or to the spa, maybe? When was the last time she'd pampered herself? Turning, she caught a brief glimpse of her reflection in the mirror hanging in the hallway opposite and winced. Forget the spa, a trip to the hairdresser's needed to be top of her new year agenda.

'As if we're going to leave you to face the dragon alone! Besides, it's only for a couple of hours. Rachel and Liam have taken the kids to the pictures and we're meeting them later at Pizza Express.'

'That sounds lovely. I've got presents in the spare bedroom for you to take back with you. It'll be chaos here trying to squeeze everyone in for lunch on Christmas Day as it is.' Sadie honestly didn't know how she was going to manage it, but she wanted to give the grandchildren a little bit of normality.

'Um, about that.' Jake took her glass and set it down the counter next to his own. 'Hang on a sec.' He stuck his head out of the kitchen door and bellowed down the hallway. 'Katie, come and give us a hand!'

Katie appeared a couple of seconds later. 'Thank God you rescued me! Gran was doing my head in moaning about everything and everyone.' She turned to Sadie. 'Did you pour her a sherry?'

'Not yet.' Sadie bent to open the cupboard where she kept the bottles she'd wanted from Pete's extensive drinks cabinet. Perhaps one day she'd feel guilty about selling his fancy whisky collection via a local auction house – perhaps not.

'Leave that a minute,' Jake said, pressing his leg against the cupboard. 'Come and sit down, Mum. There's something Katie and I want to talk to you about.'

'I thought we were doing this later,' Katie said, keeping her voice hushed as she shot a glance towards the open kitchen door.

Jake shook his head. 'Mum's already fretting about feeding everyone on Christmas Day. It's not fair to keep her worrying about it.'

Sadie looked between the two of them. 'I appreciate you two worrying about me, but it's only one meal. It'll be a bit tight but we'll manage somehow.' The truth suddenly dawned on her and, though her heart clenched, she kept her voice light. 'You want to go to your dad's for Christmas. I should've realised.' Spending Christmas in a Spanish villa with its own swimming pool, or squeezing around her tiny kitchen table? It wasn't really a choice.

'No!'

'God, no!'

It was gratifying how quickly they responded, but Sadie felt a pang of guilt too. Pete hadn't left them, he'd left her and he'd always been a great father. She appreciated their loyalty, but she didn't want her situation to permanently poison their relationship with him. 'If you wanted to go, I wouldn't blame you and I'd never try and stop you. He's still your dad at the end of the day. And don't worry about me, I'll manage just fine on my own.' A quiet couple of weeks with her feet up might not be so bad. She could catch up on her reading pile and indulge herself in all the Christmas movies she wanted. She could even go shopping in the sales and buy some new curtains.

'He's a selfish git,' Katie snapped. She sighed then shook her head. 'We don't want you to have to manage, Mum. You've been so bloody brilliant these past few months. I honestly don't know how you've held it all together.'

Sadie smiled at her daughter, feeling a little watery as she raised one shoulder in a shrug. 'There didn't seem much point in doing otherwise.' The few times she'd let herself give in and cry she'd just ended up feeling tired and terrible while still having the same awful mess to sort out. 'Besides, I decided your father didn't deserve any more of my tears.'

'And he doesn't.' Jake put an arm around her shoulders and gave her a quick hug. She felt tiny tucked up against his big, broad frame. 'I remember when you were little enough to pick up,' she said as she looked up at him. 'What happened to my baby boy?'

Jake grinned. 'I'm still here, Mum.'

Leaning against him, Sadie held out her hand to Katie. 'However things ended, I'll never regret a day I spent with your father because we raised two of the very best people in the world.'

'Oh, Mum.' Katie curled an arm around Sadie's waist so she was standing between them. 'The reason we won't be spending Christmas Day here with you is because you won't be here.'

Sadie shot her a bemused look. 'Oh, really? Where exactly do you think I'll be instead?'

Letting go of her, Jake turned to where he'd slung his jacket over the back of one of the kitchen chairs earlier and pulled something out of the pocket. He handed it to Sadie. Intrigued, she unfolded a flyer for a twelve days of Christmas event at somewhere called Juniper Meadows. 'What's this?'

Katie squeezed her waist. 'It's our gift to you. Two weeks at a luxury hotel and spa in the Cotswolds.'

'The activities are optional, but they have a really good reputation as an artists' retreat and we thought you'd enjoy that,' Jake added. 'Plus you'd travel down on the Thursday so you won't even need to take any time off work.'

Sadie couldn't quite believe what she was hearing. 'I haven't done art for years!'

'I know, but you used to love it. I still remember how much fun you had helping with our school projects. Just imagine it,

Mum. You won't have to lift a finger and they've got acres of beautiful grounds to explore. You can wrap up warm and walk as much as you want.'

It *did* sound wonderful. 'But what about you guys?'

Jake and Katie exchanged a look. 'The four of us have talked about it and we'd really like Christmas in our own homes for once. We've always shuttled the kids between you and Dad and their other grandparents. That wasn't so bad when they were younger, but we'd like to make some memories at home for a change.'

'Liam's already ordered matching onesies for us and Isla,' Katie said with a grin.

Sadie laughed. 'You'll have to promise to send me a photo.' She turned to include Jake. 'Lots of photos.'

'We promise. And you'll have to do the same. You'll be back on the Thursday before New Year's and Rachel wants to have everyone for lunch that Friday so we can celebrate together then.'

'It sounds like you've got everything all planned out.'

Katie frowned. 'You don't mind, do you?'

'Oh, darling, of course not! Honestly, it sounds absolutely wonderful, but are you sure you can afford it?'

Her daughter shot her what could only be described as an evil grin. 'Pete the Perv sent us both some money for Christmas and told us to spend it on whatever we wanted, and we all decided that we wanted to spend it on you.'

'Then it's all settled.'

'What's all settled?'

Sadie's joy drained away as she met her mother's unsmiling gaze. 'We... ah, we were just making plans for Christmas, Mum.'

Margaret sniffed. 'Well, I hope you're not expecting me to spend it cooped up here with you in this awful rabbit hutch. I've already made plans to visit Celia in Harrogate, so you'll just have to manage without me.'

Katie leapt into action before Sadie had the chance to say anything. 'That sounds brilliant, Gran! Here, let me sort out that sherry for you and you can tell me all about it.'

Once she and Jake were alone in the kitchen, Sadie turned to face her son. 'Which one of you called Aunty Celia, and what did you have to promise her?'

Jake's grin was entirely unrepentant. 'I did. Rachel and I are taking the boys to stay with her at Easter and we've already booked Bettys tea rooms to treat her.'

'You really have thought of everything.' Though they'd taken her by surprise, it was touching how much effort both he and Katie had gone to.

Jake frowned, reaching out to put an arm around her shoulders. 'None of this is set in stone, Mum. If you don't want to be on your own, then you can come to us.'

Sadie shook her head. 'No, darling. You are right to put Rachel and the boys first.' When he opened his mouth to protest, she placed a gentle hand on his chest. 'Children grow up so fast that before you know it your boys will be making plans for you.'

Jake laughed. 'It'll be a few years yet.'

She patted his chest. 'It'll be here before you know it.'

His face grew serious once more. 'I meant what I said, Mum. Rachel and I would be happy to have you.'

She picked up the leaflet Jake had shown her earlier and studied it. The front cover was dominated by a beautiful painting of a stately home surrounded by snowy fields. It looked like something out of a fairy tale. She folded the pages out, took in the opulence of the bedrooms, the gleaming marble of the spa, the classical elegance of the dining room laid out for a function. It was a million miles from her little box of a house. On the back page were images of a woodland trail covered in lights, a court-yard of little shops packed full of smiling people. Sadie imagined herself there, walking through the woods, enjoying a massage in the spa, relaxing in the heated depths of a claw-footed bathtub before dressing for dinner – a dinner she hadn't had to lift a finger to prepare. She could please herself. Stay in bed all day reading if she wanted to, beholden to nothing and no one. It was something she'd never have dreamed of booking for herself, but now the opportunity had arisen?

'As lovely as staying with you, Rachel and the boys would be, I'm afraid I shall have to decline as I'll be spending Christmas at Juniper Meadows.'

3

So much had changed since Dylan had last been back that time had rendered most of the drive from Heathrow to the Cotswolds unrecognisable. As they passed the black on white sign marking the boundary of the village of Stourton-in-the-Vale that sense of discomfort and unfamiliarity faded at the sight of the first row of chocolate-box stone and thatched cottages. *Home.* It shouldn't be possible given he'd been nineteen the last time he'd passed along this same road, though travelling in the opposite direction, and yet it was as if a missing piece of his soul clicked into place. He steered the car to the kerb and sat for a minute, drinking it all in.

The grip of winter's harshness on the bare tree branches had been softened by the subtle golden glow of fairy lights. Wreaths of black-green holly leaves adorned with red berries, pine cones and splashes of brightly coloured ribbons hung from front doors painted glossy black. A pair of Christmas trees stood sentry on either side of the front door of the village pub. The Stourton Arms had been the source of more than one hangover and Dylan was overwhelmed with a sudden wave of nostalgia as he remembered the pride he'd felt walking through the door with Ziggy and Zap on his eighteenth birthday to a round of applause from the locals. The applause had been mostly for the fact he'd pulled out his wallet and declared that the drinks were on him than any particular deference to the youngest child of the local bigwigs. Though always conscious of their privilege, their generation of the Travers family had worked hard to distance themselves from the patrician attitude of their grandfather and considered the villagers friends and neighbours.

'Well, here we are,' he said. When there was no response Dylan glanced in the rear-view mirror to find Theo had his head-phones on, his eyes glued to his phone, while Avery was fast asleep, her head resting on a makeshift pillow Theo had made by rolling up his hoodie. 'After all that fuss you guys made about wanting to come here, too,' Dylan grumbled to himself with a chuckle.

He checked around him, ready to pull out to complete the final short drive to the gates of the estate when a flurry of movement caught his eye. Three men stood under the bright light over the entrance to the pub, laughing about something. *What the hell?* Though that mane of white hair had been dark the last time he'd seen it, and the belly resting on the waistband of his jeans much expanded, Dylan would've known his father anywhere, even if he weren't still wearing the same patchwork jacket he'd bought at some festival back in the seventies. The warm glow of nostalgia faded and Dylan set his jaw as he pulled away from the kerb and drove off a little faster than was polite for the quiet village streets.

Throughout the short drive from the village to the estate, Dylan turned over in his mind the messages he'd exchanged with Ziggy about their trip. Their communication had mainly focused on making arrangements, including asking if the children had any particular interests or dietary preferences. Funny how he hadn't found time to mention their parents being back on the estate. Probably because he knew how Dylan would react to the news. The last he'd heard in one of his elder brother's infrequent updates, their parents had been somewhere in South America and he'd had the impression their visits home were very few and far between. So what was Monty doing here now?

Their father had made it clear from a young age he had no intention of taking on the responsibilities of the estate, leaving Ziggy to take the strain of their grandfather's expectations. Dylan had wanted to do the right thing and set his heart on doing a business course at university but had hated almost everything about it. Only his desire to not let Ziggy and Zap down had kept him on track and, when the incident with his brother and Rowena had happened, Dylan knew he'd made a bigger deal about it than it had needed to be because it had given him the chance to run away too.

As bad as the old man.

Before he had time to fully jump on board that particular guilt train, the entrance to the estate, including the grand wrought-iron gates, came into view. Dylan slowed as he turned, coming to a complete halt just after entering the gates. He glanced in the rear-view mirror at the kids sprawled on the back seat. 'Hey, we're here.'

Theo glanced up, his scowl at being interrupted fading into a look of wonder as he caught sight of the impressive vista over Dylan's shoulder. He sat forward in his seat, his phone all but forgotten. 'Oh my God.'

'Not bad, eh?' Dylan replied with a grin before turning his attention to Avery, who had been woken up by Theo moving. 'Hey, sleepyhead. We're here.'

Avery rubbed her eyes then let out a squeal of delight as she took in the view. 'It's so pretty!'

'Isn't it just?' Leaning back in his seat, Dylan tried to take it all in. The tall trees lining the main avenue were bedecked with lights and he could only imagine how impressive they would look once the sun went down. As the original estate's designers had intended, the line of the trees drew the eye to the enormous pale-stone mansion sitting on an artificially created rise in the landscape. The Cotswold stone seemed to glow in the rays of the late morning sunshine, a beacon to draw visitors. And not just visitors, because the urge to see it up close for the first time in thirty years was almost overwhelming. 'Come on, let me show you where I used to live.'

The fountain at the centre of the circular driveway had been turned off, the deep basin that he'd paddled in as a little kid was hidden under a cover, the statue of a Grecian goddess and her pouring jug removed and åno doubt tucked safely away in storage somewhere. In its place stood a collection of small wire sculptures, each one representing one of the twelve days of Christmas, covered in sparkling white lights. Dylan didn't pay it too much attention, his eyes continually drawn towards the grand marble steps leading up to the front door. The peeling paint he'd remembered was gone, replaced by a slick shine of black gloss he thought he might be able to see his reflection in if he stood close enough. The sagging gutters and slipped tiles had been repaired, the tangles of ivy burrowing into the brickwork removed. He couldn't begin to estimate how much money they'd have to have spent on the place.

When he was growing up, the hall had been the world's most exciting playground. Hide and seek games could last an entire day, the curving banisters on the main staircase only shined thanks to the friction of sliding bottoms. Moth-eaten bed drapes, a lingering smell of cold damp in long closed-up rooms, hints of the glory days of the family shrouded under yellowing dust sheets. Every time he'd returned from boarding school for the holidays it had seemed as though the number of rooms the family used had dwindled, as had the number of staff to look after them. And in amongst all that crumbling splendour, his grandfather had refused to change. No safari park for them or jousting knights and tea rooms that other grand families had resorted to in order to keep the roof over their heads from falling down around their ears.

'You really used to live here?' Avery's question was full of wonder as they got out of the car to stand at the foot of the steps.

'Yep. But it was a lot different back then.'

The front door opened and a slender woman with short silvering hair smiled down at them. 'Welcome to Juniper Meadows! Are you checking in today?' The woman frowned for a moment. 'Dylan?'

His heart thumped in his chest. 'Stevie?' The last time he'd seen her he'd been maybe sixteen or seventeen, when she'd moved to London. Dylan hadn't been the only one keen to escape, but he couldn't blame his sister for wanting to live elsewhere because their grandfather had shown little to no interest in her. With a small cry, she flew down the stairs towards them and Dylan found his throat catching as she threw her arms around his neck. As his arms closed around her, the years seemed to fall away and he was transported back to the last time he'd clung to his sister like this. He'd been six and Stevie nearly nine and they'd just watched Zap and Ziggy be driven away to start at boarding school. Their parents hadn't been around to stop it, their father having one of his regular blow-ups that resulted in the pair of them disappearing for months on end. They'd gone touring around Australia, that time, if he remembered rightly.

'Don't worry,' Stevie had murmured as she'd soothed his recently cropped hair. 'I'll never leave you alone.' She'd meant it, too, but what was one little girl supposed to do in the face of their grandfather's iron will? Two years later, she'd been packed off herself, though to a girls-only school because grandfather had had no time for new-fangled nonsense like co-educational boarding. And Dylan had been left to run wild until it was finally his turn to go. At least he'd had Zap and Ziggy to show him the ropes, but they'd been too busy with their friends and thinking about exams to do much more than show their faces in the first-year common room now and again to make sure Dylan wasn't being bullied.

'Dad?'

The question in Avery's voice was enough to pull Dylan back to the present and he released Stevie. Looking down, he saw he wasn't the only one with wet cheeks and he gave an embarrassed laugh as he dabbed his eyes with his sleeve. He turned to face Theo and Avery, who were watching them with curious smiles. 'Theo, Avery, this is your aunt, Stevie.'

Stevie stepped forward and raised a hand to gently touch the dark curls tumbling over Avery's shoulders. 'I'd know this hair anywhere.' Her hand shifted to cup Avery's cheek. 'And those eyes. Hello, darling, it's so lovely to finally meet you.'

Avery ducked her head, a blush warming her cheeks. 'Hi, Aunt Stevie. Thank you for having us to stay.'

'It's our absolute pleasure.' Stevie turned to Theo, her smile deepening as she extended her hand towards him. 'And you, young man, are the spitting image of your father at your age.' She glanced back towards Dylan. 'A Travers to his bones.'

'In looks, maybe, but he's got his mother's brains and temperament, thank goodness!' He didn't know if it was a genetic thing, or just that natural inclination of each generation to kick against the previous one, but Theo was one of the most grounded, sensible people he knew. A little too sensible, sometimes, and Dylan worried his divorce from Jen had left him feeling scared to do the wrong thing. He sighed. That Philip Larkin poem had it right about getting effed up by your mum and dad, that was for damn sure.

'Come on in and I'll show you to your rooms.' Stevie leaned closer and lowered her voice. 'Look, we didn't want to overwhelm you with the whole clan so thought you'd like the chance to settle in and get used to the idea of being back here. We've planned a family dinner for later in the week, but if that's not what you want, just say the word.'

Dylan appreciated the thoughtfulness. 'That sounds good. I'll catch up with Zap and Ziggy before then – and Rowena, of course.' When he caught a flash of concern in his sister's eyes, he leaned in and kissed her cheek. 'It's all good, Stevie, I promise. Hey, did I imagine it or did I see Monty coming out of the pub earlier?'

Stevie's lips quirked in a not-quite smile. 'He's here, but that's a story for another day.'

Dylan raised an eyebrow, but didn't push it. Seemed as though he wasn't the only chicken come home to roost.

4

'May I help you with that?'

Sadie turned from where she'd been apprehensively eyeing her suitcase on the top shelf of the luggage rack to find a young woman with the most beautiful head of chestnut curls she'd ever seen smiling at her. 'Oh, I love your hair!' Sadie burst out, unable to help herself. 'I always wanted curls when I was younger, but mine's as straight as a poker.' Having not got around to getting it cut, Sadie had dragged hers back into a low ponytail that was practical for travelling, but not exactly her most flattering look.

The woman laughed, clearly pleased. 'Thank you.'

'Oh, and yes, if you wouldn't mind helping with my case, I'd be so grateful. I'm worried I'll clatter someone with it.' It had been absolute carnage at Paddington station, and even though Sadie had been poised beneath the big display screen for her platform to come up, she'd been no match for the speedwalking commuters. By the time she'd boarded, the rack had been almost full and she'd blocked the aisle while trying to work out where to squeeze her case in. An exasperated man behind her had grabbed it without a word and heaved it up out of the way before pushing past her to claim one of the last remaining seats. Though she'd booked her seat online, the young man occupying it had given her a blank stare before turning his attention back to a video playing at full volume on his phone. Not up to a fight, Sadie had retreated to the corridor and tried to hold her breath every time the door to the toilet had swung open and shut. Thankfully the train had thinned out at Reading and she'd been able to find a seat. Another crowd of humanity had belched out onto the platform at Swindon and the person next to her had moved onto an empty table of four.

With the friendly woman's help, Sadie got her case down with no disasters. Having thanked her good Samaritan, she shuffled into the corridor to wait for the train to pull in at Kemble station. A moment later the connecting door to the carriage popped back open and her friend from the luggage rack appeared, laughing with two other women around her age. Sadie exchanged another smile as she tucked herself into the corner to make room for them and their luggage. The train lurched and slowed, forcing her to grab for the safety handle with one hand and her suitcase with the other. It seemed to take an age but eventually the light on the door control illuminated and one of the women pressed it. Sadie stayed in her corner, waiting for the others to disembark before making her way down the steep steps, bumping her suitcase behind her.

A gust of cold wind threatened to cut her in half and Sadie yanked her hat from her coat pocket and tugged it on as she looked around to orient herself with the exit. It was a little two-platformed station much like the one she'd departed from that morning in her home town. The gods must have been smiling on her because she'd disembarked on the station-exit side so wasn't faced with the prospect of carting her luggage up and over the footbridge. The three friends from the train were just a little ahead of her and Sadie followed in their wake as she recalled the instructions from the email she'd received from the Juniper Meadows team coordinating her arrival. They'd told her not to worry about a taxi, that they were running their own shuttle service from the station and to look out for a black Range Rover with the company logo on the door.

As promised, a vehicle was waiting. A broad-shouldered man she judged to be around Jake's age stood beside it, bundled up in a blue quilted jacket and a black knitted hat. He stepped towards the three women, a broad smile on his handsome face. 'Ladies! I think you might be looking for me.' He laughed as he seemed to catch his words. 'Goodness, that didn't come out quite as I intended! Are you headed for Juniper Meadows?'

'Yes, we're booked in for the long weekend package,' Sadie's helper from earlier said. 'I'm Charlie, and this is Anna and Jane.'

'I'm Rhys and, when I'm not running a taxi service, I look after the farm on the estate. Leave your bags and jump in out of the cold.' He frowned. 'Mum said I should expect four of you?'

'I think I'm your fourth.' Sadie raised her hand, resisting the urge to shrink back as the other guests all turned to look at her. She'd been feeling a bit apprehensive about her trip as it had loomed closer, but she'd given herself a pep talk. She had no baggage, other than her literal suitcase. No one would know her, or know about how Pete had humiliated her. She would not be prejudged or seen as a bystander, or an appendage, not someone's wife or someone's mother. Just herself – whoever that might be. *Maybe that was something she could work on over the next couple of weeks.* She straightened her shoulders and smiled. 'I'm Sadie Bingham.'

Rhys beamed at her. 'Sadie, of course! It's a pleasure to meet you. Am I right in thinking you're joining us for the whole of Christmas?' He stepped back as he spoke to open the front passenger door for her as the three younger women climbed in the back.

She smiled in thanks as she took her seat. 'Yes. I'm here until the 28th.'

'Oh, lucky you!' One of the women, Jane she thought, said, leaning between the seats to grin at her. 'We're going home again on Monday.'

'It took most of the year to coordinate a weekend that worked for all three of us,' Charlie said with a laugh. 'Imagine trying to plan for a fortnight.'

'Still, a weekend is better than nothing,' Anna said, her perfectly spoken English carrying a European accent Sadie couldn't immediately place. 'And we're celebrating your birthday!' The three of them laughed as though at some private joke.

'Happy birthday,' Sadie said as Rhys climbed onto the driver's seat.

He glanced around. 'Whose birthday?'

'Mine,' Charlie replied. 'Although not really as it was back in May. It's just taken us this long to sort it out.'

'We're not completely disorganised,' Jane interjected. 'We did have a weekend booked for the summer, but the spa had a burst pipe and cancelled at the last minute so we decided to wait and have a pre-Christmas treat instead.'

'Well, I can promise that we'll do everything to make sure it was worth the wait,' Rhys said. 'Right, everyone got their belts on? Then let's get going so you can start those birthday celebrations.'

Sadie was content to listen to the other three chat, her gaze fixed on the window as they left the town. The view changed, the shops and houses giving way to the Cotswold countryside. The landscape was almost monochrome, the fallow fields brown, the stone walls separating them washed out beneath a pale afternoon sun that was already edging towards the horizon. She tried to overlay what she was seeing from the photos on the Juniper Meadows website full of rolling green hills and dancing fields of waist-high wheat. If she had a good time, perhaps she could treat herself to another visit next year. It wasn't as if she had anyone else to please. Perhaps she could get Jake and Liam to look after the children and treat Katie and Rachel to a weekend away, just the three of them. Or they could all come during the summer holidays and rent a couple of the eco-pods on the estate. The kids would love the chance to run around and explore, and Sadie could babysit in the evenings and give their parents a chance to spend some quality time together. As the car slowed to turn into a pair of impressive ornamental gates, Sadie felt her pulse quicken in excitement.

5

'It's too much,' Dylan murmured to his sister as they watched the kids roam wide-eyed around the stunning accommodation they'd been given. The three-bedroom suite wouldn't have looked out of place in a top London hotel. It had a separate lounge that was bigger than most of the rooms he'd stayed in over the years and two bathrooms. The en suite connected to the master bedroom had a walk-in shower large enough that Dylan could throw a party in it. The second bathroom interconnected between the other two bedrooms and had a fancy roll-top bath in addition to a waterfall shower cubicle.

'Oh, hush,' Stevie said. 'If I can't spoil my family then what's the point?' She reached out and squeezed his hand. 'The presents you ordered are all wrapped and hidden in the bottom of the wardrobe in the master bedroom.'

Though they would be celebrating when they were back home with Jen and Eric, they'd wanted the kids to have a few things to open on Christmas Day. With Ziggy's help they'd bought presents online via UK retailers and had them delivered to the estate. 'You didn't have to go to the trouble of wrapping them.'

'It wasn't any trouble, it was fun.' Stevie brushed a quick kiss on his cheek. 'There's a couple of things in there with your name on too.' When he raised an eyebrow at her she gave him a mischievous grin. 'Big sister's prerogative. Right, I'll leave you to it. Welcome drinks will be in the lounge at five.' With another grin she headed for the door and pulled it closed behind her.

Shaking his head over his sister's antics, Dylan turned his attention back to the room to find it was empty. 'Hey, where are you guys?'

'In here!' Theo poked his head through an open door on the opposite side of the suite. 'This is Avery's room,' his son continued once Dylan joined them, 'and mine is next door. Yours is the big one, of course.'

'Seems like you've got it all figured out.'

'You never told us you lived in a palace, Daddy!' Avery exclaimed as she flopped on her back on the bed, her arms and legs splayed like a starfish.

Dylan grinned. 'It didn't look like this the last time I was here. And my room was a lot smaller than this.' It hadn't escaped his notice that the family suite Stevie had allocated them was miles away from the chilly top-floor nursery rooms they'd all occupied when the family had lived in the hall. Even when they'd far outgrown them, their grandfather had never suggested moving them onto one of the lower floors. He didn't need to get into all that, certainly not with the kids. He sat on the edge of Avery's bed and grinned at them. 'I think your aunt Stevie might be guilty of a little family favouritism.'

'If this is an example of the strings Aunt Stevie can pull, then I'm really glad we persuaded you to bring us here,' Theo said, leaning against the wall.

'Don't even think about trying to push that advantage.' Dylan looked between the two of them. 'I'm serious, guys. It's one thing to accept her generosity, but we have to remember that the other guests will have paid a lot of money to be here, so let's be discreet, okay?'

'I was only joking,' Theo protested, coming to sit beside him.

Dylan patted his leg. 'I know, pal, I just want everything to run smoothly while we're here.' *Well as smoothly as possible anyway.* It was another thought he needed to keep to himself. He reached out and placed his free hand on Avery's lower leg. 'You're sure you'll be okay sharing a bathroom?' They didn't fight about much, but accusations of bathroom hogging were a big bone of contention between the two.

'We'll be fine, won't we, Avie?' Dylan's heart did one of those funny little flips at Theo's use of the nickname – his first attempt at pronouncing his sister's name.

Avery sat up, curling her arm around Dylan so the three of them were connected. 'We'll be fine, Daddy. Besides, if you meet someone nice while we're here you might need the privacy.'

Laughing, Dylan untangled himself from their group embrace. 'I don't think there's much chance of that!' As he rose, he saw the children exchange a look. 'What?'

Theo looked at Avery again. 'You raised it...'

Avery shuffled to the edge of the bed and let her legs dangle over the edge. 'We just thought that now Mom and Eric are married—'

Dylan cut her off. 'You don't think I was hanging around hoping your mother and I might get together one day, do you?'

Avery rolled her eyes. 'Of course not, silly! We just thought...' She glanced back over at her brother. 'We just hoped that perhaps you'd start thinking about yourself for a change. Theo's going to be a senior next year and then off to college and I won't be far behind him.'

Dylan sank back down on the bed between them. 'Look, I know you guys won't need me forever, but I haven't stayed single because of that.' Well, perhaps a bit of him had because he'd seen too many of his co-workers and parents of the children's friends struggle to balance their blended families. He counted himself lucky that Jen had been very clear with Eric that she and Dylan parented the kids equally and that wouldn't change. It had taken them a long time to transition into a fully committed relationship and Dylan had been only too happy to accept Eric's invitation to go out for a few beers so they could talk frankly. That wasn't to say there hadn't been a few bumps in the road, but they'd worked them out for the sake of the kids.

Theo placed a hand on his arm and that thing inside Dylan did another funny little shift. They were growing up so fast, moving beyond the childish phase where their world understandably revolved around what they wanted and needed. They were both displaying the kind of understanding and compassion he could see they would carry with them into adulthood. 'We're always going to need you, Dad, one way or another. It's not about that. It's about wanting you to be happy. You work so hard and when you're not at work you're ferrying us around from this club or that activity.'

'That's what dads do,' Dylan protested.

Avery snuggled into his side. 'Not all of them. We know you only want what's best for us, but we want what's best for you too.'

Dylan put his arm around her shoulders. 'I appreciate that, sweetheart, more than you can know.' He dropped a kiss on the top of her head then lifted his other arm as he looked at Theo. 'Come on, pal. No one else is looking.' He winked.

Theo huffed out a laugh but he tucked himself against Dylan's side as well. 'I know I probably sound like a cracked record, but, damn, I'm lucky to have you guys as my kids. You make me so proud.' They all clung on for a few seconds, as if they each sensed that time was moving on and this might be one of the last times they got to be away together. 'And now,' Dylan said, after easing his hold, 'I reckon it's time we headed downstairs and met a few of the other guests. Your aunt Stevie said there's welcome drinks starting in...' He raised his wrist to check his watch. 'Half an hour so we've just got time to unpack.'

6

'Oh, this is beautiful!' Sadie exclaimed as the porter stepped back to allow her to enter her room. The first thing she noticed was the chandelier glistening overhead. The crystal teardrops seemed to dance as they caught and reflected the flames from the fire burning in the grate beneath the ornate marble fireplace. Thick ruby-red velvet drapes framed a huge picture window overlooking the neat hedges and paving of a formal garden. The far side of the room was completely dominated by an enormous four-poster bed stacked with pillows and cushions. It was much higher than her bed at home and she wondered how she was going to climb onto it.

'May I come in for a moment, ma'am?'

Sadie startled, having forgotten the porter was there. 'Yes, of course.'

Smiling, he wheeled her suitcase in and over to the chaise longue at the foot of the bed. 'Shall I place this here so you can unpack?'

'That would be lovely, thank you.'

He lifted her case up then walked past the bed to open a door.

'This is your bathroom.' He left the door open as he moved back to her end of the room and indicated a leather-bound folder on the coffee table. 'There's an information guide, which should hopefully answer any questions you have, but if you need anything, just dial zero on the phone and someone on the team will be happy to help you.'

'Thank you.' Goodness, she sounded like a stuck record. 'Sorry, I didn't catch your name.'

The young man smiled. 'It's Justin.'

'Well, it's very nice to meet you, Justin, and thank you for making me feel so welcome.'

'It's my pleasure. As I said, if you need anything just pick up the phone and don't forget there's welcome drinks in the lounge starting in about half an hour.'

She nodded, because honestly how many times could she say thank you in under five minutes? 'The lounge is just off Reception?'

'That's right. Straight down the stairs and it's on your left. There's a map in your information pack with a plan of the hotel until you find your way around. If that's everything for now, I'll leave you in peace.' He turned to go.

'Oh, wait a minute!' Sadie grabbed her handbag and fumbled for her purse. It'd been so long since she'd been anywhere that required a tip she wasn't sure where to start. A couple of coins felt a bit measly so she opened the notes flap to find she didn't have anything smaller than a twenty-pound note. Everything was chip and pin these days, and, although she'd brought extra cash with her because there'd been mention of a Christmas market, she hadn't had a chance to break anything down into smaller denominations. She shot Justin an embarrassed smile. 'I don't suppose you have any change?'

He smiled back. 'Reception will be happy to sort some out for you, but please don't worry about individual tips.'

She frowned, not sure if he was just being polite. 'Well, as long as you're sure.'

'I really am.' He paused at the door with a cheeky grin. 'On a completely unrelated note, there's a jar behind the bar for our post-Christmas party fund and any donations to that would be gratefully received.'

Sadie laughed. 'Noted, thanks again, Justin.'

With time to kill before the welcome drinks, Sadie decided she might as well unpack. Every little thing seemed to have been thought of, from pretty scented bags in the drawers to keep clothes fresh, to the selection of luxury toiletries lined up neatly on the bathroom counter. A basket next to the sink contained cotton wool, a miniature nail-grooming set, even a little sewing kit.

Having finished putting everything away, Sadie cleaned her teeth and brushed her hair, securing the messy strands back out of the way with a butterfly clip. She wished now that she'd taken the time to get her hair done before her trip. Since moving, she hadn't got around to sorting out a new hairdresser and going back to her old one would've meant being both the subject of and subjected to all the local gossip. She'd looked through the window of a few salons in town on her lunchbreak, but by the time she finished work all she wanted to do was get home so it was another thing she'd put off for another day.

Sadie shook her head and pushed the sneaky voice of her inner critic away. Her hair was fine and she was just looking for an excuse not to go downstairs.

Wandering back into the bedroom, Sadie perched on the edge of the chaise longue. What was there to be afraid of? Those girls she'd shared a lift from the station with had been lovely, as had

Rhys. The hotel staff were friendly and full of smiles. The next
two weeks were the perfect chance to relax and recharge and it
would be a waste of her time, never mind the money the kids had
spent, if she hid away in her room. She was here to have a good
time, not to worry about the past – or the future. Sadie rose.
Maybe she could put her new-found skill with personal pep talks
to good use and start a new career as a motivational coach. The
thought of it was enough to make her laugh out loud and she was
still smiling as she walked along the corridor and down the stairs.

Even without Justin's simple directions, there was no chance
of Sadie not finding the lounge. The sound of conversation and
laughter reached her before she'd made it to the bottom of the
stairs and a pair of smiling women were waiting beside a younger
one who was holding a tray full of glasses of champagne. The two
women were as different as chalk and cheese. The taller of the
pair had silvery hair cut in a flattering crop that highlighted her
excellent bone structure. She was wearing the kind of clothes you
didn't find on the high street. A simple skirt, the same shade of
dark green as the branches of the Christmas tree, fell in an
elegant drape to mid-calf, teamed with a white pleated silk blouse
with fitted sleeves. Lifting a glass from the tray, she took a step
forwards, her face lit with a welcoming smile. 'Sadie, isn't it?'

'Yes, that's right.'

'I'm so sorry I wasn't here when you arrived but we had a
sudden influx of arrivals and it was all hands to the pump.' She
offered the glass. 'I'm Stevie and this is Rowena.' She gestured to
the woman beside her who was wearing a shimmering kaftan the
jewelled colours of peacock feathers. Her wild fall of hair had
been dyed a rich shade of purple and her bright blue eyes
sparkled with good humour to match her broad smile. 'And we
are so thrilled you've decided to celebrate Christmas with us here
at Juniper Meadows.'

'Yes, you are so welcome!' Rowena held out her hand with a clatter of silver bangles and squeezed Sadie's fingers. 'And if you don't mind me saying—' Rowena lowered her voice to a conspiratorial whisper '—I admire you enormously for coming on your own.' She squeezed again and Sadie found herself returning the gesture, welcoming the little show of support. In a normal tone, Rowena continued, 'I promise we've got a lovely group of guests staying with us. A real mix of singles, families and friends. And we've got so many activities planned you won't have to worry about being bored.'

'The activities are *purely* voluntary,' Stevie added, with a wry smile. 'This is your holiday and you must please yourself.'

'Well, yes, of course you must,' Rowena agreed, still holding Sadie's hand. 'But I'm sure when we were in correspondence you mentioned an interest in art so I think tomorrow will be right up your street. We're going to make a centrepiece for the entrance.' Turning, Rowena gestured with her free hand to the large round table standing empty in the centre of the impressive vaulted room. 'We'll be working in the orangery, which is one of my favourite rooms in the entire hall. It'll be very relaxed.'

Sadie smiled at the other woman's attempts to reassure her. 'I have decided I am going to make the most of my visit. It's my intention to say yes rather than no to most things so I would love to join you tomorrow. I must warn you that what skills with a paintbrush I might once have laid claim to are very rusty.'

'Oh, I'm so pleased! And don't worry about anything, it's designed to be fun for everyone from absolute beginners upwards, and it's not just painting, there's going to be a whole range of things to choose from.' She released Sadie's hand with one final squeeze. 'Now, come on, let's introduce you to a few people and you'll feel at home in no time.'

The lounge was a great deal grander than the name implied

and a million miles away from her little box at home with not much room for more than a sofa and chair, a coffee table and a TV stand. Not forgetting those curtains her mother hated so much. Sadie found herself smiling as she looked around at the Chesterfield-style sofas and wide cushioned armchairs grouped around tables. A few chairs had been set on their own in quiet corners of the room so guests would have a choice about mixing or not. There was one near the fireplace Sadie made a note of as a potential reading spot if the weather let them down one day. A wooden bar ran half the length of the back wall, an impressive array of bottles filling the shelves behind it. Subtle Christmas touches had been added everywhere, from little table pieces of pine cones, holly and dried citrus slices to a garland of greenery and sparkling lights dressing the front of the bar.

'Sadie!' She turned to find Charlie, Anna and Jane sitting at a table over by the window. Charlie waved. 'Come and join us if you like.'

'Oh, you've made some friends already.' Rowena beamed.

'We met in the car earlier, when Rhys collected us from the station.'

'My son.' Rowena's smile broadened even more.

'He mentioned something about running a farm here, so Juniper Meadows really is a family business, then?'

It was Stevie who laughed. 'We've definitely kept it all in the family. Ro' is my sister-in-law and we run this place together. Her husband, Zap, is our master brewer over at the distillery and my other brother, Ziggy, is in overall charge of the estate. My son and daughter work here too, and their partners are all involved with the estate one way or another.'

'That must be lovely. I've a son and daughter of my own and I never feel like I see enough of them. Not that I'm complaining,' she added, hurriedly. 'I'm delighted they're settled and have their own families. They're the ones who treated me to this break, actually.'

'That's lovely. I hope you won't miss them too much over Christmas?' Stevie's expression was sympathetic.

Sadie smiled. 'I'm sure I will miss them terribly, but I also know what it's like to have too much expectation placed on your time. They both wanted a quiet Christmas with their children while they're still young enough for the magic to really mean something. We're having a lunch party at my son's after I get back and, as I'm not the one having to do the hosting, it'll be a double treat.'

Stevie touched her arm. 'Well, then, I'm even more delighted that you've chosen to celebrate with us. If you'll excuse me for a moment, I need to go and check everyone's got a full glass.'

'Of course. I'm sure you've got plenty to be doing as well,' Sadie said as she turned towards Rowena, but the other woman wasn't looking, never mind listening. Her attention was fixed on the doorway behind them, her mouth slightly open as she stared as if seeing a ghost. Sadie turned to see what she was looking at. A man was standing on the threshold, a teenage boy and girl at his side. He was tall, that was the first thing Sadie noticed. Handsome too, with his thick dark hair and strong, even features. He reminded her of someone, but she couldn't think who. Glancing back at Rowena, she noticed a tear glistening on her eyelash. Whoever he was, Sadie was intruding. Murmuring a quick 'Excuse me,' she headed over to the table where Charlie and her friends were sitting.

7

'Dad, why is that woman staring at you?' Avery nudged Dylan's arm.

He looked around, his eyes locking with Rowena's. Her face was softer, those curves of hers he'd always found so attractive a little more generous. The hair, though, and her bright, flowing outfit were the same splash of colour he remembered. 'She's an old friend of mine,' Dylan answered. 'Why don't the two of you go and grab us a table and I'll be over in a minute?'

'Can't we meet her?' Avery asked, full of curiosity.

Though it would be easier to use the children as a shield, there were things the two of them needed to say to each other. Things that should've been said a long time ago. 'Do as I ask, please.' He didn't play the 'stern father' card often, but his tone said it wasn't a request.

'Come on, Avie,' Theo said, tugging his sister by the hand. 'There's a table over there near the window.' He glanced back at Dylan. 'Take your time, Dad, we'll be fine.' There it was again, that streak of empathy that ran right through his son's core.

Dylan waited until the kids had moved away before turning

his attention back to Rowena. She hadn't moved from the spot, and didn't look as if she had any intention of doing so even after he sent her an encouraging smile. *Looked like it was up to him then.* He took a step forward and then another and another until they were separated by less than a couple of feet. 'Hey, Ro', it's good to see you.'

'Is it?' Her voice wasn't much more than a whisper.

He nodded. 'Yeah, it really is.' Time to bite the bullet. 'How's Zap?'

'He's okay.' Her lips quirked in a wonky smile. 'Worried to death about seeing you again.'

Dylan raised a hand to rub at the sudden pain in his heart. 'He has no need to be.' He closed the distance between them and touched her hand. Just the merest brush of fingers. 'Everything's good between us, Ro', I promise. I'm sorry I stayed away so long. I didn't do it to punish you.'

Her throat bobbed around a visible swallow. 'We missed you.'

'I missed you too. All of you, but the longer I stayed away, the harder it was to reach out.'

She glanced down at where their fingers were still barely touching. 'You're home now, and that's all that matters.' When she looked up, tears glistened on her dark lashes like diamonds. 'Have you been happy, though?'

He nodded. 'Yes. I sulked around for a few years, but then I met a wonderful woman who helped me get back on track. Our marriage didn't last the course, but we have two brilliant children together.' Dylan tipped his head towards the table where Avery and Theo were pretending to play with their phones, but he could tell they were watching everything.

Rowena glanced over her shoulder. 'Is that them?' When she turned back her expression had softened into one of sympathy. 'I'm sorry about your divorce.'

Dylan shrugged one shoulder. 'Don't be. It was a long time ago and the best thing for all of us. Come and say hello to the kids.'

He led Rowena over to the table. 'Hey, guys, this is your aunt Rowena. She and I were at university together a lo-o-o-ong time ago.'

Theo immediately stood and offered his hand. 'I'm Theo. It's really good to meet you.'

'You too, Theo.' Rowena looked from him to Dylan. 'He's the spitting image of you.'

Dylan grinned as he ruffled his son's hair. 'If people keep telling him that, the poor boy will get depressed!' He held out a hand to Avery as she came around from the other side of the table. 'And this beautiful angel is my daughter, Avery.'

Avery made a gagging sound. 'Honestly, Dad, you're so embarrassing.'

'Hey, it's my job,' Dylan said with an unrepentant laugh.

Giving him the kind of look of disdain only a teenage girl could manage, Avery deliberately turned her back on him to face Rowena. 'Hello! You run this place with Aunt Stevie, right? It's *so* amazing, I love everything about it!'

Rowena smiled at her. 'That's right. I look after the spa and organise the art classes. We're going to make a centrepiece tomorrow if that's something you'd like to help out with? And if you want a massage or a manicure and pedicure...' she quickly glanced over to Dylan, clearly seeking his permission, and he nodded his approval '...then it'll be my treat. Consider it an early Christmas present.'

Avery lit up. 'That would be great, thanks, Aunt Rowena!'

Rowena turned to Theo. 'What about you, dear? I know young men are much better at taking care of themselves these days – can we tempt you with one of our specially designed men's facials?'

Theo shook his head. 'No, thanks, but I'm definitely up for the art session tomorrow.'

'Oh, yes, me too!' Avery piped up. 'What about you, Dad?'

Dylan shook his head. 'I've got a few things I need to do in the morning, if you guys will be okay with Rowena?'

'I'll be happy to keep an eye out, though you both look more than capable of looking after yourselves. You'll have the chance to meet your cousin Ben, as well, as he'll be helping out. Now, will you excuse me as we're going to do a bit of briefing in a minute?'

Dylan touched Rowena's arm as she turned to go. 'I'd like to see Zap in the morning. Will you let him know?'

She nodded. 'I think that'll be good for both of you. He'll be in the distillery from about nine as usual. It's part of The Old Stable Yard complex – do you remember where that is?'

'I saw a sign for it as we were driving in earlier. I'll find my way. You sure about the kids tomorrow?'

'Of course.'

_____

8

'Hello again,' Sadie said as she approached Charlie and her friends. 'Are you all settled in?'

Charlie nodded. 'All unpacked, thanks. How's your room? Is it amazing?'

Sadie laughed. 'It's incredible! I've got the most enormous four-poster bed. Only trouble is, I'm not sure how I'll get on it.'

The others joined in with her laughter. 'Here, sit down,' Jane said, pulling out the empty chair.

'Oh, I don't want to intrude on your special weekend together...'

'It's fine. Please, join us.' Anna gestured towards the chair. 'My bed is enormous too, and so comfortable. I made the mistake of lying down on it and wanted to stay there.'

Sadie settled into the seat with a grateful smile. 'So what do you all have planned for the weekend? Rowena was just telling me about a group art project planned for tomorrow, which I think I'm going to check out. Are you coming along or are you going to make the most of your access to the spa?'

Charlie slid a leaflet she'd been looking at across the table. 'I was just reading about it in here and it sounds like it might be fun. We can go together if you like because I think these two are booked in for some spa treatments.'

'Well, only if you're sure?' They were incredibly kind but Sadie didn't want them to feel obliged to look out for her.

'Definitely. I'd rather walk in there with someone I know, anyway.' Charlie raised her glass and Sadie clinked hers against it. 'There, we're friends now!'

Sadie took a sip then glanced down at the leaflet. 'Oh, is this what they have planned for the weekend?' She picked it up for a closer look. The front page was all about the art workshop, with the plan being to create a partridge in a pear tree using a range of different techniques from crochet to metalworking and everything in between.

Reaching out, Charlie tapped the back of the leaflet. 'There's a murder-mystery dinner on Saturday. We have to sign up for a table if we want to take part.'

'What's a murder mystery got to do with the twelve days of Christmas?' Sadie pondered aloud as she turned the sheet around. The answer became apparent as she read the description.

A terrible crime has been committed at Staunton Hall. Inspector Turtle and Sergeant Dove are on the case and will need all the help they can get to track down the dastardly murderer!

'Sounds like it might be a laugh,' Jane said beside her. 'Though I'm not sure I'll make a very good detective.'

'Me either,' Sadie agreed.

'They want groups of eleven as we have to leave a space at each table for a mystery guest,' Charlie added. 'So, us four and...'

She nodded at the table next to them. 'Maybe we could see if they want to join us as well?'

Sadie glanced over to see she was gesturing towards the man and the two teenagers she'd noticed arriving earlier. The man looked up, catching her eye before she had the chance to look away. *Goodness, it ought to be illegal to be that handsome.* When he quirked an eyebrow at her, Sadie realised to her horror she was still staring and, in a panic, she thrust the leaflet towards him. 'We... uh, we were wondering if you wanted to join us for dinner on Saturday evening.' Oh, dear, how forward did that sound? 'All th-three of you, of course,' she added, quickly, trying to ignore what she was sure was a blush rising. 'For the murder-mystery dinner, I mean.'

The man leaned over and took the leaflet, glanced at it briefly, then showed it to the teenagers. 'What do you think?'

'Sounds fun,' the boy said.

'Is it going to be like Clue?' the girl asked.

Her father nodded. 'Yeah, like a live-action version with actors playing the parts. You want to give it a go?'

She nodded. 'Sure, why not?'

The man turned back to Sadie, offering her the leaflet back. 'Count us in.' He smiled. 'I'm Dylan, and this is Theo and Avery.'

'I'm Sadie.' She turned to the others, feeling a little awkward about introducing them when they were all but strangers, no matter how friendly they'd been. The three women said their names in turn and waved across. 'It's nice to meet you,' she added, not sure what else to say.

Her blushes were saved as someone tap-tap-tapped on a microphone and they all looked around to see Stevie and Rowena standing with three younger women in front of the bar. A hush fell over the guests and a few shuffled their chairs around so they were facing the right direction. Dylan picked up his chair and moved around to the other side of the table, placing it between Sadie and Avery. 'Do you mind? I don't want to crick my neck.'

'Not at all.' Sadie shifted over so he had a bit more room then turned her attention to the women at the front.

Stevie smiled. 'Thank you, everyone. We won't disturb you for long, we just wanted to outline the plan for the weekend and give a bit more information for those of you who will be with us for the full fortnight Christmas experience. As you will see from the flyers we left on the tables, the plan is to celebrate the twelve days of Christmas with a special event each day. We are conscious of making sure you all have time to relax and do your own thing, so please be assured that participation in all the activities is voluntary and will only ever take up a portion of each day. I'm going to hand over to Hope, who will explain a bit more.' Stevie smiled at a young woman with thick dark hair and a bright smile as she passed her the microphone.

'Good afternoon, everyone. I'm the deputy manager here at Juniper Meadows, and I'd like to quickly introduce you to Tasha, our events manager—' a woman with curly red hair raised her hand '—and our activities consultant, Lydia.' The other woman, with thick glossy hair held back with a red Alice band, smiled and nodded. 'While Mum, sorry, *Stevie*, and Rowena will be looking after every aspect of your stay here at the hotel, the three of us are your points of contact for the twelve days' events. At least one of us will be present at each of the activities to make sure everything runs smoothly. If you look over towards the door you'll see there are two tables with information packs on them. The ones on the left are for those of you who are here for the long weekend, and the ones on the right are for everyone else who is here for the full fortnight. Please help yourselves once the briefing is over. They should tell you everything you need to know, but you'll also find contact details for myself and Tasha in them so if you have any questions, feel free to send us a Whats-App, or give us a call if it's anything urgent.'

She turned and handed the mic to Tasha, who stepped forward with a smile. 'Welcome, everyone, I promise I won't keep you for too much longer. We have aimed for a mix of daytime and evening activities, both indoor and outdoor. Outdoor activities are weather dependent.' Tasha held up her hand to show she'd crossed her fingers and a ripple of laughter went around the room. 'But the forecast is looking pretty promising. I just wanted to cover off a couple of practical things. There's plenty of hanging space in the downstairs bathrooms just off the entrance hall so you won't need to carry wet coats and things up and down to your room if you'd prefer not to. We also have a boot-room facility behind Reception with spare wellies, hats and gloves, umbrellas and waterproof jackets. Please help yourselves, but we do ask that borrowed items are returned in case someone else needs them. Other than Christmas Day, the only event meal we have planned is the murder-mystery dinner this Saturday evening. There's a blank table plan also by the door, so please pop your names down on it. We hope you will all choose to join us for what should be a fun night, but supper will be available for anyone who would prefer a quiet meal instead, and that will be served in the blue drawing room.' Tasha paused and looked at Hope and Lydia. 'I think that's everything?' They both nodded and Stevie stepped forward to take the microphone once more.

'All that remains is for us to thank you for choosing to spend time with us here at Juniper Meadows and we wish you all a wonderful stay. There's plenty of champagne so please don't be shy if you would like another drink. Dinner will be served in the main dining room this evening between six-thirty and eight-thirty.' There was a polite round of applause.

Avery jumped up. 'Shall I get our packs, Dad?' she asked, her expression eager, and Sadie couldn't help but smile at her excitement.

'Sure, sweetheart. Why don't you get some for the ladies here while you're at it?' He turned to Sadie. 'Are you here for Christmas as well?'

She nodded. 'Yes.' She looked at Avery. 'Can you get us one Christmas pack and three weekend ones, please?'

'Sure thing!'

Dylan frowned. 'You're not all together?'

'No. I met Charlie and the others when we were picked up at the station earlier and they were kind enough to invite me to join them for a drink.' She leaned slightly closer and spoke in a lower tone. 'I'm trying not to gatecrash their weekend too much.'

Dylan grinned. 'Try having two teenage children, then you'll feel like a permanent gate-crasher.'

She laughed. 'Ah, I well remember those days. I swear my son only communicated in grunts for about three years. Once they fly the nest, you'll miss them, though.'

'I'll take your word for it! Theo isn't that bad, but he spends too much time in his room for my liking, and when he's not hiding away—' Dylan nodded towards his son, who was tapping away on his phone '—he's glued to that.'

'I hate to tell you, but if you look around that's exactly what 90 per cent of the room is doing.'

He chuckled. 'Good point. So, your children aren't joining you here for Christmas?'

'No. They both have young families of their own now and they're each having a quiet Christmas with their children.' She hesitated, wondering how much to share. 'I was quite relieved when they suggested it, because I've hosted for as many years as I can remember. And when they told me they'd booked me in here, it was simply the icing on the cake. We're all getting together at my son's just before the new year, which will be fun.'

'Sounds like the best of both worlds,' Dylan said. 'We're here because I promised the children they could do whatever they wanted for Christmas while their mom and stepdad are on their honeymoon.'

'Mom? Your ex-wife is American? I thought Avery had an accent.'

'Yeah, I've lived there for nearly thirty years. I bummed around for a few years on various working holidays and found myself in Florida and somehow never left.' His smile said he didn't seem to mind how things had turned out.

'Florida to the Cotswolds seems like a bit of a leap for your kids to make. What's the attraction?' The luxurious surroundings of Juniper Meadows were perfect for her, but it seemed an odd choice for a couple of teenagers.

Dylan gave a funny kind of half-shrug and she wondered if her question had made him uncomfortable, though for the life of her she couldn't figure out why it would. 'We have family in the area,' he said eventually before taking a large mouthful of his champagne.

Avery returned at that moment, a stack of information guides in one hand, her other clinging tightly to the woman who'd introduced herself as Hope during the announcements. 'Look who I just met!' Avery announced, her blue eyes shining with excitement as she dumped the guides on the table.

Hope smiled at Dylan. 'Mum said you'd arrived safely. Are you settling in okay?'

Sadie found herself looking between Hope and Avery, noting the same dark, glossy hair and blue eyes. Blue like Dylan's. Blue like Stevie's.

Oh.

As Dylan rose to greet Hope, Sadie reached for the abandoned packs and quickly sorted out one for herself and the three weekend ones for Charlie and the others. 'Let's see what else is going on,' she said in a bright voice as she shifted her chair back to its original position and handed them out. Soon the four of them were deep in conversation and making plans for the next few days. Well, the three women were making plans. Sadie did her best to focus on them and ignore the nosy bit of her brain that was hyper-fixated on what was happening behind her. When Dylan had said he had family in the area, that had been one hell of an understatement.

9

When Dylan opened his eyes the next morning, it felt as though
it had been only moments since he'd finally managed to close
them. While it would've been nice to pretend it was only the jet
lag that had messed up his sleep, he was through with lying to
himself. It had taken ages for Avery to calm down over the excitement at meeting, not only her aunts, but one of her cousins, and
she'd sat in bed chattering away to Theo, who had sprawled
across the end of his sister's bed as she'd speculated on what the
rest of the family might be like. She seemed to be taking it in her
stride, but, always quieter, Theo was proving harder to read. Guilt
had wracked Dylan as he'd lain in bed on the other side of the
suite. Their voices had carried across the sitting room and
through the door they'd left open because Avery had wanted a
night light in case she had to get up and Dylan had wanted to
make sure he heard her if she did.

The book he'd held had remained unread as he'd silently
berated himself for keeping the children apart from his family all
these years. They'd never behaved as though they felt like something was missing from their lives, and Jen's parents, Frank and

Nancy, had been the most attentive of grandparents any children could have wished for. Throw in a gaggle of cousins and second cousins who all lived within an hour's drive and they'd not been short of familial ties and affection. Still, it was clear they'd wondered about his family and it pained him now that they'd clearly felt unable to ask him about it. How much courage had it taken for them to ask him for what he should have done for them years before?

Too much.

Well, there was no point in lying there worrying about it, all he could do was try and smooth the way and make the rest of the introductions as easy as possible. Which meant getting his arse in gear and facing Zap and then Ziggy. Climbing out of bed, he gathered the clean T-shirt and underwear from where he'd left them out the previous night and headed towards his bathroom. Showered and dressed, he entered the sitting room to find he was the first one up. He poked his head around Avery's door, and was surprised to find Theo propped up against the headboard next to his sister, the soft blue glow from his phone illuminating his pale face. He looked knackered, poor kid, though he gave Dylan a thumbs up when he noticed his presence. Avery, on the other hand, was out like a light, her hands tucked under one cheek just the way she used to sleep when she was tiny. His heart felt too big for his chest as he watched her for a few moments before she rent the air with an enormous snore that made him grin and Theo roll his eyes. Dylan tilted his head, indicating for Theo to join him, and stepped back into the sitting room.

'She's been like that all night,' Theo grumbled as he padded in. 'She didn't want to sleep on her own so I agreed to stay with her.'

'Sorry, pal, you should've come and got me.' Perhaps he'd slept better than he'd thought.

'You were flat out too, snoring even louder.'

Oops. 'Look, it's still early so why don't you go to bed and see if you can grab a couple of hours' sleep? That art thing you guys want to do doesn't start until ten, so there's no rush.'

Theo nodded, then frowned. 'What about breakfast?'

With a smile, Dylan put an arm around his shoulders and steered his son towards his bedroom. 'Don't worry about it. I'll sort something out when you're ready. I've got connections with the staff, you know?'

Theo managed a sleepy chuckle. 'Good point.' He let Dylan pull back the pristine covers then settle them around his shoulders, and didn't even flinch in that too-grown-up-to-be-fussed-with way when Dylan stroked the messy fringe from his forehead. 'You don't mind being back here?' he murmured, already sounding more than half asleep.

'No, pal. I don't mind. I just wish we'd done it sooner.' Chancing his luck, Dylan leaned over and pressed a kiss to Theo's cheek. There was no response, the boy's breathing already slow and steady. Moving as silently as possible, Dylan tiptoed across the room and pulled the door closed behind him.

Showered and dressed, Dylan nipped back into his daughter's room to leave her a note letting her know that Theo was not to be disturbed and he was going for a walk. Downstairs, it was still pretty quiet. There was a sign on Reception with a number to call for assistance and a helpful arrow pointing towards a coffee machine in the lounge where they'd had drinks the day before. The chugging and hissing as it prepared his cappuccino seemed loud in the empty room. Dylan retrieved his takeaway cup, resisted the temptation of a basket of single-serve biscuits as he helped himself to a lid to secure his drink before heading back into Reception and out of the front door.

It was barely dawn. That strange grey haze that was neither

dark nor light and he was grateful for the low-level security lights marking out a footpath. He followed it around the side of the hall, admiring the clean lines of the stone façade where once he remembered a thick layer of ivy and flower beds choked with weeds. He could still remember his grandmother's tears at having to let the gardener go. She'd done her best to keep things going, but it had been an impossible task on her own. They'd have been able to help out more if their grandfather hadn't packed them all off to boarding school. How much had the fees cost, even back then? And for what – to make four children miserable and rack up more debt just to meet some kind of standard only the old man had cared about. Dylan had loved going to the village infant school, would have happily piled onto the diesel-belching double decker that took the local children to the middle school in town once he'd outgrown it, but he hadn't been given the option.

He shook his head as he took a sip of his coffee. Churning over that old ground wasn't going to get him in the right frame of mind for the day ahead. The past was the past and he needed to stop drawing comparisons and make the most of the opportunity to see what his siblings had done with the place in his absence.

The path followed the perimeter of the hall, eventually bringing him around to the back where the low walls and hedges of the formal gardens were dark shadows in the mist rising from the damp grass. Dylan's breath added another white cloud to the air and he nestled down into the collar of his jacket. It wasn't exactly freezing, but it also wasn't Florida. Resisting the urge to pull out his phone and check the temperature back home, he took another mouthful of coffee and continued his circuit around the hall.

The blinds were open in the orangery, a low light burning in one of the corners. Intrigued, Dylan cupped a hand to his eyes as he peered through the window. A figure was curled up in one of the wide armchairs, a blanket tucked around their knees as they read by the dim light of a lamp. Recognising Sadie from the previous day, Dylan rapped on the glass with a knuckle and raised a hand when she glanced up with a start. He was about to continue on his walk when she shifted, setting the blanket aside as she stood up and walked towards the patio-style doors. Dylan moved to stand opposite them, pointing upwards to show her where the bolts were as she tried the handle. She stretched up on tiptoe, the soft material of her cream jumper riding up to the waistband of her jeans as she reached to loosen the bolt. Dylan stepped aside as she pushed open the door. 'Good morning. I didn't mean to disturb you. I was just waving hello.'

'Oh, I thought you wanted to come in.' She glanced at the cup in his hand. 'Is that coffee? There's a kettle in my room but I can't be bothered to go back upstairs.'

'There's a machine in the lounge.' Dylan gestured with his now empty cup towards the other end of the room where a door led back to the main part of the building. 'I'm going to get myself a refill so I can get you something if you like?'

'If you don't mind? I'll take anything that's got caffeine in it.'

She had a gorgeous smile, he realised, one that lit her whole face. 'I can vouch for the cappuccino.'

'That would be lovely.'

His feet led him unerringly from the orangery, through the length of the picture gallery that ran like a spine through the centre of the hall. Generations of his ancestors bedecked the walls; marble statues of Greek gods and goddesses gathered in small groups here and there; replica Chinese vases decorated large plinths. Dylan knew they were replicas because his grandfather had flogged the originals at Christie's to pay down some of the crippling mortgages he'd taken out on the estate. Dylan didn't need to look up, he knew the faces staring down at him as well as he knew his own because this had been his playground once upon a time. Countless rainy hours he and his brothers and sister had spent playing hide and seek behind curtains and in shadowy alcoves.

He counted off the rooms in his head as he passed them. Ballroom on the right, his grandmother's private sitting room, the library, with his grandfather's study beyond that and the blue drawing room, which they'd been allowed to enter only on Sunday afternoon for high tea, on the left. Dylan found himself tugging at the neck of his jacket, an echo of the little boy he'd once been fiddling with an over-starched uncomfortable collar as he waited outside the door to be summoned. He quickened his pace and was soon back in the reception area. A young man was behind the desk and he smiled as he spotted Dylan. 'Good morning, Mr Travers. You're up and about early this morning. Is there anything I can get for you?'

'Morning. No, I'm fine, thanks. I'm just going to grab a couple of coffees from the lounge.'

'Of course. Breakfast starts in about half an hour and they're just setting up now. Continental and light bites in the lounge or there's a full hot service in the blue drawing room.'

'Thanks again.'

A couple of teenage girls dressed in black trousers and T-shirts looked up as he entered the lounge. 'Good morning, sir,' the girl nearest to the door said. 'Breakfast won't be long.'

'I'm just after a couple of coffees.' Dylan pointed towards the machine.

'Oh, I can do that for you,' she replied, setting aside a handful of cutlery. 'What would you like?'

'I can help myself,' he assured her, but she had already beat him to the machine and arguing would only make it awkward. It was clear Stevie wanted the staff to be attentive towards the guests so best to go with the flow. 'Two cappuccinos, then, please.'

As she turned to the machine, Dylan noticed the logo on the back of her T-shirt. It was a simple roundel design with two sprigs of greenery covered in dark purple berries framing the words Juniper Meadows. He'd seen the same branding on a few things, including the complimentary toiletries in the bathroom. The look might be a bit more casual than other hotels he'd stayed in, but Dylan liked it and he bet the staff did too, especially youngsters like the girl in front of him who was probably earning a bit extra for herself in the school holidays. She'd just finished putting lids on the drinks when her colleague arrived bearing a small basket filled with a selection of breakfast pastries and a couple of napkins. 'Something to tide you over until service starts,' she said with a grin.

'That's really kind of you.' Before Dylan could wonder how he was going to juggle two cups and the basket, the first girl had retrieved a small tray from a stack he hadn't previously noticed on the table. 'You two really are the dream team,' he said, earning a pair of bright smiles. 'Thank you.'

'Our pleasure. Are you sure I can't carry the tray for you?'

Dylan shook his head. 'You've done more than enough. Please don't let me keep you from setting up any longer.' With another pair of cheery smiles, the girls returned to their tasks and he beat a retreat back to the orangery.

He found Sadie back in her corner, legs once more tucked up under the blanket. 'I come bearing gifts,' he said with a grin as he set the tray down on the table in front of her. 'Courtesy of two very efficient young ladies in the lounge.'

'Oh, what an unexpected treat!' Sadie gestured to the chair that was set at right-angles to where she was seated. 'Are you going to join me, or carry on with your walk?'

Dylan glanced towards the windows. It was definitely lighter outside, but the mist rising from the ground had formed a chilly-looking blanket that made it impossible to see more than a couple of feet beyond the glass. 'I think I'll save my walk until later.' He tugged off his jacket and tossed it over a free seat before taking the one she'd offered him. 'We got interrupted last night,' he said as he reached for the two coffees and handed one to Sadie.

'You looked a bit busy.' Sadie glanced down at her cup and then back up to meet his eyes. 'I'm sorry if I was prying yesterday, about your family, I mean.'

Ah. He smiled. 'I think I was the one who raised the subject of families in general. How did you make the connection?'

'When Avery brought Hope over, I couldn't help but notice the resemblance. Again, I didn't mean to pry so I won't say anything.' She laughed. 'Not that I've anyone to say anything to.'

It was his turn to look away as he sought out the right words. 'I've been away a long time, but it's important to the kids to get to know my side of the family. They've a stack of relations on their mother's side, but they asked and so here we are.'

Sadie nodded. 'It's natural for them to be curious. You mentioned their mother is on her honeymoon. That can't be an easy thing to deal with.'

Dylan laughed. 'You'd be surprised how easy it's been, actually.'

Sadie's eyes widened. 'I'm sorry, I didn't mean to imply anything.'

Dylan held up his hand to forestall any further apology. 'A poor attempt at a joke on my part. Jen and I have been divorced for over a decade now. I'm very happy she's found someone and Eric is a good guy. I even gave Jen away at the wedding last week because her dad's not been so well.' He found his eyes straying to where her left hand clutched her coffee cup. There were no rings, but the pale indent at the base of her fourth finger said that hadn't always been the case. 'What about you? You mentioned your children and grandchildren...'

Sadie's mouth twisted in a not-quite smile. 'My ex-husband is in Spain shacked up with his much younger girlfriend.'

Unlike his situation, he got the impression this was a much more recent state of affairs. 'I'm sorry.'

She shrugged. 'There's really no need to be. I'm feeling less sorry about it with every day that passes.'

Dylan took the time to really look at her. She was an incredibly attractive woman and the few lines she had on her face suited her because they spoke of her ready smile. There was a quiet calmness about her, and she was such easy company he felt as if he'd known her for ages already. 'His loss, I reckon.'

She flicked startled eyes up at him, a faint hint of a blush colouring her cheek as an impish smile stretched wide. 'I reckon so too.'

Something warm and lazy stretched inside him. It had been a long time since a woman had smiled at him like that. Whoever her husband was, he really was an idiot. He was just reaching for the basket of pastries to offer her one when his phone beeped. 'Excuse me.' He pulled it out of his pocket and barely suppressed a grimace when he read the message from Avery. He put his phone away then stood. 'Our timing doesn't seem to be very good, does it? Avery's awake and I need to go and check on her.'

'No, of course, you must go.' Sadie smiled and raised her cup. 'Thank you again for the coffee... and the company.'

'Thank you for letting me disturb your peace and quiet. I hope we can catch up later?'

'I'd like that. Are you coming to the art class?'

Dylan shook his head, more than a little regretful. 'The kids will be there, but I need to go and catch up with my brothers. There's a reunion dinner planned for a bit later in the week but I don't want to wait until then to see them. Maybe we can have a drink before dinner, though?'

'That would be nice. I'll be in the lounge from around six-thirty.'

He bent to gather his coat, then pinched a pain au chocolat from the basket with a grin. 'I'll come and find you later.'

10

'And then he said, "I'll come and find you later,"' Sadie said to Charlie in hushed tones a few hours later. She was back in the corner of the orangery, having decided to let the more enthusiastic members of the group get stuck in. In the centre of the room, Rowena was guiding the group in charge of painting the impressive model of a tree that would form the heart of the centrepiece, while the rest of them focused on creating decorations to hang from its branches. A young man called Ben – another Travers, by the look of him – was showing half a dozen people how to paint some ceramic leaves he'd pre-made in his pottery. In another corner, Carrie-Ann, who had been introduced as a silversmith with her own workshop on the estate, was leading a group who were using stamps and templates to cut out and shape leaves from different types of metal.

Sadie's attention had been caught by a basket of yarn and several printouts with crochet patterns on them. It was something she hadn't done in ages, but the sight of them had conjured many happy hours she'd spent making blankets, jackets and hats, first for her own children, then more recently for her grandchildren.

When Charlie had seen her pick up one of the patterns she'd asked if Sadie would mind if she joined her and the pair of them were settled happily on the sofa. The mist had lifted, offering a lovely view out over the gardens, and Sadie had already promised herself a walk after lunch to explore them. She wasn't quite sure how they'd got onto the topic of Dylan, other than Sadie mentioning she'd woken early and their ending up having a cup of coffee together. Before she knew it, the words were out of her mouth.

'Sounds like you've got yourself a date,' Charlie replied with a grin as she worked her crochet hook through the next stitch of the leaf she was making.

Sadie yanked the yarn she was working, cursing under her breath at the tightness of the stitch. She removed her hook and unravelled it. 'A casual agreement to meet for a drink with a fellow guest is *not* a date.'

Charlie's face fell. 'It was a joke. I didn't mean to imply anything by it.'

Of course she hadn't, but Sadie hadn't been able to get it out of her mind. 'I was saying it more to remind myself than anything. It's been playing on me, wondering if I've given Dylan the wrong impression, but then I think I'm probably overthinking it.' *Well that stream of consciousness was going to reassure precisely no one.*

The smile Charlie sent her was sympathetic. 'I'm sure he was just being friendly. If you're both going to be here for the full fortnight then it'll be nice for you both to have some companionship, especially if his children want to do their own thing from time to time.'

Sadie nodded, feeling relieved. 'I'll have to scope out if there are any other single people staying and we can maybe set up an informal group for anyone who wants company.'

'That sounds like a plan, and you've got us three for the next couple of days as well.'

Sadie finished off her leaf, stitching the loose ends of the yarn into the back before snipping them off and smoothing it out. 'That's turned out quite well, I think.'

'It looks beautiful. I'm nearly done with this one.'

Sadie laughed as she picked up a different shade of yarn. 'I'm amazed at how quickly it's all come back to me.'

Charlie smiled. 'It's fun having someone to chat with while we work. I'm more used to being curled up on my sofa alone. I'm glad I decide to give the spa a miss.'

'Me too, because I'm enjoying your company,' Sadie said, her hands moving almost unconsciously as she crocheted the chain for her next leaf. 'Now, I was wondering how the three of you met.'

The rest of the morning passed in easy conversation. A few other guests drifted over from what they'd been doing to try their hand at crocheting, including Tara and Jon, a couple she guessed were around her age who were going to split their time between the estate and visiting their son and daughter-in-law and grand-children, who lived on one of the military bases in the area.

Sadie found she rather enjoyed her unofficial role as leader of the group, and she gained in confidence as the morning went on and they turned to her for help. It was also just nice to spend time getting to know people, something she hadn't done in a long time. Before Pete had left, she'd had little in the way of a social life. When they'd been younger, they'd been out all the time, but then the kids had come along and her friendship group had revolved around the school run, play dates and afterschool clubs. There'd still been work dinners with Pete, but those had stopped. Pete had claimed at the time that they were a chore and she'd done more than enough to support him over the years, but now she wondered if he hadn't wanted her around for more nefarious reasons. If she started worrying about how long and how often he might have been carrying on behind her back, she would drive herself up the wall. Best to focus on the gift of potential new friendships than keep harking back to the past.

By the time the session had ended, there was a good collection of leaves ready for decorating the tree. Ben had collected all the painted ones to take back to his kiln for glazing and firing. Rowena gathered them into a group around the main work area where a tray of Buck's fizz and sparkling fruit juices waited to reward them for their hard work.

'I hope you've all had fun this morning.' There was a general murmur of agreement, smiles and nods. Rowena smiled. 'Lovely. Now, the plan is to carry on over the next few mornings until we have everything complete. As ever, those sessions are entirely voluntary and you are welcome to drop in for an hour, stay for the whole thing or spend your time doing other things. The choice is entirely yours. Tomorrow we're going to start making the pears and there will be a variety of different techniques we'll be using, all of which are suitable for absolute beginners.' She pointed to Ben, who was lurking at the back of the group. 'Ben will be back to help with decorating, together with his partner, Amelia, and I'll be here, of course.'

Ben stepped forward with a shy smile. 'It's a bit more hands-on tomorrow, as we'll be sculpting the pears, not just decorating them. We'll be using modelling clay, and for those of you with fond memories of your school art classes, we're going to use papier mâché, although the recipe we use these days is a lot less messy.' A ripple of laughter greeted that pronouncement, though Sadie wasn't sure she fancied doing either because she didn't want to ruin her nails, apart from anything else.

Rowena drew their attention back to the front and gestured

towards Carrie-Ann. 'And you're going to be focused on making the partridge, isn't that right?'

Carrie-Ann nodded. 'I'll need a couple of volunteers and it'll be quite fiddly work so anyone who has tried their hand at jewellery-making at home, or is handy with a pair of pliers, let me know.' To Sadie's left, Jon raised his hand. 'I can do a couple of hours tomorrow before our family joins us at lunchtime.'

'Brilliant, thanks.' Carrie-Ann looked around. 'Anyone else?' A couple of other people volunteered and they finished their drinks and broke up for lunch.

'I'm not sure I fancy any of that,' Tara said, echoing Sadie's own thoughts as they placed their glasses on the tray.

Charlie shook her head. 'I want to explore the estate more tomorrow so I'll give it a miss. I had a lot of fun today, though. I'm going to find Anna and Jane, see how they got on in the spa.'

'Have a lovely afternoon, and thanks for your help. We wouldn't have achieved half of what we did without you,' Sadie told her.

'I'm not sure about that, but I did enjoy it. Might see you in the bar for a drink later?' Charlie raised her eyebrows, a knowing grin on her lips.

'I'll be there,' Sadie replied, refusing to rise to the bait.

'Are you coming through for lunch?' Tara asked her once the younger woman had left to find her friends. 'You're very welcome to join Jon and me.'

'That would be lovely, thank you.'

They were halfway to the door when Rowena swept up to them in a jangle of bracelets. 'Ah, my crochet queens! I was just having a look at what you've done this morning and I'm very impressed. I wasn't sure if we'd have any experienced hands but I've got the cutest template for a pear if you're not all stitched out?'

Sadie turned to Tara. 'What do you think? I haven't got anything planned for tomorrow, if you want to give it a go?' It was the sort of project she could carry around afterwards and do the odd extra hour here and there as the fancy took her.

Tara nodded. 'Why not? Jon'll be here anyway.'

Rowena beamed at them. 'Oh, you are brilliant. I'll bring it with me tomorrow and you can see what you think.'

11

As soon as he'd got the kids dropped off with Rowena ready to start the morning craft session, Dylan headed out. The early mist was beginning to lift, leaving a blanket of watery diamonds laid over the grass. It was fresh rather than chilly, so Dylan decided to walk across to the distillery where Rowena had said he would find Zap. Though there were signs of improvement and development everywhere, the layout of the estate was as he remembered it. As he followed the main road away from the hall, he found himself intrigued by odd structures scattered seemingly at random across the open land. Some kind of temporary trackway had been laid down and he realised he must be seeing part of the layout of the Christmas light trail. Several of the larger trees he passed had spotlights positioned at the base of their trunks, confirming his suspicions.

He wondered if the kids could be persuaded to check it out later. They were growing up so fast, and he wondered if they were already too old to embrace the magic of it. He wasn't too proud to beg, he found himself realising with a grin, because he would need the memories they made over the next couple of weeks to sustain him once they flew the nest. They were already starting to slip away from him, his allocated time with them spent either chauffeuring them from place to place, or in the kitchen preparing endless snacks and meals for the friends who descended like hungry locusts to take over the lounge with their gaming or movie marathons. Not that he minded, but this precious time where it was just the three of them wouldn't come around again. Which made it even more important that he put the past to rights so he could focus on what was most important, making sure Avery and Theo had the best holiday he could possibly give them.

When he reached The Old Stable Yard it was almost beyond recognition. The transformation was truly remarkable. The slightly tumbledown collection of buildings he remembered was now a vibrant collection of welcoming spaces. The stables themselves had been converted into a row of workshops. A newer building, constructed to blend sympathetically with the rest, housed a large café with bright welcoming windows full of sparkling lights. To the right stood the old carriage house, which according to the signage over the double-height wooden doors was the home of the Juniper Meadows distillery, and his destination.

The door to the distillery stood half open and Dylan took that as an invitation to poke his head around the edge and look in. The open-plan space was dominated by a pair of shiny stills with complicated pipework leading to and from each one. Brass plaques declared their names as William and Mary. Dylan couldn't help but smile, wondering if it was a brewing tradition or simply a quirk of his brother's. Gentle music filled the air, some sort of instrumental piece that reminded him of one of the soothing tracks he listened to when sleep eluded him. To the right of the room sat an array of workbenches covered in bottles and boxes and machines he had no idea the purpose of. On the left stood an impressive display filled with bottles. Dylan wandered closer and soon found himself lost in admiration of Zap's imagination because at least half of the flavour combinations the labels boasted of were things he would never have put together.

The sound of claws pit-patting across the tiled floor made Dylan turn and he bent to greet a scruffy little dog with hair around his jaw and chin that looked like an old man's unkempt beard, and bright, black button eyes. 'Hello, who are you, then?' Dylan asked, keeping his voice soft as he extended a hand for the dog to sniff.

'His name's Hercule. Hello, Dyl.'

A lump came to his throat at the sound of that old nickname and he wasn't sure if it was his age or the wellspring of emotion that caused his knees to wobble as he straightened up. 'Hello, Zap. You look good.'

'I look old,' his brother said with a laugh as he scrubbed a hand over the stubble on his cheeks. 'And I've got nearly as much grey in my beard as Hercule there.'

'You still look good,' Dylan insisted. Sure, there was lots of grey speckled through his brother's dark hair, but he was as broad and rangy as the fit young man he remembered from their youth.

Zap grinned. 'Nice twang you've developed there.'

It was Dylan's turn to laugh. Most of the people he met back home never mistook him for anything other than an Englishman, but being here had made it more obvious to his own ear that he'd picked up more than a touch of a Floridian drawl. 'You should hear the kids.'

'Ro' said they're a couple of smashers. I'd love to meet them.'

Dylan took a couple of steps closer. 'And you will, I promise. I needed it to be just you and me first.'

Zap nodded, his face creasing in pain. 'Dyl—'

'No.' Dylan held up a hand to stop the man who had always meant more to him than anyone else, well, until his children had come along, but there was no love in the world to match that. He closed the gap between them until they were less than a couple of feet apart. 'It's not on you to make this right, Zap, it's on me.'

Zap's head jerked up, his blue eyes flashing wide in surprise. 'What are you talking about? If I hadn't been so selfish, you never would've left.'

Dylan shook his head. 'That's not true. You kissing Ro' might have been the catalyst, but I was already desperately looking for a way out.'

'I don't believe that. For whatever reason, you're just trying to spare my feelings.'

Reaching out, Dylan gripped Zap's shoulder. 'There's a lot of stuff you don't know. Things were going badly for me at university and I was basically failing my course.' Dylan closed his eyes briefly as the ghosts of old shame tugged at him. 'I knew how much you guys needed me to step up and I knew I'd never be able to do it, so I took the easy way out.' Just as their father had always done.

Zap broke his hold but only so he could step in and put his arms around Dylan. 'You're my baby brother and you should've been able to talk to me about anything. The fact that you couldn't then, the fact it's so hard for you even now, means I failed you, Dyl, and for that I am eternally sorry.' Dylan couldn't speak, he just clung to the at once strange and yet achingly familiar strength of this man he had missed so much. Zap turned his head to kiss Dylan's cheek, his voice choked with tears as he spoke again. 'We never needed you to be anything other than happy. If we pressured you into trying to be something you're not, then that's on us, not you. We should've seen you were unhappy. *I* should've seen.'

Dylan loosened one hand only to wipe the tears from his eyes. 'I should've told you.' So many regrets. So many years convincing himself they were all better off without him. As he let the warmth and love seep into his bones, Dylan swore to himself he wouldn't waste one more minute of his life on being afraid of rejection.

* * *

If he'd thought his reunion with Ziggy might be easier, Dylan had a nasty shock when he knocked on the back door of the farm-house and opened it as Zap had instructed him to after dropping him off on the way to run an errand in the village. The laughter that had filled the room fell silent as three sets of eyes turned to look at him. At the head of the long, sturdy kitchen table sat the mirror image of the man who had just driven off, though this incarnation had shorter hair, and a smart shirt with sleeves rolled to the elbows instead of an old sweatshirt and jeans more hole than denim. To his right sat a woman Dylan found vaguely familiar and from the way the pair were holding hands he assumed this to be Daisy, an old girlfriend with whom Ziggy had recently reunited.

It was the woman at the other end of the table who commanded most of his attention, though. Smaller than he remembered, her crease-lined face was tanned to a shade that wouldn't look out of place on one of the Floridian matrons who lived in the apartment complexes a stone's throw from the port, packed suitcase always by the door ready to jump on one of the multitude of cruise ships that circulated in and out of Fort Laud-erdale every day. 'Hello, Mother, I heard you were back.' He tried and failed to keep the stiffness out of his voice. He'd known he would have to see her at some point, Monty too, but he'd wanted to do it on his own terms.

Alice Travers gave him a sad smile. 'I thought it was past time I reconnected with the family. Ziggy and the others have been gracious enough to let me stay for a few months.'

Dylan nodded, acutely conscious of Daisy trying to slip quietly from the room. He knew they were making the most awkward tableau, but things between him and his mother had always been strained. When he was little, he'd relied on his brothers and sister for affection, and not just because their parents had kept too unpredictable a timetable to be relied upon. Dylan had been a mistake, an unplanned surprise and not a pleasant one because Alice had almost died giving birth to him.

'How's Monty?'

'His usual bloody-minded self,' Ziggy said, rising from his chair and coming around the table to greet him. 'Come here, you.'

Once again, Dylan found himself engulfed in that strange-familiar warmth of an embrace long missed. Ziggy's hands moved over his back, an unconscious soothing gesture that was second nature to the family peacemaker. 'It's good to see you,' Dylan murmured.

'It's good to have you home.' Ziggy released him and stepped back. 'How are the kids enjoying things?'

Dylan smiled. 'They're having fun. Ro' and Stevie are taking good care of them. They're at the decorating thing up at the hall.' He pulled his phone out and opened his photo app, scrolling through until he found the picture he'd taken of the pair of them at Jen's wedding. 'You can tell they're part of the family.'

Ziggy took the phone and laughed as he studied the image. 'I see what you mean. Avery is the spitting image of Hope at that age.' Ziggy spoke Avery's name as though speaking of someone well known and well loved, and not a stranger at all. 'Your Theo's a fine-looking lad, too,' he added as he handed back the phone.

'If he keeps growing, I think he'll be taller than all of us. They're looking forward to meeting everyone.'

'May I see?' Their mother's voice was tentative, a hint of something pleading in the question.

'Of course.' Sliding into the seat nearest her, Dylan handed her his phone.

Ziggy placed a hand on his shoulder, causing Dylan to look up at him. 'Cup of tea?'

'Yeah, that'd be good, thanks.'

As Ziggy crossed the kitchen to the kettle, Dylan once again appreciated the easy way his eldest brother took control of the situation. He, more than anyone, knew why things were difficult – after all he'd been the one to sit Dylan down when he was barely old enough to understand and tried to explain in as a kind a way as possible why their mother never hugged him and why their father could barely look at him. 'Mummy was very poorly when she had you and it made her very, very sad for a long time afterwards. Daddy took her away to help her get better. He was scared when she was so ill and seeing you reminds him of that, which upsets him all over again.'

Dylan looked at his mother as she zoomed in on the children's faces. Her expression was hard to read, but there was no mistaking that smile. 'There's loads of them on there. Feel free to look through,' he found himself offering.

She glanced up at him, a hunger so bright in her eyes it was almost painful. 'Are you sure you don't mind?'

Dylan shook his head. 'Not at all.'

They spent the next few minutes going through the ridiculous amount of photos he had on his phone of Theo at various sporting events, with his nose stuck in a book, shouting with glee as he punched the air after absolutely demolishing Dylan on one of his computer games. The next picture was one of Avery, delicate and graceful on the balance beam in gymnastics, the one after of her looking far too grown up for his liking in a pretty peach organza dress with a matching corsage on her wrist for her first school formal dance. The third was one of his personal favourites, Avery grinning around a mouthful of hotdog as she sat between her mother and Eric at a baseball game the five of them had gone to the previous summer.

'You have a beautiful family,' Alice said, when she finally dragged her eyes from the screen and up to his face. 'I'd love to meet them.' He could tell she was being completely sincere and he wondered again at her comment from earlier about trying to reconnect with the family.

'You'll be here for dinner on Sunday?'

Alice didn't answer immediately, glancing over at Ziggy instead. 'Of course she will,' Ziggy said, giving their mother a warm smile that said whatever issues his eldest brother might have had about being lumped with the responsibility of not just the estate but his siblings' welfare had been forgiven. 'Daisy and I are in charge of the cooking. We're going to make a couple of big pots of curry and loads of sides.'

'Sounds great. I'll pop into the village tomorrow and get some wine.' It felt like the least he could do.

Ziggy shook his head. 'Zap's in charge of the drinks and Ben and Amelia have said they're sorting out dessert so you don't need to bring anything other than yourself and the kids.'

Their mother rose from the table with a smile. 'I shall look forward to it, but in the meantime I'll leave the two of you to catch up.' She seemed to hesitate before reaching out a tentative hand to touch a finger to Dylan's cheek. He felt his breath catch because he could almost count the number of times she'd volunteered first contact between them. 'I'm glad you're back, Dylan, even if it's only for a little while, and thank you for sharing your photos of the children with me. I can't wait to meet them.'

'It was good to see you again, Mum.' Dylan was surprised to find the words were true and not just a polite effort on his part. 'Maybe we can do something, just you, me and the kids? The café over at The Old Stable Yard looks nice – perhaps we can have afternoon tea there one day?' He couldn't bring himself to include his father in the invitation, and it hadn't slipped his attention that his mother had made no mention of him either.

Her entire face lit up, as though he'd offered her something infinitely precious. 'Oh, that would be wonderful! Whatever day or time suits you, just let me know and I'll be there.' She was still beaming as she left the room and closed the door behind her.

'That was kind of you,' Ziggy said, coming to sit down, bringing with him a fresh round of drinks.

'It seemed like it was important to her, and if she wants to make the effort to get to know them then I'm not going to stand in the way.' His mother might not have been able to love him in the way a child deserved, but he wasn't that hurt little boy any more. She seemed eager to forge a bond with the children and, at the end of the day, they were what mattered.

Ziggy nodded. 'She's been trying really hard. I won't make excuses for what went on in the past, but it took a lot for her to stand up to Monty and insist on staying home for a while.'

'How long have they been back?'

'Since the spring. She'd been on at him for ages to visit and I think he broke her heart when she found out he was only coming home because he thought he'd found a way to sell the estate out from under us.' Ziggy's mouth twisted into a bitter grimace.

Dylan rocked back in his seat. 'Sell the estate? You can't be serious!'

Ziggy lifted his tea to his lips and blew across the hot surface before setting it back down with a sigh. 'Technically, it all belongs to him, but I'd have fought him tooth and nail if he'd tried to go ahead with it. I know he always hated the place, but I didn't think his desire for revenge over Grandfather would run so deep as to try and do a deal behind our backs. He only gave up on the idea when Mum threatened to leave him, and things are still pretty dicey between them. He's gone travelling a couple of times over the past few months, but she's stuck to her guns and stayed put. She won't stay in that camper van of theirs and he refuses to give it up so they're at something of an impasse.'

Dylan's head reeled as he tried to understand what Ziggy was telling him. In the end he latched onto the most trivial bit of information. 'You don't mean he's still got that same old VW van?' Unlike his brothers and sister, Dylan had never been sad when the rainbow-coloured vehicle had chugged off down the drive, taking their parents away for another of their trips to far-flung places. No one had ever admitted it but, after the initial tears, they had all been happier when their parents were away. Or perhaps it had just been him.

Ziggy smiled, but there was little warmth in it. 'The very same one. We've offered him use of one of the holiday lets, but Monty's as stubborn as ever. I'm amazed he's stayed as long as he has.'

'Will he be here for the dinner?'

His brother shook his head. 'No. My anger towards him is nothing compared to how Hope, Rhys and Ben feel about it. Rhys hasn't spoken a word to him. His partner, Tasha, got caught up in the whole mess and he nearly lost her over it. If Monty would apologise then it might go some way to thawing things between them, but you know what he's like.'

Dylan shot his brother a wry grin. 'Still no good at taking responsibility, I take it?'

'He's worse, if anything. I don't think Mum has it in her to actually divorce him after all the years she stood by him, but sometimes I think she's just waiting for him to leave and not come back.'

'You think that's likely?'

Ziggy shrugged. 'He doesn't seem interested in mending any fences. He spends more time down the pub than he does around here.'

'I saw him coming out of there when we arrived,' Dylan recalled. 'He was all smiles.'

'He always was better at getting on with strangers.' There was no bitterness in his brother's words, just a simple statement of fact.

Dylan reached across the table to grasp Ziggy's hand. 'We don't need him. We never did because we always had each other.' Until he'd chosen to walk away, that was. Perhaps he was more like their father than he liked to admit. It was an uncomfortable feeling.

Ziggy's grip tightened as their eyes locked. 'I'm not letting you go again, Dyl. My heart won't take it.'

12

The lounge was already busy when Sadie entered just after six-thirty. A fire crackled in the hearth and the lamps were turned low, creating a warm, intimate air. The brightest spot in the room was the bar, where white fairy lights twinkled and danced in ever-changing patterns in amongst the thick garland of fir branches that had been pinned along the top. Someone had been rear-ranging the furniture so the tables formed a long row down the middle of the room with the sofas and chairs surrounding them to make one big, sociable area. There were still a few quieter spots for couples who preferred their own company, but most people had joined the central group.

'Here, Sadie!' Tara waved from where she and Jon were sitting with half a dozen other people, including Dylan and his children.

Dylan came to meet her. 'I was hoping we'd have the chance to chat but seems like everyone had the same idea about having a drink.'

Sadie smiled. 'We'll have to work on that timing issue, won't we?'

'Definitely.' The way he said it made something warm bloom

inside her. Before she could process her reaction, he gestured for her to go ahead of him and they went to join the others. 'Have you had a good day? What can I get you to drink? We've got a couple of bottles of wine on the go, but I'll grab you something else if you'd prefer it?'

'Oh, white wine will be perfect as long as it's something vaguely dry, thank you. And I've had a lovely, lazy day, although I made a mistake of treating myself to a bath this afternoon and it was a struggle to get out!'

He laughed as he gestured towards the space next to where he'd been sitting, only taking his seat beside her once she'd settled. 'Theo ended up using my shower because Avery spent so long in the tub in the main bathroom. I had to threaten to go in and pull out the plug in the end.'

'There was loads of time,' Avery huffed from the other end of the sofa, not even looking up from her phone.

Dylan grinned, not looking the least bit put out at his daughter's grumpy response. 'I did it for your own good. You nearly had more wrinkles than me.' He turned to Sadie. 'White wine, you said?'

'Yes, please.' She accepted the glass he filled with a smile of thanks. 'How was your day?'

'Good. Lots of catching up.' There was a slight tightening around his eyes, but his smile seemed genuine.

She recalled that he had mentioned he was seeing his brothers and how long it had been since he was last home and decided not to pry further. 'Well, you missed out on all the arts and crafts fun.' She raised her glass towards where Tara and Jon were sitting opposite. 'Tara and I are now officially the crochet queens, aren't we?'

'We are indeed,' Tara replied, returning her toast. 'And Jon was telling me earlier how impressed he was with Theo's dexterity.'

The mention of his name caused Theo to raise his head, though he looked a little unfocused as he pulled out an earbud. 'Did somebody want something?'

Tara sent him an indulgent smile. 'We were just praising your artistic skills earlier. Go back to whatever you're watching. I didn't mean to disturb you.'

The boy smiled. 'It was fun today. I might come and hang out again for a couple of hours tomorrow.'

'You can help us with the partridge, if you like?' Jon offered. 'Your fingers are a lot more nimble than my old stubs.' He held up a hand to show a collection of nicks and scars accumulated over many years.

Theo nodded. 'That would be sick, thanks.' He popped his earbud back in and returned his attention to his screen.

'I guess that was a yes,' Jon said, with a slightly baffled expression, making them all laugh.

'I've given up trying to keep up with the current vernacular,' Dylan said. 'It's incomprehensible.'

'That's kind of the point, Dad,' Avery deadpanned.

'Our grandchildren need to come with a translation guide,' Tara chipped in.

Sadie grinned. 'Mine haven't got to that stage yet, but, goodness, they are growing up fast!'

They spent the next few minutes chatting about ages, names and dispositions of their children and grandchildren and once again Sadie was struck by how long it had been since she'd spent time getting to know new people. She would have to make a concerted effort when she got back home to socialise a bit more, though she wasn't sure quite where to start with that.

A tall man with striking white hair walked into the bar and looked around. Sadie had noticed him the previous evening, but they hadn't crossed paths for her to speak to him yet. She watched him glance at their group but he looked away before she could catch his eye and headed to the bar. 'Do you know him?' Dylan asked.

'What? No, I haven't met him yet, but I saw him last night and I got the feeling he was on his own as well. Do you think we should ask him to join us?'

'I'll go and speak to him, shall I? That way he can have the option, as he might prefer to be on his own.' Dylan stood and retrieved the empty bottle of white wine from the cooler. 'Anyone else need a refill?' His smile widened. 'Ah, ladies, just in time. Red, white or something else?'

Sadie turned in her seat to see Charlie, Anna and Jane had just arrived. 'We were going to have negronis,' Anna said, 'but I'll get them.'

'My treat tonight,' Dylan said with another smile as he walked past them.

'Come and sit,' Sadie said, gesturing to one of the free sofas nearby. She leaned towards Jane, as she took the seat nearest to her. 'Dylan's on a mission to scope out the chap at the bar so getting in drinks is a good excuse. We think he might be on his own and we want to give him the chance to join us, but without him feeling pressured to join a big group of strangers.'

Jane shot a discreet glance towards the bar. 'That's a nice idea. We went out for a walk earlier and I think we passed him. If it was him then he was definitely by himself.'

They had their answer a few moments later when Dylan returned with the white-haired man. Both were smiling as Dylan directed the man to set a cocktail jug down on the table in front of Charlie, Anna and Jane. 'Everyone, this is Marcus. I've promised him that we're mostly harmless so he's agreed to join us.'

'Best behaviour, then!' Tara said with an impish grin. 'Lovely to meet you, Marcus. I'm Tara and this is my husband, Jon.'

Jon bobbed up from his seat and offered his hand to Marcus to shake. 'Good to meet you. Here, you can sit with us if Tara budges up a bit.'

After some shuffling around and a barrage of greetings, Marcus settled on the sofa opposite Sadie. 'I am hopeless with names, I'm afraid, but I shall do my best.'

'It's always harder when faced with a big group at once,' Sadie said, giving him a sympathetic smile. 'How long are you staying for?'

'I'm here for the full two weeks,' Marcus said. 'My wife died a couple of years ago and Christmas last year was so awful that I simply couldn't face being alone again.'

Sadie's heart went out to him. 'I'm so very sorry for your loss. This is the first Christmas I'll be by myself, though not for the same reasons. As nerve-wracking as it is meeting new people, I'm glad I decided to come here. I hope you'll find this year a little easier.'

Marcus smiled. 'So far so good.'

'There's a few of us on our own,' Dylan said to him. 'So there'll always be someone around for a bit of company when you want it.'

'Hey! What about us?' Avery piped up from beside him.

Leaning over, Dylan put an arm around her and kissed her cheek. 'You are the apple of my eye and one of the two best things in my life, but you don't want your old man hanging around you all the time, do you?'

Avery wrinkled her nose. 'Definitely not. I'm glad you've found some friends your own age to play with.' Sadie wasn't the only one who burst out laughing. Avery was smart as a whip and Sadie loved her spirit.

'Well, that's me told,' Dylan said with a rueful grin as he turned back to them. 'Looks like I'm free to join you guys whenever I like.'

'Maybe we can have a bit of a planning session each evening,' Sadie suggested. 'A check in on what plans we have for the following day and link up as things suit us.' When he nodded in agreement, she turned her attention back to Marcus. 'Do you have any particular interests?'

He shook his head. 'I think I'll just go with the flow. This is your first Christmas alone too, you said?'

Sadie cringed a little inside. She hadn't meant to blab about her situation to everyone, but she'd felt so sad for Marcus when he'd mentioned losing his wife she'd wanted him to know he wasn't the only one in the same boat. Oh well, not much she could do about it other than be straight with him. 'My ex is off sunning himself in Spain with my much younger replacement.' It was easier to be honest about her situation than she'd expected and her loss felt so much smaller in comparison to his. 'My children decided to treat me to a break here in lieu of presents and I have to say I think I've lucked out.'

Marcus nodded. 'I agree. I wasn't sure about the organised activity programme at first but then I decided it was the sort of thing I need to spur me into joining in. I've become something of a loner, I'm afraid, as my wife and I tended to do everything together. I knew I needed to do something to shake me out of the habit before I got too insular.'

'Well, I'm very glad you decided to come and I for one will be grateful of the company. I was only thinking to myself earlier how long it's been since I had to make the effort to make new friends. I'm going to have to sort myself out when I get back home, although I'm not really sure where to start.'

Marcus nodded. 'I know what you mean. Perhaps we should

do a bit of research while we're here and it might be motivation enough for us both to make an effort in the new year.'

'An accountability pact? That sounds like a very good idea, because, honestly, the thought of January looming is so depressing!'

'A pact it is.' Marcus raised his glass and Sadie leaned over to tap hers against it.

'I joined a thing called the University of the Third Age, or U3A,' Jon said, leaning in to join the conversation. 'I've gone part-time at work as a step towards retirement but, once I'd sorted out all the odd jobs, Tara got fed up of me moping around the house.'

'He was always under my feet,' Tara said with a laugh and a shake of her head. 'I was making up DIY projects just to give him something to do!'

Jon shrugged, though he was smiling as he did it. 'She's a great one for clubs and makes friends everywhere we go, but it's never been as easy for me. I had a couple of false starts at U3A and it took me a few attempts to find something that suited me, but I go to a tinkerers club once a month. We do everything from repairing old clocks to reviving our old woodworking skills from school. I meet up with a couple of the chaps from the group and we go walking once a week now too.'

'Walking to the nearest pub, usually,' Tara said, leaning in to give Jon a hug. 'Seriously though, it's been great to see Jon rediscovering hobbies he used to love.'

'That sounds like my sort of thing. Perhaps I can pick your brain some time before I go home and find out a bit more about it?' Marcus asked.

'Absolutely.' Jon's smile included Sadie. 'There's lots of women's groups and mixed activities, too. I can show you both how to navigate the website and find out what's in your area.'

'That would be lovely. The only thing I could think of was the

WI and my mother is a very vocal member of the local group. I get bossed around by her enough at home so I'm not keen on incorporating that into my social life.'

Jon grinned. 'We'll find you something that's mother-free, don't worry.'

They wandered into dinner about half an hour later where Sadie's good intentions to watch what she ate were immediately cast to the wind at the sight of a huge bubbling tray of lasagne sitting on the heated display. She added a couple of slices of garlic bread for good measure – something else she could indulge in now she didn't have to put up with Pete moaning about the smell. Being single had its advantages after all. She did resist dessert when the time came, but only because she didn't have room for even a tiny sliver of the tempting-looking opera cake. She was happy to sit and chat while others tucked in, though as the minutes ticked by she felt ever more full. Perhaps the garlic bread had been a step too far. By the time they left the dining room, all she wanted to do was go upstairs, take her trousers off and lie on the bed.

'Nightcap, anyone?' Jon asked as they paused in the hallway.

Dylan shook his head. 'The children want to speak to their mom, so I think we're going to call it a day.'

Sadie pressed a regretful hand to her full stomach. 'The only thing I'm going to drink is a big glug from a bottle of Gaviscon.'

Tara laughed. 'I know the feeling!' She turned to her husband. 'I'm going to go up and read, but you stay down here for a while if you want to, darling.'

'I'll join you for a coffee, Jon,' Marcus said. 'And maybe a small brandy.'

'Sounds good to me.' The pair headed towards the bar while the rest of them started for the stairs.

'What time are we crocheting tomorrow, Sadie?' Tara asked.

'I'm happy to start after breakfast because you and Jon have afternoon plans, I think you said?'

'Yes, that's right, we've got family visiting and we're going to explore the estate and take the children to see the lights as soon as it gets dark. The dinner isn't until seven-thirty so we'll be back well in time for that.'

'Can I try some crochet tomorrow?' Avery asked, her voice somewhat hesitant in comparison to the sparky energy Sadie was used to from her.

'Of course you can. Have you done it before?'

The young girl shook her head. 'I've seen it on TikTok but I don't have anyone to show me. My mom isn't into crafting and my grandmother only does cross stitch.'

'Well, I'll be happy to teach you the basics. Come and find me when you're ready in the morning and we'll make a start.' Sadie glanced over at Dylan. 'If that's all right with you?'

He nodded. 'Theo wants to do some stuff with Jon tomorrow morning, isn't that right?'

'Yeah, we're going to work with Carrie-Ann on making the partridge.'

'Great, well, I'll come along and find something to keep myself occupied as well.' Dylan gave Sadie a cheeky grin. 'I might even try my hand at crochet if you think this old dog can be taught a new trick or two.'

She laughed. 'We'll have to see how it goes. I'm good but I'm not a miracle worker.'

13

The next morning, Dylan woke to the sound of rain hammering against the window of his bedroom. Still groggy, he reached for his phone by the bed and squinted at the screen: 4.30 a.m. He dropped his head back against his pillow with a groan and closed his eyes. Maybe if he was lucky he'd be able to drift back to sleep before his brain caught up with his body. He was focusing on his breathing, letting the rhythm of his inhale and exhale lull him closer to that blissful darkness, when his bladder decided to make its presence felt. With another groan, he fumbled for the beside lamp then tossed back the covers.

With the most urgent of his morning needs met, he washed his hands and poured himself a glass of water to take back to bed. He really wanted a coffee but the kettle in the sitting room was louder than a jumbo jet taking off and he didn't want to disturb Theo and Avery. He did peek into their rooms to check on them and was pleased to see they were both fast asleep, though less pleased to see Theo's room bathed in a blue glow from the wall-mounted TV. Theo's game controller rested on the bed near his hand and Dylan wondered how late into the night he'd been messing around on the damn thing. Looked like some ground rules were in order. He retrieved the controller and turned off the TV before returning to his room. The controller went into the bottom drawer of his bedside cabinet, then he slid into the lingering cocoon of warmth beneath his covers. He fiddled with his phone to turn off the alarm he'd set out of habit for seven-thirty and then spotted a few new emails had come in overnight. *Probably nothing but best to check...* Fifteen minutes later, Dylan leaned over to yank the drawer back open and tossed his phone inside. Theo wasn't the only one who needed screen-time rules setting.

The rain against the window had settled from a hard drum to a gentle patter and Dylan rolled on his side. Who needed sleep app sounds, when he had the real thing? Within moments he was fast asleep.

The next time he awoke it was to the fantastic smell of coffee and the less fantastic sound of his children bickering. The rain had stopped at some point and a pale sliver of sunshine cast a line across the room through a gap in the curtains. The sounds of arguing grew louder and Dylan hauled himself up to a seated position, fortified himself with a swig of coffee from the mug one of the kids had left beside his bed and went to head off whatever had upset them before World War Three broke out. 'Just call me Mr United Nations,' he muttered to himself.

'I haven't got it!' Avery's voice had reached a pitch normally only dogs could hear. 'I haven't even been in your room!'

'Well, it was there last night and you were up before me. Who the hell else took it, a ghost?' Theo snapped.

'Enough.' They both whipped around to face him, Avery rosy-cheeked with anger and not a little distress, Theo, dull-eyed and sullen.

'Apologise to your sister,' Dylan demanded, holding Theo's

glare with a hard stare of his own. He looked exhausted and Dylan's anger roused anew at how long into the night he must've stayed up playing his games. 'And don't you ever let me catch you speaking to her with that tone again, or you and I are going to have a serious problem.'

'But—'

'I took your controller and I'm going to keep it because I've clearly shown too much trust in your ability to regulate yourself. What time were you up until?'

'I couldn't sleep,' Theo mumbled, but there was a hint of a blush on his pale face as he turned towards his sister. 'I'm sorry, Avie.'

'I told you I didn't have it,' Avery said, shooting a final baleful glare at her brother before coming over to cuddle against Dylan. 'He wouldn't listen to me, Dad.'

Dylan hugged her before stepping back so he could look down at her. 'Theo has apologised and you need to accept that with proper grace, okay?'

Her lips tightened in a brief signal of defiance before she sighed and nodded. 'Apology accepted.' She didn't turn and face her brother to say it, but it was good enough. Dylan kissed her forehead. 'That's my girl, and do I have you to thank for my coffee?'

She beamed up at him and nodded. 'I know how grumpy you are when you don't get enough caffeine.'

'Brat.' Dylan kissed her again then moved over to where Theo was standing hunched in on himself. 'Come here.' It took a few seconds for Theo's stiff frame to soften against him. 'I just don't want you spoiling your day by staying up so late. I know it's hard being away from all your mates, but I want us to make the most of our time together. I'm not saying you can't play your games or chat online, but we need to set some screen-time ground rules.

For me as well as you guys because I'm as guilty of having my phone glued to my hand. What do you say?'

Theo nodded. 'Okay. But I really couldn't sleep, well, at first, anyway.'

'It'll take a couple of days for the jet lag to settle down. Now let's get ourselves sorted out so we can get some breakfast. We'll chill out after lunch, maybe grab a nap if needed.' He raised his eyebrows at Theo in a meaningful look. 'We've got the murder-mystery dinner tonight and we'll all want to be fresh for that, won't we?'

The detente remained in place through breakfast and Dylan was pleased that neither of them were inclined to hold a grudge. It was a big change for them to be away from home at this time of year – even if it had been their choice. Perhaps he could do something nice for them? Their rooms were beautiful but a touch formal. A few decorations might make it more homely, and really help them get into the Christmas spirit. The presents he and Jen had ordered were still lurking in the bottom of his closet. Resolving to have a chat with Stevie about it, he escorted the kids to the orangery and got them settled. 'You changed your mind about the crochet, then?' Sadie asked him when he didn't sit down.

He laughed. 'Not a chance! I just need to track my sister down and sort something out and then I'll be back.'

The girl on Reception directed Dylan towards the ballroom. He walked through the door and stopped at the sight of the kind of organised chaos that spoke of a big event. A group of staff were busy dressing the tables for dinner, laying out fine china plates, silver cutlery and sparkling-clean wine glasses. A pair of florists were lifting centrepieces out of boxes, another of their team directing staff in estate-branded polo-shirts who were carrying a pair of larger floral displays to be placed on the elegant sideboards that also displayed some of the family's antique Chinese vases. Tasha and Lydia stood in front of one of the large windows, the latter holding a tablet, which they were both consulting. Behind them, a beautiful vista of rolling parkland with the dramatic stark winter branches of the woods beyond showed off the grounds at their very best. A pile of large cardboard boxes stood next to them. There was no sign of Stevie and, deciding it was best not to interrupt, Dylan took a step backwards and almost bumped into someone.

He turned with a start to find his niece smiling at him. 'Everything okay, Dylan?'

'Yes, all good, thanks. I was looking for your mum but I can see everyone is really busy at the moment so I'll catch up with her later.'

'She's around here somewhere – well, she was a minute ago.' Hope glanced around the room as though expecting Stevie to pop up from underneath one of the tables.

'It's fine, really. I need to talk to her about sorting out some decorations for the sitting room in our suite, but it can wait.'

'Decorations?'

Dylan nodded. 'A bit of tinsel and a few fairy lights. Something to make it feel a bit less like a hotel room and more homely for the kids.'

Hope frowned. 'A bit of tinsel? I'm sure we can do better than that. Wait here a minute.'

Before he could stop her, Hope was across the room and talking to Tasha. The other woman glanced across at Dylan, a smile breaking out on her face as she raised her hand to wave. He returned the greeting, feeling guilty for interrupting when they clearly had their hands full.

He felt even worse when they both approached him a few moments later. 'It really can wait until I catch up with Stevie.'

'She's with the actors who are helping out tonight,' Tasha said by way of greeting. 'They're staying overnight so she's just getting them settled in, but she won't be long.'

'Like I said to Hope just now, I can see you're all busy and it's nothing important.'

Tasha looked as unmoved by his protests as Hope. 'Nonsense. If it's about making Theo and Avery feel more at home then it's a priority. Things are quiet for me with the campsite closed for the winter so I'm seconded to the hotel team. I'm not familiar with all the rooms so let's nip upstairs so I can check out your suite.'

'I'll leave you both to it, then,' Hope said with a smile just as her phone began to ring. 'Excuse me, I need to get this.'

Dylan had no choice but to follow Tasha. 'How long have you been at Juniper Meadows?' he asked her as they climbed the winding staircase to the first floor.

'Since February. I came here to help sort out the campsite and then I met Rhys, and, well, one thing led to another.' The faint colour on her cheeks clashed prettily with the lovely red curls piled on top of her head in a messy ponytail. She paused at the top of the stairs. 'You haven't met him yet, have you?'

Dylan shook his head. 'No. I saw Ben and Amelia briefly when I collected the kids after the craft session yesterday, but Rhys and I haven't managed to cross paths yet. Hopefully I can remedy that tomorrow when we come for dinner at the farmhouse.'

'Ah, a legendary Travers family meal,' Tasha said with a grin. 'I hope you know what you've let yourself in for.'

Dylan thought about the chilly, formal dinners he'd had to endure as a child with his grandparents seated at either end of the long table and the four of them huddled together in the middle. No talking unless asked a direct question, no elbows on the table, no leaving until your plate was empty even when it was something he'd hated like liver sitting in a thick, congealing gravy. It was one rule he'd refused to implement with the children. They'd been asked to taste everything but if something was rejected then it didn't make a reappearance. It had led to a few arguments with Jen until he'd explained why and then she'd been onside.

Both the kids had been through phases of fussy eating, including a three-month period when Avery had refused to eat anything other than peanut-butter sandwiches and salted crackers, which had tested Dylan's vow not to pressure them over food to the limit. But they'd got through it, just as they'd got through everything else, and now, other than a handful of things that were definite dislikes, both of his children had a healthy relationship with food.

'I'm looking forward to it, especially since Ziggy said he's doing the cooking. I don't think he knew how to do much more than boil an egg before I left home.'

Tasha grinned. 'I can assure you his skills have vastly improved. One of the things I love about it here is that everyone pitches in and takes a turn. Plus it's always a lovely, relaxed atmosphere.'

There was something in the way she said it that made him guess perhaps that hadn't always been the case for her in the past and he wondered what her story was. 'Will you be here all over the Christmas period?'

'Yes. My family is coming to stay for a few days over the new year. Mum wanted to stay here at the hall, but my sister's kids are only small so it's not really suitable for them. With some delicate negotiations, my dad and I have persuaded her to try one of the eco-lodges, with Danni, Stu and the children in one next door.'

They were almost at the door to his suite and Dylan fumbled in his pocket for the key. 'I looked at booking one of them, but

Stevie was adamant we stay here and make the most of the festivities.'

'I can take you over to check them out if you like – maybe next time you visit you can try one then.' Tasha's face fell. 'Sorry, I know things are... umm, a bit delicate.' Her face flamed as bright as her hair when she realised what she'd said. 'Oh God, I'll just shut up and let's look at what we can sort out for your room.'

Dylan unlocked the door but didn't open it as he met Tasha's embarrassed gaze. 'Please don't feel bad. I'm the one who made things awkward by staying away for so long but I'm here to build bridges. I don't intend this to be my last visit home.'

Tasha heaved a sigh of relief. 'Oh, that is good news. Rhys has been *so* stressed out about you coming back, what with everything that happened with Rowena...' She wrinkled her nose as her words trailed off. 'I really need to shut up now.'

Dylan shoved the door open with a laugh. 'That is all water under the bridge, I promise. I'm not embarrassed about it so there's no reason for anyone else to be, even less reason to keep old secrets rattling around.'

Tasha nodded. 'In the spirit of openness I should let you know that I don't get on well with your father.'

Dylan put his hand on her shoulder and gave it a brief, comforting pat. 'Well, that only makes me like you more.'

After a quick tour of the suite and with Tasha promising she'd be able to sort something out before lunchtime, Dylan left his key with her and headed back to the orangery. He paused at the table where Theo, Jon and a blonde woman who introduced herself as Carrie-Ann were working on what looked like a tangle of old chicken wire to Dylan's untrained eye. They seemed to know what they were doing and, after a brief assurance from Theo that he was happy, Dylan made a beeline for the sofas in the corner where he and Sadie had enjoyed their early morning talk.

She was sitting in the corner, with Avery sitting cross-legged at a ninety-degree angle facing her, their heads bent so close together as to be almost touching. Not wanting to interrupt, Dylan smiled at Tara, who was sitting opposite them, working away with a long hooked needle, and sank down in a free chair that made up the group of seats. Sadie was speaking softly, her tone one of encouragement as she guided Avery's hands with her own. The pair of them were totally absorbed in what they were doing, and Dylan felt his heart swell at the obvious care and attention Sadie was giving to Avery. He'd noticed it about her the evening before, the way she was conscious of other people feeling included, the natural warmth that had drawn so many people into her orbit in a short space of time. She might have said it had been a while since she'd made new friends, but she seemed a natural at it as far as Dylan was concerned.

'That's it, yes. You're really getting the hang of it,' Sadie said. 'Do you want to try on your own now?'

Dylan watched as his daughter nodded shyly while Sadie sat back and let her have a go. She glanced up only long enough to notice him and acknowledge the finger he raised swiftly to his lips, not wanting to disturb Avery's concentration when she was intently focused. Sadie gave him the ghost of a wink before she turned her attention back to his daughter. Only once she'd completed the line of stitches she was working on did Avery lift her head with a satisfied laugh. 'I did it!'

'You certainly did. Let me see.' Sadie took the yarn and ran a finger over it. 'That's really good work. You've kept the tension even with pretty much every stitch. See how nicely they lie together. Do you want to carry on chaining or are you ready to try something new?'

'Can you show me another stitch?' As though finally

becoming aware of her surroundings again, Avery turned her head. 'Dad! How long have you been sitting there?'

'Long enough to see you're doing a grand job. Are you having fun?'

She grinned. 'Sadie is the *best* teacher!' The look she turned on the older woman was little shy of hero worship. 'You'll have to show Dad next.'

Dylan held his hands up in protest. 'I was only joking about that yesterday. I'm happy to watch.' He hadn't thought about it before now, but faced with the reality he realised he didn't want to look a fool in front of Sadie.

Avery's face fell. 'You promised, though.'

Damn, now he had the choice of looking like a fool or looking like the kind of man who let his children down. Neither was a tempting prospect, but Avery's feelings mattered much more than the prick of foolish pride. Dylan leaned forward to pat her leg. 'If it means that much to you then I'll give it a go, but don't be expecting much from my clumsy fingers. Don't worry about me, just focus on what you were doing. I'll wait until you've properly got the hang of it, and then I'll try, okay?'

She cast him a sceptical look. 'You'd better not wriggle out of it.'

Dylan set his features in a solemn expression and drew an exaggeratedly slow cross over his heart. 'I promise I'll give it a try.'

As he'd hoped, Avery let out a peal of laughter as she shook her head at his foolishness. With that mini crisis averted, he rose to his feet. 'Let me sort out some refreshments to keep us all going first.'

Dylan made his way over to the table laid out with drinks, treats and snacks. He returned shortly afterwards with a large jug of lemonade, four glasses and a plate of miniature mince pies, little squares of icing-topped Christmas cake and Battenberg bites balanced on a tray. 'Here we are.' He set the tray down.

'Sit here, Dad,' Avery said, jumping up from the sofa and pointing at her vacant seat. 'I'm ready to work on my own and you'll need Sadie to show you what to do. First I'm going to go and show Theo what I've done so far.' She headed off, her tiny patch of crochet work clutched in her hands as if it were the finest treasure.

Dylan glanced at Sadie for permission and only sat beside her when she nodded. 'Thank you for doing this,' he said as she reached for a ball of pale green yarn and a shiny metallic hook. 'I'm not sure I'll be much good, though.'

'You won't know until you try,' she said with a smile before lowering her voice to murmur. 'The important thing is that you are willing to give it a go for Avery's sake.'

They both looked over to where Avery was laughing as Theo held her little scrap of crochet up to the light and made a show of examining it. 'I thought I'd get you both making simple blanket squares,' Sadie said in her normal tone, drawing his attention back. 'They're a great beginner's practice tool and if it's something Avery wants to continue with after you go home it'll be a nice project she can expand into a throw for the end of her bed, or even a full size blanket if she really catches the bug.'

'I'm in your capable hands,' Dylan said with a smile. 'And the easier the better for me.' For the next few minutes he gave Sadie his full attention as she showed him how to get started. The terminology was a little confusing at first, but she made it look easy. Too easy, he discovered when she persuaded him to have a go for himself. The hook felt too small for his hands, the chain of stitches too narrow for him to feed the yarn through. Delicate fingers enclosed his own as Sadie stopped him from poking the hook through the wrong bit.

'Here,' she said in that same gently encouraging voice she'd used on Avery. 'Now turn the hook so it's facing away and loop the yarn like I showed you. That's it, now guide it back through. Lovely.' Her fingers brushed over the backs of his hands. 'Try not to grip so tight and you'll find it easier. Much better.'

Her tone was so soothing he felt some of the tension in his arms release and, as she'd said it would, it made his movements less stiff and awkward. 'You have such a great voice, I could listen to you talk for hours.'

14

There was something about his words that brought Sadie out of teaching mode and into the reality of the situation. She was sitting thigh to thigh all but holding hands with one of the most handsome men she had ever met in her life. And now he was telling her he liked her voice so much he could listen to her for hours! Though her insides tingled with an anticipation she hadn't felt in a long time, Sadie forced herself to laugh it off. 'You need to get your hearing checked, then.'

Dylan raised his head, his serious blue eyes seeming to see more deeply inside her than was comfortable. 'Whoever taught you to deflect a compliment like that needs to go to hell.'

Sadie swallowed around a sudden lump in her throat. 'It's been a while. I'd rather forgotten what one was like.'

'Well, I'll just have to keep going until you're used to it, because I can think of at least a dozen off the top of my head.'

She gave his hands a playful nudge. 'Now you're just being kind and that's worse for my poor ego than no compliments at all.'

'One, your voice is like warm silk.' Dylan continued as though she hadn't spoken. Sadie felt her cheeks heat. 'Two, you have the prettiest flecks of green in amongst the brown of your eyes.'

'Behave yourself,' she muttered. 'Stop looking at me and focus on your crochet.'

Dylan held her gaze for a moment longer then dipped his head back to the small patch of yarn between them. 'Three,' he murmured, his voice barely more than a whisper. 'You have lovely, soft hands and a gentle touch.' Sadie went to pull her hands away but quick as a flash he switched their position so his hands were on top of hers. His thumb grazed over the tops of her knuckles. 'Four, you have a wonderful awareness of other people and do your best to put them at ease.'

'A lesson you might try and learn some time,' Sadie grumbled beneath her breath, even as she found herself leaning closer in hopes of catching the next compliment on his list.

'Five, you're funny as hell. Six, you're patient and kind and a very good teacher.'

'Now you're cheating and rolling several different compliments into one,' she protested with a half-laugh.

'Seven,' Dylan said in a firm tone that no respectable woman wanted to have addressed to her.

Maybe she wasn't as respectable as she thought after all because her mind suddenly conjured an image of when she might like to hear him use it again. There must be something in the water because the idea of ever letting Pete boss her around in bed would've been about as sexy as getting trussed up in some of that awful underwear he'd given her as a particularly disastrous birthday present. A gift more for him than for her.

'Hey, where did you go?' Dylan stroked her knuckles again, startling her back into the present.

Not wanting to tell him she'd been thinking about a red lace thong and suspender set, Sadie shook her head. 'Nowhere, I'm right here.'

'Seven,' he repeated in a thankfully more normal tone. 'You've been wonderful to both my children, especially Avery. I know she gives a lot of attitude, but she's quite shy underneath and her confidence is easily knocked.'

'She's a sweetheart,' Sadie said, a note of desperation creeping into her voice. 'They're both absolutely delightful.' Really, she needed to put a stop to this before she gave in to some of the very alarming and quite inappropriate thoughts she was starting to have about this man. Time to turn the tables. 'They must get it from you.'

Dylan kept his head down but lifted his eyes up to meet hers, a wicked grin that did nothing to calm the growing turmoil inside her stretched across his mouth. 'Thank you. See how easy it is to accept a compliment.'

She wanted to poke her tongue out at him, the bloody infuriating, lovely man. 'Touché.' She freed his grip and pushed the yarn and hook back into his hands. 'Enough of that now, you've got chains to make.'

'We'll pick this conversation up later, because I have five more to share with you,' Dylan said, easing back into the corner of the sofa and making space between them.

Not sure if that was a promise or a threat, Sadie made herself busy, picking up her own neglected piece of work and forcing herself to concentrate on the next couple of rows.

Avery returned and wanted to see how Dylan was getting on and Sadie was glad of the interruption as it gave her time to pull herself together. Only once her heart had stopped pounding and she'd completed half a dozen rows of stitches did she risk a look up.

Dylan and Avery had returned to their own projects, both

transfixed with what they were doing, but Tara was watching her with what could only be described as an amused expression. 'Everything all right?' Sadie asked, putting just a hint of challenge in her tone.

'Everything's fine with me,' Tara replied, her smile only growing wider. 'But you look a little warm, Sadie, shall I pour you a drink?'

'That would be lovely, thank you.' Again Sadie had to fight the urge to poke her tongue out. Leaning forward, Sadie helped herself to a piece of cake, popping it in her mouth before she could make a fool of herself. *Honestly, what was the matter with her?*

By the time they were ready to stop for lunch, Sadie was stitching a little face onto her first crocheted pear. Tara was more than halfway through the one she was making and Dylan had a huge length of chain stitches strung together. Avery had most of a wonky square made and looked down-hearted about it until Sadie assured her that a lot of people spent days, even weeks, just trying to get to grips with a basic chain stitch. They were just finishing the tidying up when Charlie, Anna and Jane walked into the orangery, their cheeks red and their eyes bright. 'It's glorious out there,' Charlie said, nodding towards the clear blue sky through the window.

'But absolutely freezing,' Jane added, lifting her hands to cover her face. 'I thought my nose was going to drop off at one point.'

'Did you go far?' Sadie asked.

Anna nodded. 'We found a walking trail through the woods and, according to my phone, we've walked about six and a half kilometres.'

'Wow, that's good going. You'll have earned your dessert tonight at dinner.'

Anna laughed. 'Speaking of dinner, have you seen the costumes?'

'Costumes? What are you talking about?'

'They must mean for the actors,' Dylan chipped in. 'I was talking to Tasha earlier and she said they've got some joining us tonight to play various parts and lead the mystery storyline.'

'Oh, okay. I've not been to one of these things before so I've no idea how it works,' Sadie said.

'There are costumes for us as well,' Anna said, her tone clearly saying she was excited about the prospect of dressing up. 'I haven't cosplayed in ages. It'll be fun.'

'Cos-what?' Sadie was grateful Dylan was as bemused as she was because she felt a little less like a dinosaur.

'Cosplay,' Anna repeated. 'You know, when you dress up as a character from a film or a book.' When they both stared blankly at her, she laughed. 'It's a thing, honestly, and there's loads of different communities that meet up at conventions and stuff. That's how the three of us met – we all love the same fantasy book series.'

'I know my son's been to a couple of conventions, but he never mentioned anything about dressing up.'

'Maybe you should ask him,' Anna said with a grin.

'I might just do that!' Sadie laughed, though she couldn't help feeling a bit apprehensive. She'd never been one to put herself on show. Even walking up the aisle on her wedding day had been an excruciating experience because everyone had been staring at her and Sadie had hated the fussy mountain of lace and frills her mother had bullied her into choosing. 'Is everyone going to dress up tonight?'

'I want to!' Avery exclaimed, tugging at Dylan's arm. 'Can we, Dad?'

Dylan shrugged. 'I don't see why not.' He turned to Anna. 'Where did you find out about the costumes?'

'They've put some rails up in the lounge and there's a table full of matching accessories to choose from as well. The theme is The Roaring Twenties, *The Great Gatsby* and that sort of thing.'

Sadie pulled a face. 'I'm not sure I'll make a very good flapper girl.' The only things about her that flapped these days were her bingo wings, no matter how many sets of toning exercises she did.

Charlie came over and linked her arm through Sadie's. 'I'm going full flapper – the more sequins, the better, but there's lots of other styles there too. Think *Downtown Abbey* and those elegant dinner gowns. Come on, at least come and have a look.'

Sadie hesitated, then gave in with a laugh. 'I did promise myself I was going to try new things while I'm here.'

'That's the spirit! And remember, what happens at Juniper Meadows, stays at Juniper Meadows.'

When they entered the lounge there were already a number of other guests browsing through the rails. Hope, Tasha and Lydia were there helping match accessories to costumes. As Charlie had promised, there was a vast array of choice, including a selection of tweed suits and waistcoats with flat caps for anyone who fancied themselves a Peaky Blinder. Charlie made a beeline for a silver sheath dress that dripped with so many strands of crystals it shimmered with a life of its own. It would look stunning with her chestnut curls and a feathered headdress.

Sadie sorted through the first rail, not feeling much enthusiasm for anything she saw. The dresses were all beautifully crafted but she couldn't help zeroing in on the flaws, or rather her own flaws that would be put on display by the short sleeves and mid-calf hemlines. Oh, for a shapely ankle and not a pair of legs that seemed to go straight down from her knees to her feet without any noticeable definition. She slid the last hanger along with a sigh. Maybe dressing up wasn't for her.

Lydia must have spotted her looking downcast because she bore down on Sadie with a brisk smile. 'Everything all right?'

Sadie took in her gleaming, glossy mane of hair pulled back from her face with a black Alice band and found herself wondering if it was her trademark look. Her trim figure was shown off to perfection by a pair of cream trousers and a café-au-lait-coloured silk blouse with a pussycat bow at the neck. She looked every inch the country lady and her voice held the plummy tones of the very well brought-up. Sadie did her best to give her a smile, feeling her confidence melt away in the face of such breezy self-assurance. 'I'm just not sure this is for me, that's all.'

Lydia frowned at the rail of sequins and glitter. 'Hmm, no, that won't do at all.' Before Sadie could crumple in on herself, Lydia took her hand and led her across to another rail. 'Now then,' she said, thumbing through the dresses with a brisk efficiency. 'No, not plum, you'll look ghastly and washed out. I would say black is always a winner, but it can be so dreary when everyone looks like a flock of crows.'

'Have you thought about being a motivational trainer, Lyds?' a warm, laughing voice said behind them. Sadie turned to find Tasha smiling sympathetically at her.

'Why would I want to do that when I am already the best party-planner-slash-events-manager in the county, thanks to you?' Lydia said, not even lifting her eyes from the rail.

Tasha rolled her eyes and winked at Sadie. 'If I could bottle Lydia's confidence, I'd make a fortune.'

'I'd take some, for sure.'

'Ah HA!' Lydia exclaimed, turning to face them both with a grin of triumph. 'I knew I'd seen the perfect thing for you.' She thrust a hanger towards Tasha. 'Hold onto this a minute, there's a headband and a fan that'll work perfectly.' Lydia strode off without a backward glance.

'She's only trying to help,' Tasha reassured Sadie. 'Please don't feel forced into wearing something you don't want to.'

Sadie nodded, unable to speak as she took in the dress Tasha was holding. It was floor length, with long sleeves, both already big wins in Sadie's eyes. But it was the colour that really spoke to her. The floaty dress was a rich aquamarine with a matching lacy overlay. The sleeves were also lace and, when Tasha lifted one up, Sadie gasped in delight at the extra swathes of material that connected the sleeves to the side of the dress. The neckline was cut high enough it would sit across her collarbones and the slight hourglass shape would flatter her curves. 'It's beautiful.'

'It is rather special,' Tasha agreed. 'And the colour will work well with your hair and eyes.'

Sadie raised a hand to her hair. 'I don't know what I'm going to do about this nest. I meant to have it cut before I came but I never got around to it.'

'There's a salon in the spa. Let me see if I can make you an appointment.' Tasha hooked the dress on the end of the rail, pulled out her phone and began to scroll. 'We have a slot at two if you want it. And one of our beauticians is free so you could go the whole hog and treat yourself to a mani-pedi at the same time.'

'I have been meaning to get it done,' Sadie mused. 'I suppose I could call it a Christmas present to myself.'

'Sounds like a plan.' Tasha grinned then tapped on her phone a couple of times. 'Right, that's you all booked in. Shall we go and find Lydia and see what she's found to go with this beautiful dress?'

'I'm in your capable hands.'

15

Dylan and the kids returned to their room after lunch to find that Tasha had worked a minor miracle. The furniture in the sitting room had been rearranged to make room for a beautifully decorated Christmas tree that now stood in front of the window. The red and gold theme of the decorations had been carried on throughout the room with new cushions and throws on the sofa and armchairs. Red bows and golden lights weaved through a garland draped over the mantelpiece. Three stockings hung in front of the fireplace, and a large golden bowl sat on the grate full of baubles, pine cones and gold fairy lights.

'Who did this?' Avery gasped.

'Do you like it?' Dylan asked, feeling a little overwhelmed by the transformation. Whatever they were paying Tasha it wasn't enough because she'd wrought a miracle in a few short hours. 'I figured since we'd be waking up here on Christmas morning, it would be nice to get more into the spirit of things.'

'I love it!' Avery ran over and hugged him one-armed, the hanger holding her party costume held out of the way so they didn't crush it. 'It's perfect.'

Dylan glanced over at Theo to find his son beaming. 'It's really great, Dad.'

'Now we have a tree, I suppose we'll need to get some presents to go under it,' Dylan mused. 'Perhaps one of you should check the closet in my room.'

Avery thrust her costume into his hands with a squeal and dashed towards his bedroom. Dylan grinned at Theo and tilted his head towards the master bedroom. 'She's going to need help.'

Letting out an excited whoop, Theo draped his costume over the back of the sofa and ran to meet Avery as she struggled back into the room clutching several bulky carrier bags.

Once the kids had finished placing their presents under the tree, Dylan held out the costume he was still holding for Avery. 'You might want to hang that up so the fringe doesn't get messed up.' After much consideration and mind-changing, she'd opted for a pretty emerald-green flapper-style dress with a long fringe that took the short skirt to almost knee length. She'd also chosen one of the feathered headdresses and enough bangles for her wrists that Dylan's pockets were weighed down with them. She had black tights and a pair of ballet pumps, which would work well with it. Dylan had chosen a navy velvet tuxedo jacket so dark it was almost black until seen against the trousers, with a strip of satin running the length of the outside seam on each leg, a crisp white shirt and a black bow tie – a proper one, not pre-tied. He had his dress shoes with him as he'd brought a suit to wear on Christmas Day. Theo had opted for the *Peaky Blinders* look with trousers and a matching waistcoat and a flat cap. He'd been surprisingly enthusiastic about the idea of dressing up and Dylan had been happy to go along with it once he'd seen how excited the kids both were about it.

'Okay, Dad.' Avery came over and hugged him. 'Thanks for the gifts and the decorations, oh and, well, everything!'

Laughing, he bent to kiss the top of her head. 'It's my absolute pleasure. You'll have to remember to thank your mom later because she helped me choose what to buy.'

'Thank goodness for that!' Avery grabbed her costume and ran towards her room, giggling.

'Cheeky brat!'

'I'll go and hang mine up too,' Theo said, pausing beside him. 'You didn't need to go to all this trouble, Dad.'

'It's never any trouble to do something for you and your sister. Let's hang our stuff up and then we can chill out for a bit. Don't forget it's probably going to be a late night tonight.'

Avery appeared in her doorway. 'Can I still go and get ready with Charlie?' The three younger women had offered to take her under their wing and help with her hair and make-up.

'Of course you can, but try and have a bit of a nap first, okay? Charlie took your number, so I'm sure she'll text later when they're ready to start.' It was a relief to Dylan, to be honest, as although he'd mastered the pigtails and plaits Avery had needed for school when she was little, anything more complicated than that was firmly in Jen's realm of expertise. 'I'll send your mom a message while you're resting and see if we can fix up a time for you to chat to her before we go to dinner. You'll want to show her your costume once you're all dolled up.'

Avery grinned. 'Thanks, Dad, but don't tell her we're dressing up. I want to surprise her when we call!'

'I won't say a word, I promise.'

With both kids settled, Dylan escaped to his own room. Having hung up his outfit, he flipped off the main light, pulled the curtains and took off his jeans, shoes and socks before sliding under the quilt. Hawaii was ten hours behind but they weren't due downstairs until 7 p.m. so he sent Jen a quick message for when she woke up, saying the kids would like to arrange a chat around 8.30 a.m. her time. Setting his phone aside, Dylan picked up his book and managed about half a dozen pages before he realised he'd read the same paragraph three times and still wasn't following the plot.

Replacing his book on the nightstand, Dylan reached for the lamp and turned it off, casting the room into a shadowy gloom, and let his mind wander. It should be a fun evening, especially if everyone got into the spirit of things and dressed up. He found himself thinking about Sadie. He'd lost track of her in the busy lounge and she hadn't been in the dining room when they'd stopped to grab a light lunch. Would she be dressing up tonight? So far he'd seen her only in jeans or trousers and a variety of mostly shapeless tops. She didn't seem to go in for make-up, which was fine by him, but he couldn't help wondering what she'd look like all done up to the nines.

The way she'd deflected his compliment earlier had sparked something protective inside him, because it had been clear from the way she'd immediately resorted to self-deprecation that she was either unused to them or had been made to feel actively uncomfortable about accepting praise. He hadn't missed the comment she'd made the previous evening about wanting to avoid her mother and he wondered if that was the root of it. Having an asshole for a husband who'd junked her for a younger model couldn't have helped her confidence either. What an idiot the man must be, chasing some stupid fantasy of his own youth. Well, his loss might just be Dylan's gain. It had been a long time since Dylan had felt this kind of attraction and he couldn't deny being eager to spend more time with her.

Hopefully, she was going to enter into the spirit of the evening, which would give him the excuse to dish out a compliment or two more and maybe earn him another one of those beautiful smiles that warmed him from the inside out. He rolled

onto his side, a hint of a smile playing about his lips as he drifted
off to sleep.

* * *

The nap had left them all refreshed and while Avery headed off
with Charlie, who'd very kindly come to collect her, Dylan and
Theo had a bit of guy time sprawled side by side on Theo's bed
shooting zombies in one of his computer games. They came to an
agreement over screen time and Dylan decided he trusted Theo
enough to let him keep the controller in his room. By the time the
party finished tonight they'd hopefully all have burned off
enough energy to go straight to sleep afterwards and their body
clocks would finally be over the last of the jet lag.

Showered and dressed apart from his jacket, which was
folded over the back of the sofa, Dylan waited for Theo to emerge
from his room, which he did a few minutes later holding his own
bow tie in one hand. 'Can you help me with this stupid thing?'

With a laugh, Dylan rose and crossed the room. Taking the
tie, he looped it around his son's neck and then realised he didn't
know how to do it backwards. 'Come with me into the bathroom.'

They stood in front of the mirror with Dylan reaching around
Theo from behind, watching their reflections in the mirror.
'You're getting almost too tall for me to do this,' he said with a wry
grin. 'What happened to my little lad?'

Theo blushed, a shy smile on his face as he replied, 'I'm still
here, Dad.'

With patient hands, Dylan showed Theo how to tie it. 'I
remember when my brother taught me how to do this.'

'Not your dad?' Theo's eyes were curious as they met his in
the mirror.

'No. He wasn't around much when I was growing up. He never

got on with his father – your great-grandfather – so he stayed away from the estate a lot.'

'So your grandfather raised you, instead?'

It was no wonder the boy had questions, given how little information he'd shared with them about his past. 'He laid down a lot of rules we had to live by, but we were raised mostly by our grandmother, who was kind in her own way but not very tolerant of noisy children charging about the place. I was left to my own devices and it was my brothers and sister who had most of the care of me together with the few servants my grandfather could still afford to pay.'

'Is that why you stayed away for so long?'

Dylan pulled the two loops of the bow at his son's neck, teasing them straight until they matched each other, then stepped away. 'Juniper Meadows doesn't hold a whole lot of happy memories for me, and once I had a new life with your mother and then with the two of you, there was never any reason to come back. I had everything I needed.'

'Are you angry that we wanted to come here?' Theo's final question was very quiet.

Dylan stepped forward and gathered him in his arms. 'No, not at all. I'm glad you wanted to know where you came from, and don't let my experiences taint yours. Your uncles and your aunt are wonderful people, your cousins too from what I've seen of them so far. I still have some fences to mend, and in order to do that I've realised I have to let a few things go. It's time to forget about the past and focus on the future and that's what my aim is while we are here, starting with dinner with everyone tomorrow.' He pressed a kiss to Theo's cheek. 'You and your sister have given me a chance to get my family back and I'm not going to squander that with old memories that don't matter any more.'

There was a knock on the suite door and they broke apart so

Dylan could go and answer it. Avery stood there, almost all traces of the little girl hidden beneath a layer of dark kohl eyeliner and bright red lipstick. Her hair had been coaxed into thick waves held back from her forehead by the sparkling feathered headband. Dylan had to swallow for a moment before setting his features in a mock frown. 'How can I help you? I think you might have the wrong room.'

Avery broke into giggles, the little girl still there behind the sophisticated mask. 'It's me, Dad!'

'Oh, of course it is! I almost didn't recognise you, you look so grown up. Did you have fun?'

Avery nodded. 'It was brilliant. Charlie even found some varnish to match my dress.' She held out her hands to display glittering green nails.

'They look fantastic. And did you behave yourself?' He raised his gaze to where Charlie and her friends were watching, indulgent smiles on their faces.

'She was a delight,' Charlie said, stepping forward. The movement made her silver dress shimmer and catch the light, casting dazzling sparkles everywhere. 'We had a great time.'

'Well, thank you for taking such good care of her, and I must say you all look wonderful.' He glanced back down at Avery and nodded to the open door behind him. 'Why don't you and Theo see if you can get hold of your mom?'

'Okay.' She turned to the others. 'Thank you!'

'Our pleasure,' Anna said, a vision in a red silk drop-waisted dress paired with some sort of cape around her shoulders studded with beads of jet. 'We're going to go down to the bar, because we promised to meet Sadie.' She looped arms with Jane, who had eschewed a dress for a pair of wide-legged striped trousers, a white shirt, thick braces and a trilby tilted at an angle that could only be described as jaunty. 'We'll save seats for you guys, okay?' Anna continued as she offered her other arm to Charlie.

'Sounds good. We won't be far behind you.' He watched the three women head towards the stairs before he returned to the suite and closed the door.

Bright laughter greeted him as Avery twirled in front of the tablet Theo was holding up. 'You look gorgeous, baby girl,' Jen said from the screen. 'So beautiful! Eric, come and see!'

Her image on the screen shifted slightly so Eric could peer through the camera. 'Wow, Avery, look at you, sweetheart!'

Dylan moved closer so he was also in their eyeline. 'Hey, guys, sorry for the early start but I knew you'd want to see them.'

'We were getting up early anyway as we have a hiking tour booked this morning,' Jen said. 'But thanks so much for your message because I would've hated to miss this.' She eyed him with a grin. 'You're looking pretty fine and dandy yourself there, mister.'

Dylan laughed. 'Well, I couldn't let them have all the fun, now, could I? Here, give me that,' Dylan said, circling around to take the tablet from Theo. 'What do you make of our very own Peaky Blinder, then?' he asked as Theo moved to join his sister. The British TV show had become a cult classic in the States.

'So cool,' he heard Jen say. 'That cap really suits you.'

'You look great, Theo, man,' Eric said. 'Just like you've stepped out of the TV screen.'

Theo fiddled with the brim of his cap, looking pleased if a little shy at the attention. 'I might get one of these to bring home.'

They chattered on for a few more minutes until Dylan checked his watch. 'We need to be downstairs in about five minutes, guys, and your mom and Eric have a busy day planned so say your goodbyes, okay?'

Avery did a final twirl, sending the fringe on her skirt fanning out while she blew kisses towards the screen. 'Love you guys!'

'Love you too, baby. Message me tomorrow and tell me all about it, and don't forget to take lots of photos.'

'Bye, Mom, bye, Eric.' Theo clasped the brim of his cap between thumb and forefinger and tugged it in a gesture that made them all laugh.

Dylan packed away the tablet and reached for his jacket. 'Pee if you need to pee,' he reminded the kids. 'It'll be easier now.'

'Geez, Daddy, we're not five years old any more,' Avery grumbled while Theo took the hint and dashed off to the bathroom.

Dylan raised his eyebrows at her. 'I'm just saying...'

'Well, you don't need to, okay, I'm fine,' she insisted.

'Okay, then.' Dylan crossed to where a large mirror hung above the fireplace and checked his reflection. He shrugged his shoulders to settle his jacket just right and tweaked his bow tie so it sat straight. Theo returned and Dylan eyed them both. 'Got your phones and whatever else you need?' They both nodded. 'Let's go, then.' He tucked his own phone in his trouser pocket, picked up the room key and pulled open the door. 'It's party time!'

They got five steps down the corridor before Avery let out a groan of frustration and held her hand out to him. Dylan placed the key on her palm and couldn't help grinning as she marched back to their room and let herself in. Theo laughed. 'She hates it so much when you're right.'

'She sure does,' Dylan agreed. 'But she'll get over it.'

16

The first person Sadie saw when she reached the bottom of the stairs was Rowena. Dressed in a burgundy smoking jacket over a pair of wide-legged satin trousers and sporting a silver turban over hair now dyed to match her jacket, she lit up in delight as she spotted Sadie. 'Look at you!' she cried, opening her arms to sweep Sadie into a hug. 'Don't you look splendid?' Rowena stepped back, an admiring smile on her face as she took Sadie by the shoulders. 'And this cut! Turn around so I can see the back, and I love these highlights. You look like a different woman, Sadie!'

Sadie raised a tentative hand to check the short bob was still smooth. 'It's a lot shorter than I usually have it.'

'It's perfect! And you have such a lovely swan neck, it deserves showing off.' She spotted someone behind them and called out. 'Stevie, come and see Sadie's fabulous new haircut.'

Sharp heels clicked on the tiled floor and Sadie turned towards the sound. Where Rowena always loved to make a state-ment, Stevie was understated elegance in a simple black gown that fitted her slim frame to below the knee before flaring out in a stunning ostrich feather skirt. She held open her arms as she took in Sadie's outfit. 'That colour is perfect on you, and Rowena's right, your hair is gorgeous. Tasha told me she'd booked you in at the spa. Did you have a lovely time?'

Sadie held out her hands to show off her manicure. 'They pampered me to within an inch of my life. Honestly I'm so relaxed I feel like I've been here for a week rather than a couple of days.'

'That's exactly how we want every guest to feel,' Stevie said, linking their arms. 'Shall we go through and find you a drink?'

Sadie was grateful for their company as they walked into the lounge. She was getting better at coming out of her shell but it was still a lot to walk into a room on her own. She needn't have worried because Charlie, Anna and Jane were waiting just inside and they came over, Charlie handing her the second glass of champagne she was holding. After another round of compliments about her new hair, Sadie felt as though she was floating on cloud nine and was more than happy to pose for photos.

They were standing around admiring everyone else's outfits when Sadie felt a warm hand against her back. 'You look beautiful.'

Recognising Dylan's voice, Sadie turned and found herself speechless as she stared into his blue eyes. He'd done something with his hair, the curls tamed into the sleek waves of a matinee idol. The velvet jacket he was wearing looked so soft she found her fingers straying to his shoulder to brush at an all but invisible spot of lint. Realising what she'd done, she pulled her hand away. 'Sorry.'

'You look beautiful,' he said again, catching her hand and giving it the briefest squeeze before he let it go. 'Sit next to me at dinner?'

She barely had time to nod before his children bowled up.

Trying to ignore the fluttering inside her, she did her best to focus on them, admiring how handsome Theo looked and clapping when Avery did a twirl to show off the fringe of her dress. Their group expanded as first Tara and Jon and then Marcus joined them and before she knew it Dylan was on the other side of their loose circle deep in conversation with Rowena.

An earth-shattering scream pierced the air, and Sadie wasn't the only one to clutch a hand to her chest as a young woman dressed in a short black and silver dress with a matching feathered headband ran into the room. 'He's dead!' she cried out, gesturing towards the hallway with a hand clutching a long cigarette holder. 'The duke is dead! Come quick, everybody, there's been a murder!'

As she ran back out of the room, a ripple of relieved laughter followed her as they realised it must be the start of the evening's entertainment. 'I guess we should go and see,' Tara said to Sadie with a shrug.

'I guess so!' They followed the rest of the guests, pausing to deposit their glasses on the trays of the wait staff who had appeared at the edge of the door. By the time they got into the hallway there was a circle of people gathered and Sadie had to stand on tiptoe to see what was happening. The young woman was on her knees wailing at the top of her lungs. Next to her on the large Turkish rug was the body of an older man, the front of his crisp white evening shirt soaked red, a very realistic-looking knife sticking out of his chest. 'That'll be the dead duke,' Sadie murmured to Tara as she shuffled to one side to let her see.

The front doors burst open and a man around his mid-thirties wearing a long dark overcoat and a black hat pushed his way in. On his heels was an older man, dressed in a period policeman's uniform and sporting a very impressive handlebar moustache.

'Nobody touch anything!' the younger man called out. 'I'm Inspector Turtle and this is Sergeant Dove. Where's the body?'

'Here, he's here!' The young woman stood and Sadie noticed with a smile that not a spot of her make-up was out of place for all that supposed weeping and wailing.

'Stand aside!' Inspector Turtle declared and the guests moved back, widening the circle enough that gaps appeared so Sadie and the others on the outside could see more clearly what was happening. The inspector went down on his knees by the body. 'My God, it's the Duke of Nortington, Sergeant Dove, lock the doors! No one is leaving until the murderer has been found.'

The sergeant made a big show of closing the doors and sliding the bolt across. 'Right then, ladies and gentlemen, that's enough gawping. Follow me so I can take everyone's name.' Weaving through the group, the sergeant led them into the dining room. It had been dressed beautifully, with flowers and candles on every table. A large plan stood just inside the door indicating which tables they'd been assigned to and the guests soon dispersed to take their seats. Sadie had just reached their table when Dylan appeared at her side. He pulled out a chair for her then quickly claimed the one next to hers, sending her a ghost of a wink as he unfastened the napkin on his plate and laid it across his lap. Theo and Avery had already taken empty seats on the opposite side of the table, leaving room for Tara and Jon to claim the chairs to Sadie's left. 'Is this free?' Charlie asked, pointing to the seat beside Dylan.

'Not any more.' He rose in one smooth motion, pulling out her chair, before moving to make sure Anna and Jane were also both comfortable in the seats next to her.

That left three empty places at the table. One was claimed by Marcus, who asked Jane if he could sit beside her. A few moments later Stevie arrived and took the seat next to him with a smile.

'Rowena and I decided we could keep an eye on things and still enjoy ourselves at the same time,' she said.

'Who's missing?' Sadie asked, nodding to the final chair.

'You'll see,' Stevie said with a secretive smile. 'Now then, shall we open this wine?'

They'd all got drinks and the wait staff had been around and laid out mixed mezze plates for everyone as a starter when a young man wearing a straw boater and a candy-striped blazer rushed over and took the empty seat. 'Sorry, I'm late! Took blooming ages to get back from Oxford. Bad news about the old man, what?' He turned to Theo, who was sitting next to him. 'Good to meet you, I'm Lord Monckton, but you can call me Dickie, everyone does.'

It didn't take long to establish that Dickie was in fact the dead duke's eldest son and heir to the title. The three younger women seemed more au fait at how the evening was meant to go and they peppered him with questions about his background, his relationship with his father, etc. The crying woman they found out was a former showgirl who the duke had taken up with following the untimely demise of Dickie's mother. 'Millicent, she calls herself now,' Dickie said with a clear sneer of disdain. 'As if any of us are going to forget about Millie the Minx's speciality act involving a shot glass, a golf ball and a peacock's feather.'

'The mind boggles,' Stevie said, and Sadie wasn't the only one to turn a laugh into a hasty cough as she caught the look of confusion on Avery's face. Theo opened his mouth, but thankfully closed it again when Dylan shook his head once.

'So, your father's acquaintance with Millicent is a relatively recent one?' Jon asked, thankfully diverting the conversation away from the anatomical creativity of Millie the Minx. He'd got right into the spirit of things, taking a pen from Tara's handbag and using the back of one of the menus to scribble down anything he considered might be a clue.

Sadie was happy to let the others get on with it while she focused on her food and the warm heat of Dylan's leg pressed against hers. The first time he'd brushed against her, she'd assumed it was an accident, but when he'd reached for his fork as she'd reached for her knife, his little finger had touched hers. When she'd looked up at him, he'd held her gaze for a long moment before moving his hand away and turning his attention to his meal. His foot had touched hers beneath the table and when she hadn't moved away, Dylan had shifted towards her just enough she could feel the heat of him through the thin silk of her skirt.

Not trusting herself not to blush if she looked at him, Sadie concentrated on chatting to Tara, who was happy to have an audience as she described the lovely day she and Jon had enjoyed with their grandchildren. She couldn't put her mind to anything more serious than that because too much of her attention was caught up in her awareness of the man beside her. What if she was reading something into nothing and his gestures were entirely accidental? She could be sitting there all hot and bothered about something of which he was entirely unaware. How embarrassing, how desperate, if that was the case.

It had taken her ages to get used to sleeping on her own, not that she'd missed Pete all that much, but she'd missed having *someone*. Waking up in silence had meant lying awake for hours missing the sound of his breathing, the strangeness of all that empty space beside her. It had been better once they'd sold the house and she'd moved into her own place. Buying new furniture might have been a luxury her budget couldn't really afford but she'd refused to take anything from the old house with her, most especially the bed. Her new double was smaller than the old super-king, but it was hers and hers alone. The first night in her new place she'd made a point of sleeping not on her usual right side but in the middle and now she enjoyed having the space to spread herself out, to seek a cool bit of the bed in the heat of the summer, to roll herself up in the quilt like a sausage in a bun on chilly nights simply because she could.

There was only one way to find out if she was imagining things... Sadie knocked her napkin 'accidentally' off her lap and in the ensuing flurry of activity to retrieve it, she took the opportunity to shift her chair further away from Dylan. 'Okay?' he asked as she settled back into her seat.

'Yes, everything's fine, thank you.'

There was no time for any more conversation as the staff came to clear the plates and Dickie excused himself from the table. His seat wasn't empty for long as Sergeant Dove sat down. He cast a suspicious look around the table, then took a notebook out of his pocket and began to quiz them about what the young master had had to say for himself.

And so the evening continued: as each course was delivered and cleared a new person came to join the table, dropping hints and casting aspersions on each other with abandon. Sadie had no idea who the murderer was, and honestly she didn't really care, it was enough to enjoy the atmosphere, the good food and the even better company. When they came around with coffee and dessert, Sadie was too full but, after a quick, pleading look from Theo she accepted the slice of cake she'd been about to refuse and sent it around the table to him. With no more mystery guests to join them, Jon shifted into the empty seat next to Stevie so he could consult with her, Marcus and the three younger women.

'So what's your theory?' Dylan asked her as they settled back in their seats with coffees in hand.

'I don't really have one. They all seemed pretty suspicious to me. What about you?'

'I kept getting distracted thinking about Millie's stage act,' he said with a wicked grin.

'Oh, don't!' Sadie set her coffee down on the table before she spilled it. 'You know you're going to get questions about that from Theo, don't you?'

Dylan mock shuddered. 'I'm already dreading it.' His smile returned. 'Have you had a nice evening, though?'

She nodded. 'It's been wonderful fun.'

His expression grew serious and his voice lowered so only she would be able to hear him. 'And you didn't mind me wanting to sit next to you?'

'Not at all.' He stared at her as though expecting her to say something more. Perhaps those touches hadn't been accidental after all. But how to ask without just blurting it out? God, she was so out of practice with this kind of thing. 'I like your company very much.'

'I like yours too. Perhaps we could go for a walk some time? Just the two of us.'

She didn't have time to answer because Avery was suddenly there between the two of them, whispering something urgently. Quick as a flash, Dylan was up and out of his seat and helping a rather green-looking Theo out of the room, Avery following at their heels.

Not sure if she was feeling relieved or disappointed, Sadie bit her lip as she and the others looked at each other after watching the abrupt departure. 'I feel awful for giving him my dessert,' she confessed.

Stevie shook her head. 'Don't blame yourself, he had mine too and several of the chocolates that came with the coffee.'

'It is rather warm in here,' Tara added, lifting her fan from the table to waft her face. 'I think I might leave the super sleuths to it and retire to the lounge.'

'I need to go and check on a few things,' Stevie said, rising. Marcus stood to ease her chair back and Sadie didn't miss the brief touch the other woman laid on his arm before she departed. Perhaps she wasn't the only one finding herself in the middle of a flirtation. That had to be what it was, right? Having someone make her feel attractive again was a heady experience and Sadie felt as if she were walking on air as she and Tara said goodnight to the others and left the ballroom. They parted at the bottom of the stairs, Sadie demurring on the offer of a night cap. She didn't need anything else to cloud her judgement, she needed to think about what was potentially happening between her and Dylan because they seemed to be heading along a path that both excited and frightened her.

17

Dylan was still rueing his bad luck the next morning. Thanks to Avery's quick actions they'd got Theo back to their room without disaster and once he'd lain down with the window open and a cool flannel on his forehead the sudden bout of queasiness had eased off. Dylan didn't have it in him to be annoyed with his son. The poor kid had been ready to die with embarrassment even after many reassurances that it wasn't a big deal and no one would think less of him.

'At least you didn't puke on the table,' Avery had told him in a somewhat tactless attempt at reassurance. 'Cos that would've been *really* humiliating.'

Dylan had shooed her off to bed at the point, leaving Theo in peace shortly afterwards with an emergency bowl on his bedside table that he'd hastily emptied some pretty dried flowers from. It was probably an antique, but Dylan had figured he could negotiate a family discount if anything happened to it, and better one bowl than the lovely bedsheets, or the carpet.

In the end the bowl hadn't been required and a slightly delicate, still repentant Theo had emerged from his room the next morning no worse for wear. Mention of breakfast had made him pull a face so Dylan had decided the best thing to do was to get him out in the fresh air. They'd spent most of their time cooped up in the hall and it was a glorious blue-sky morning so they might as well get out and explore. Avery had been happy to wait to eat, with the promise of a breakfast bap at the café later, so they'd piled on their warm layers and headed out.

Dylan stuck his head in the lounge door on the off chance, but there was no sign of Sadie so he decided to leave it for now. He'd thought he might have blown it when she'd moved her leg away from his the evening before, but there'd been no mistaking the heat in her eyes when she'd told him how much she enjoyed his company. Even if they never progressed beyond what they had now, it was still nice to spend time around a woman he felt attracted to again. He'd almost forgotten what it was like.

Following his split with Jen there had been one or two awkward incidents with a couple of the mothers in the neighbourhood who had wrongly assumed arranging a play date between their children might lead to something else. After letting them down as gently as possible, he'd left those arrangements for Jen to sort out and stuck to escorting the children to group activities. In the end, he'd kind of got used to his own company and with the kids in the mix he just hadn't felt like starting anything serious. They'd adapted well enough to Eric coming into the family but adding someone else might have upset the delicate balance they'd all achieved.

Flirting with Sadie didn't carry the same edge of risk. Not only were the kids older, there was no way of carrying anything on beyond the next couple of weeks as they'd both be returning to their own lives. Long-distance relationships rarely worked out so just getting to know her better, having someone to chat to and feel a bit coupley with for things like going into dinner, would be more than enough for him. He wondered if she liked to dance. He'd always loved dancing and that was one of the things he'd truly missed when he and Jen had split up. He hoped he'd get the chance to find out.

By the time they'd made it across to The Old Stable Yard, Theo was fully recovered and declared himself starving as they entered the café. Christmas lights sparkled everywhere, and from hidden speakers Brenda Lee was urging them to rock around the Christmas tree. Though it wasn't much past the ten o'clock daily opening time, the café was already busy so Dylan sent the kids to claim one of the last remaining tables while he queued up to place their order. The woman behind the till smiled at him. Then her eyes widened and she *really* looked at him. She shook her head when she realised she was staring. 'Sorry, you just look very familiar.'

'Being the younger brother of the owners will do that,' he said with a grin. 'I'm Dylan.'

Her face broke into a broad smile. 'Of course you are! Zap was only in here yesterday saying how lovely it had been seeing you again after all this time. I'm Sandra. Now, what can I get for you?'

'It's lovely to meet you, Sandra. Can I have three bacon and egg rolls, a large cappuccino, an apple juice and a hot chocolate, please?' He paused then added, 'I assume you know what Zap likes to drink? Can I pay for a large one of those and I'll pick up a takeaway on our way out.'

'Of course. He's partial to a latte and he was eyeing up the date and pecan slices yesterday.'

Dylan had to give her credit for the upsell. 'Then I'll take one of those for him as well.'

Breakfast done, they returned to the counter to collect the takeaway items and Dylan led them across the courtyard to the distillery. A small queue trailed out of the door and Dylan edged past them to have a look. Zap was standing at a counter near the display stands, wrapping a couple of bottles. Hope was next to him, processing the sales. 'I'm not buying anything,' Dylan said to the woman standing nearby who was giving him a 'you'd better not be pushing in' look. 'Just dropping something off.' She raised a suspicious eyebrow but turned towards her companion and Dylan took the chance to get past her and went to stand at the end of the counter where he wouldn't be in the way.

Zap looked over, his face lighting up when he saw Dylan. He handed over the wrapped bottles then abandoned his post to come over. 'Hello! This is a nice surprise.'

'Rubbish timing on my part,' Dylan said. 'I didn't think about you having customers. I just wanted to introduce you to the kids and leave you this.' He put the coffee and the little pastry in its brown paper bag on the counter. 'Sandra assures me they're your favourites.'

'Oh, lovely,' Zap said after peeking inside the bag. 'And there's no such thing as rubbish timing when it comes to family.' He smiled at Avery and Theo, who were standing just off to Dylan's left. 'Aren't you two a sight for sore eyes? I must say I was looking forward to meeting you both later but this is such a treat.' He held out his hand. 'You must be Theo.'

'Hello, Uncle Zap. This place is amazing! Do you really make your own stuff?'

'I do. I can give you a tour if you like? You'll have to wait until the queue calms down a bit, but I'd love to show you around.'

'That would be great, thanks!'

'I'm Avery! Can I look around too?'

'Of course you can, my darling,' Zap said, beaming at her. 'You can help me come up with a new flavour idea if you like. How about that?' And just like that, Zap had them eating out of the palm of his hand.

Dylan noticed Hope glance over and, not wanting to interrupt while the children were peppering Zap with questions, he slipped past his brother and took his place behind the counter. 'Am I wrapping this for you?' he asked the woman, indicating the bottle Hope had just rung through.

'No, I have a bag already, thank you.' She lifted it onto the counter and held open the handles to display several other items she must've purchased at the workshops outside.

With a careful hand, Dylan moved a couple of things aside to make a gap and slid the bottle inside. 'How's that?'

'Lovely, thanks. Merry Christmas!'

'Merry Christmas to you too!'

'You'll do me out of a job,' his brother said with a laugh as he returned to his post. 'I've suggested you all come back in about an hour and things should've quietened down by then.'

'Can I stay?' Theo asked.

Dylan shook his head. 'We'll come back as Zap suggested. I thought you wanted to look around the workshops and the market stalls.'

'It's no bother if the lad wants to stay,' Zap said. 'I'm always happy to exploit a bit of child labour.'

Dylan laughed. 'Well, it's up to you.' He glanced down at Avery. 'What about you?'

'I want to look for a gift for Mom and Eric.'

'All right, then.' He raised a finger towards Theo. 'No touching anything unless your uncle says it's okay and no sampling the products.' He added a wink to the last bit.

'This is nice, Dad,' Avery said a bit later, snuggling into his side as they strolled between the little wooden huts of the Christmas market that had been erected next to the café.

Dylan put his arm around her shoulders. 'It's lovely getting to spend a little time just the two of us, isn't it?'

'I hope everyone else is as nice as Uncle Zap this evening,' she said, her voice a little quieter.

'Are you nervous about meeting the rest of the family? I don't think there's any need to be as you've met most of them already.'

'I know, but there'll be a lot of people there all at once.'

Dylan led her over to an unoccupied picnic table that had been set up near the food stalls and they sat down. 'You've met a lot of new people over the past couple of days. Is it getting a bit much?' Avery was so cheerful and friendly it was hard to remember sometimes that she was still so young.

'I'm having a good time,' Avery protested.

'I didn't say you weren't.' Dylan reached out to stroke her hair. 'But it's okay if you're feeling a little bit anxious too.' He glanced over the crowded stalls. 'Would you rather wait until it's quieter to look for something for your mom?'

She shook her head. 'No, it's not that. I just know how important this is for you and I don't want to make a mistake or say the wrong thing.'

Oh, hell. Dylan scooted closer so he could put his arms around her. 'You are the kindest, most thoughtful lovely girl in the world.' He kissed the top of her head then pulled back so he could look down at her. 'You don't have to be anyone other than yourself, not tonight, not any time. You are not responsible for me and you are definitely not responsible for making sure I make up with everybody, okay?' When she bit her lip, Dylan leaned in to kiss her temple. 'You saw just now how everything was with your uncle Zap, right?'

'He's really funny,' Avery said with a smile. 'Do you really think he'll let me make a new flavour?'

'I'm sure he will. And your uncle Ziggy is just a quieter version of him. You like Hope, Ben and the others, yes?' She nodded, quickly. 'Then I promise there isn't anything to worry about. I'll make a deal with you, okay? We'll go and check it out tonight but, if at any point it feels like it's too much and you want to leave, then you let me know and I'll take you straight back to the hotel. I promise you no one will get upset because, like your uncle Zap said just now, there's no such thing as rubbish timing when it comes to family.'

Avery leaned against him. 'I love you, Dad. I just want you to be happy.'

He folded his arms around her. 'I'm already the happiest man in the world because I have you and your brother, so, please, no more worrying about me. Come on, now, let's go and find something nice for your mom.'

* * *

The children had a blast with Zap as he showed them around the distillery. Avery was overwhelmed by the choice of different ingredients in the stock room and couldn't settle on an idea for a new flavour but she promised to think about it. Dylan found time to have a quiet word with Hope and forewarn her about Avery's anxiety about dinner. She was completely understanding and promised to talk to Stevie so between the three of them they'd be able to keep an eye on her and not let things drag on too late into the evening.

When they returned to the hall there was still no sign of Sadie – in fact there was no sign of anyone other than Marcus, who was sitting in the corner of the lounge deeply engrossed in a book. Dylan tried not to feel too disappointed. He just hoped she didn't think he was avoiding her. As soon as that thought occurred to him, he wished it hadn't because then he started to worry that perhaps she was avoiding *him*. He couldn't just lurk around waiting for her to appear because that would definitely put her off! Resigned to sorting things out at a later date, Dylan followed Theo and Avery upstairs, where he'd promised them a couple of hours of screen time before they headed back out for dinner.

Just after six they were back downstairs and this time there were more signs of life. Stevie and Rowena had arranged to give them a lift across to the farmhouse so the three of them waited in the hallway in one of the seating nooks. They weren't waiting long before Rowena swept through the door that led to the spa, her smile lighting up when she saw them. 'Give me five minutes and I'm all yours! Any sign of Stevie yet?'

Dylan shook his head. 'Not yet, but no rush, I know you've both got a lot going on.'

'She's probably in the office and forgotten the time. I'll go and chivvy her along.'

It took ten more minutes before they were both ready. 'I'm parked around the back,' Stevie said, still in the process of tugging on her coat, her handbag dangling from her elbow.

'Here.' Dylan took hold of her collar and helped her settle her coat on her shoulders.

'Thank you.'

They were passing the stairs when they saw Sadie descending and Dylan paused. 'I'll catch you up.'

'Off out somewhere?' Sadie asked as she drew level with him.

'It's the big family reunion dinner. I think I mentioned it the other day.'

'Oh, yes, that's right. Well, have a lovely time. Will you be back for the entertainment later? It's some sort of Moulin Rouge-style show, apparently.'

He'd forgotten all about it. 'I'm not sure what time we'll be back.'

'Dylan?' Stevie called from the far end of the corridor.

'I'm coming.' He turned back to Sadie. 'I've got to go. Can we catch up tomorrow some time?'

She smiled. 'Of course. I'll be in the conservatory before breakfast and after that I'll be in the lounge. I've got a couple of pears I need to finish off ready for the tree.'

'I'll find you,' he promised. 'Sorry, I've got to run. Between last night and tonight, we have the worst timing.'

'We'll work it out. Go, go!' She shooed him away, her laughter following him down the corridor.

Dylan caught up with the others, ignoring the pointed look from his sister as she held the door open for him. 'Everything okay?' she asked.

'Everything's great, thanks.'

'Hmm.'

18

The kitchen at the farmhouse was almost full to bursting even before they arrived. The back door was open and someone had lit a couple of space heaters and placed them next to a pair of wooden benches in the courtyard. Dressed in warm jumpers and gilets, Hope, Amelia and Ben were sitting on the benches, talking to a sandy-haired man in glasses Dylan didn't know. 'Cameron, darling, you made it!' Stevie cried, hurrying over to greet the man, who rose with a smile to give her a hug. 'How's your mum and dad?'

'They're great, thank you. They said to say thanks for the hamper you sent them – you shouldn't have.'

Stevie waved him off. 'Of course I should. It's the least I can do as we won't be seeing them for Christmas and they're letting us steal you away.'

'Dad's sorry he couldn't get the time off, but the overtime will come in handy and he's promised he'll put in a request for next year as soon as the new leave year starts.'

'Oh, that will be lovely. Come here and meet my brother and

his children.' Stevie led Cameron over to them. 'Dylan, Theo, Avery, this is Hope's partner, Cameron.'

'Call me Cam,' the tall man said. 'Only Stevie and my mum call me by my full name.'

They shook hands, then Dylan put an arm around Avery. 'We should make name badges for everyone.'

Cam grinned. 'I know what you mean. The first time I came here it was like a new member of the family popped up every time I turned around.'

'Well, now you've met us I think that's a full house.'

'Speaking of which,' Stevie said, 'come on in and you can say hello to the others.' She turned to Hope. 'Are you all right out here?'

Hope raised a tall glass of something sparkling. 'All good. Poor Ziggy was tearing his hair out with everyone in his way so we beat a retreat. We're still waiting on Rhys to finish and Tasha's going to be late because Lydia texted her about a last-minute problem with tonight.'

Stevie froze in her tracks. 'Do I need to go back?'

Hope laughed as she shook her head. 'Not unless you can do the cancan. One of the three French hens has twisted her ankle. Tasha's the first aider so it makes sense for her to go and see if there's anything she can do. If she thinks it's more serious than a strain she'll take her up to A & E to get checked out.'

'Oh dear, the poor girl, I hope she's not badly hurt,' Stevie said, looking concerned. 'Maybe I should go and see...'

Hope stood and came to hug her mum. 'Everything's in hand. It didn't sound serious from what Lydia was saying, only that she might not be able to perform. They're due on right at the end of the show, and I'm sure no one will mind if there's only two dancers.'

'I suppose you're right,' Stevie agreed, hugging her daughter.

'It's just such a shame because Lydia worked so hard to design unique things to suit our twelve days theme. Make sure you let me know when you get an update, will you?'

'Of course.'

Stevie led them inside and Dylan could see why the others had decided to brave the cold. The kitchen was a chaotic blend of noise, delicious food smells and heat. Ziggy was on the far side next to the oven, dressed in jeans, a casual shirt and wearing a striped butcher's apron. Daisy paused in the process of setting the table to say hello. Zap was sitting at the top end of the table, their mother beside him, the pair of them deep in conversation. Both had chopping boards and were slicing things to go in the huge salad bowl in front of them. Somewhere in the background a radio was playing.

'What should we do with our coats?' Dylan asked.

'You can hang them up through here,' Stevie said, leading them towards a closed door.

'No!' Ziggy, Zap and Daisy all chorused, Daisy hurrying around the table to block access.

'The dogs are in there,' she explained. 'And I cannot begin to tell you how long it took us to corral them all into one place.' She pointed towards the door behind Ziggy. 'You're welcome to leave your things in our sitting room.'

With that sorted out, Dylan led the children over to Alice. 'Mum, say hello to your grandchildren.'

There were tears glistening in Alice's eyes as she stood up. 'It's so lovely to finally meet you.' She held her arms out and Dylan felt his heart flip as both children stepped in to hug her. His eyes met his mother's and she mouthed 'Thank you' to him over their heads.

Pulling out his phone, Dylan opened his camera app. 'Give us a smile, guys.'

'Oh, that's a lovely shot,' Rowena said, peering over his shoulder. 'Here, give me that and go and join them.'

Not given any other option, Dylan handed her the phone and went to stand beside his mother, with Avery slightly in front of them and Theo on Alice's other side. Dylan felt his mother's tentative touch on his back and found himself smiling down at her as he extended his arm around her shoulders.

'Perfect, don't move!' Rowena called out. 'Yes, oh, look, that's perfect.'

Dylan took his phone back. As he stared at the photo Rowena had taken, something shifted inside him. He was still looking down but his mother had turned towards the camera. Her expression was full of such need and longing it made him want to cry. Time and circumstances had stolen so much from them all, but it wasn't too late to change things. Moving back to his mother's side, he put his arm around her waist and bent to kiss her cheek. 'It's good to be home, Mum.'

Her hand raised to press over his heart. 'I'm so glad I got this chance to see you again.'

'It's only the beginning, I promise.'

'Something smells good. I'm starving.' Dylan glanced up to see a tall, broad-chested man who could only be his nephew, Rhys, filling the doorway. He was holding a little brown dachshund under one arm and a large collie stood so close at heel Dylan was surprised Rhys didn't trip over him. 'No, don't come near me, Mum, I stink!' Rhys laughed as he stepped back from Rowena who was moving towards him.

'I wasn't coming for you, I was coming for this precious darling.' She scooped the dachshund from his hold and cuddled her against her chest. 'Hello, beautiful Delilah.'

'Well, that's me told,' Rhys said with a grin. 'Right, I need a shower, like yesterday.' He glanced around. 'Where's Tasha?'

'She's sorting out something up at the hall,' Stevie replied. 'Hopefully she'll be back by the time you're done.'

'Okay.' Rhys walked towards Dylan and the children, the collie still shadowing his every step. He made a big show of giving them a wide berth as he approached the door behind them. 'I'll say hello properly in a minute, I promise.'

He reached for the door handle, the cries of 'No' from his father and uncle too slow to prevent him from opening it. A streak of black shot past him, followed by a second and the kitchen was filled with a cacophony of barking as two black Labrador puppies bounced around the room trying to greet everyone at once. A smaller Dalmatian, all floppy ears and paws too big for the rest of his body, entered the room, took one look at everyone and shot underneath the kitchen table. Hercule, Zap's little terrier, sauntered in looking as if he couldn't understand what all the fuss was about.

One of the puppies paused in his mad circuit to jump at Avery, all eager tongue and scrabbling claws against her jeans. Dylan was about to intervene when Hope ran in. She grabbed the nearest Lab by the collar, her arm straining towards the one trying to give Avery a tongue-bath as she shouted, 'Sooty! Sooty, down! Get down!' The puppy immediately flattened his body to the floor, his enthusiastic barking quietened to a gentle whine.

Hope reached them and took the dog by the collar with her free hand, tugging him towards her as she sat in a chair. She issued a command for the puppies to sit, only releasing her grip on them when they'd obeyed so she could fuss and hug them both. 'Good boys, yes, yes, you are.' She glanced up at Avery over their heads. 'I'm so sorry, are you okay? We've been doing obedience classes but they still get excited when there are lots of people around.'

'I'm okay.' Avery crouched down next to her. 'Hi, puppies.'

She giggled when Sooty licked her chin as she began to pet him. 'They're so cute...'

'No,' Dylan said before she could give voice to the thought. 'I am not getting a dog, so don't even start.' Eric was allergic to animal fur so having a dog at home was out of the question. Still, every now and again Avery waged a campaign for Dylan to get one.

'But don't you get lonely when we're not around, Daddy?' she said, all big eyes and a hopeful smile.

'No, not really.'

'The only Travers without a dog,' Zap said as he bent down to scoop Hercule up. 'Talk about letting the side down.'

'Leave him alone,' Ziggy admonished, pointing a sauce-covered spoon at his twin. It was as if the clock had turned back forty years, Zap always the one with a laughing tease, Ziggy the protector there to intervene. Still holding the spoon, Ziggy cast a glare around the room. 'If you want a chance of eating before midnight I need you all to go away. Right now.'

They dispersed with a laugh. Hope, Zap and Rowena went to secure the dogs in the sitting room, while Rhys headed upstairs for his much-needed shower. The rest of them moved outside to huddle under the heaters and chat. Rhys joined them a few minutes later and a much calmer Ziggy popped his head out shortly afterwards to say they were all welcome to come in and sit down.

It was a squeeze, but they managed to all get around the big table. There were a few laughs and elbow clashes but with a bit of cooperation everyone soon had a bowl filled with fragrant curry and rice in front of them. The back door opened and Tasha came in. 'So sorry I'm late.' She edged around the table to the sink so she could wash her hands before claiming the empty chair next to Rhys.

Rhys kissed her in greeting. 'Everything okay?'

She nodded. 'All good. It's just a slight strain and I've left her with an ice pack and she's keeping her foot up. She had her own painkillers and she said it was already starting to feel a bit better. They were working out a modified routine with chairs so she seems determined to go on if she can.'

'Well, it sounds like you've done all you can, thank you,' Stevie said. 'I'll give Lydia a quick call once we've eaten and just make sure she's okay.'

Tasha did her best to hide her smile. 'Good idea, but, yes, let's eat. I'm so sorry if I held things up.'

'We've only just dished up,' Ziggy assured her. 'Now, what would you like? There's a chicken korma, a vegetable masala or a beef madras if you're feeling brave.'

'I think I'll have a bit of the korma and the masala, please.'

Dylan decided to go for a spoonful of everything. He wasn't the only one who was enjoying his food as there was a general lull in the conversation as everyone focused on eating. He was just contemplating whether he could manage an extra spoonful of korma to go with the chunk of naan he had left over when there was a quick knock at the kitchen door before it swung open.

Monty stood there, dressed in faded jeans, a once-white, now slightly grey wool jumper and that patchwork coat Dylan had recognised when they'd been passing the pub. Cutlery stilled as they all stared at him. 'I came to speak to Alice, but I can see I'm interrupting,' Monty said, a hint of peevishness in his tone.

'We've just been welcoming Dylan and his children home,' Ziggy replied, his own voice a flat monotone.

Their father scanned the table, his gaze settling on Dylan for a long moment before he looked away without offering any acknowledgement of his youngest son. 'Yes, well, it seems I missed the invitation. I'll leave you in peace.'

Dylan felt a hand against his back, and knew without looking it was Zap offering him comfort. He appreciated the gesture, but he didn't need it because Monty's rejections had stopped hurting a long time ago.

'I'm finished,' Rhys said, pushing to his feet. 'Thanks for dinner, Ziggy, but I appear to have lost my appetite.' Without another word, he left the room, Tasha rising with a muttered apology to follow him.

'Something I said?' Monty shrugged as if it were no big deal, but telltale spots of red on his cheeks said otherwise. 'Anyway, I didn't mean to interrupt, I just came to let you know that I'm going to head off for a bit. I was going to wait until after the holidays, but there's obviously no point in waiting. Have a nice Christmas, folks.' He walked out, the kitchen door slamming behind him.

'Oh, goodness, I'd better go after him,' Alice said, standing up.

Stevie put out a hand to stop her. 'It's what he wants, Mum, to keep you running after him.'

Her eyes filled with anguish, but she nodded as she sat back down. 'You're right. He's never going to change if I give into him.'

'He's never going to change, full stop,' Rowena said. Alice nodded again, her eyes filling with tears.

There was a harsh scrape of chair legs across the tiled floor. 'I've damn well had enough of this,' Ziggy snapped as he marched towards the kitchen door and yanked it open. The noise it made as he slammed it closed behind him silenced them all.

Dylan exchanged a look with Stevie and Zap and the three of them rose in unison. 'Zap, darling, wait,' Rowena protested, placing a hand on her husband's arm.

'No. This has gone on for too long and I'm not leaving Ziggy to deal with him alone.' He moved to the door where Stevie was already waiting and they both went outside.

Anger like he hadn't felt in a long time surged inside Dylan. All these years and Monty was still manipulating everyone. 'I'll be back in a minute,' he assured Theo, who was watching him with wide worried eyes, before following his brother and sister.

He heard angry voices before he was halfway across the yard. 'If you're really leaving, Monty, I'm telling you now it's for the last time,' Ziggy said in a tone as hard as iron.

Monty turned to face him, his features harsh in the bright beam of one of the security lights. 'You think you can tell me what to do, boy? This is *my* damn estate and I'll come and go as I bloody well please!'

'No,' Stevie said, moving to stand beside Ziggy. 'Enough is enough. You've walked out on us once too often and we won't play this game with you any more.'

Monty's lip curled in a snarl. 'Who are you to lecture anyone on walking out on their family?'

Stevie's gasp was one of pure pain as she flinched and stepped back. Dylan had to clench his fists against the urge to punch Monty in the mouth. It was Zap who stepped forward next, shaking with a rage Dylan hadn't known him capable of. 'You spiteful, childish bastard. If Stevie hadn't come home when she did, that monster she was married to could've killed her.'

Shoving his own anger down, Dylan put his arm around Zap and pulled him back. 'He's not worth it. Let him leave – we're better off without him.'

Monty looked him up and down, an ugly sneer twisting his features. 'And you'd know all about leaving, wouldn't you? Don't try and judge me, boy. We're the same and you know it.'

Dylan snorted, unable to hide his contempt. 'I'm nothing like you. *Nothing.* Yes, I left, but at least I had the decency to stay away until I got my shit together. I'm home to make amends, but you, you wouldn't know the meaning of the word.'

Zap pushed him gently towards Stevie, always the protector. 'Just go, Monty, no one wants you here. You do nothing but cause harm. Every time things settle down you come back only long enough to sow your chaos. As soon as things get tough you piss off again and leave us to pick up the pieces. Well, no more. You're done. *We're* done.'

Monty shook his head. 'You don't know what you're talking about! None of you do! You have no idea how hard it is for me to come here, not after everything your grandfather put me through!'

Ziggy's ugly laugh echoed around the yard. 'Excuse me if I don't reach for a violin. You knew what he was like, but you were happy enough to leave us here to deal with him. And that's exactly what I did.' Ziggy jabbed a thumb in his own chest. '*I* did what you couldn't do. I took care of this family. You're fighting a war that ended long ago. You're trying to punish a dead man, but all you're doing is punishing us!'

Unable to let his brother shoulder all the responsibility, Dylan moved to his side and addressed their father. 'If you stopped putting yourself first for one second, you'd see the damage you're doing. I couldn't care less what you do because I got over the fact you've never loved me a long time ago, but the others aren't like that. They're still clinging to some forlorn hope that you can change, but we both know you're too bloody selfish.'

All Monty's righteous anger seeped away, leaving him looking old and shattered. 'How can you say I never loved you? You're my son.'

'Your son you can barely bring yourself to look at.'

Monty took a step towards him, but stopped in his tracks when Dylan held up a hand to ward him off. He needed no comfort from this man. Monty's head dropped, his voice a husky whisper as he said, 'When I look at you all I can see is your mother lying there, all the life drained out of her. She was so ill for such a long time afterwards.'

The pressure in his chest was so strong, Dylan wanted to scream in frustration. 'None of which was my fault!' He shook his head, wondering why he was even wasting his breath. 'I'm done. I don't care enough to fight with you about this any more.' He turned away, straight into Stevie's waiting arms. A moment later he felt Zap's hand settle on his back, then Ziggy's and the four of them were locked together. A united front. Together they had made a stand to protect the people who meant the most to them in the world – their children.

Ziggy shifted to address their father over one shoulder. 'Think hard on what you do next, Monty, because you've run out of bridges to burn.'

19

Sadie was feeling a little delicate when she entered the lounge the following morning and set her coat down on the nearest sofa. The show the previous evening had been great fun, perhaps a little too much fun. The ballroom had been transformed into a nightclub, the walls covered in dark hangings, small tables dotted around the room illuminated with soft-glow lamps. A temporary stage had been erected, and they'd been treated to a cabaret with singers, acrobats and a magician. The show had ended with a marvellous rendition of the cancan and Sadie's hands had been sore from clapping along to the music. Dylan hadn't made it and, although it would've been nice to see him, his absence had given her the opportunity to have a final evening with Charlie, Jane and Anna before they departed this morning. They'd had a brilliant time, shared more champagne than was good for them and finally staggered up to bed some time after one in the morning.

Sadie walked over to the coffee machine as though she'd spotted a long-lost friend and made herself a cappuccino with an extra shot. The lounge was quiet, unsurprisingly, as they hadn't been the only ones late to bed. Clutching her coffee, Sadie settled on one of the sofas near the door so she could keep an eye on who went past. She'd already checked with Reception and she hadn't missed the girls leaving. No doubt they were finding getting up a struggle too.

They appeared about half an hour later, all looking just a shade worse for wear. They made a beeline for the coffee machine just as Sadie had. Each clutching a large takeaway cup, they came over to hug Sadie. 'It's been so much fun,' she said as Charlie stepped back.

'You've got my number,' Charlie replied, reaching out to take hold of her suitcase handle. 'Send me a message when you're home and let me know how the rest of your holiday goes.'

'I will. And once the weather improves we'll fix a Saturday and I'll come into London so we can have lunch.' It had been ages since she'd visited the capital, but there was nothing stopping her now. She'd found her way across country on the train by herself and the one advantage of moving home was she was now within walking distance of the mainline station.

'I'll look forward to it.' Charlie leaned in for another quick hug. 'I hope everything goes well with you and Dylan.'

Sadie pulled back to stare wide-eyed. Oh, goodness, what had she said to them last night. 'Whatever I said, it was just the champagne talking.'

'Our lips are sealed,' Anna said, pretending to zip her mouth closed. 'It's been lovely,' she added, taking her turn to hug Sadie. 'Though I feel like someone is doing the cancan inside my head this morning!'

'Me too. I hope you'll be okay on the flight home.'

'A couple more of these, and I'll be fine.' Anna raised her coffee and took a sip.

Tasha walked into the lounge, her face lighting up as she

spotted them. 'Ah ha, there you are. I'm parked just outside if you're ready to go, ladies?'

'Take care, Sadie.' Jane gave her a quick hug. 'And have a really lovely Christmas. Take lots of photos for us, won't you?'

'Yes, share them in the group,' Anna urged. 'Though it'll only add to my terrible FOMO. I'm going to start saving so I can stay for the whole fortnight next time.'

Sadie walked with her friends to the door, standing on the top of the steps to wave them off. A shiver ran through her and she looked up at the sky. Yesterday's blue skies had been replaced with heavy clouds and there was a yellow warning of snow from a storm moving in from the west. The worst of it looked to be centred mainly on the north-west and Wales, with only the edge of the area on the map skimming the Cotswolds, so it would be a case of waiting and seeing. A dusting would be nice, just enough to cover the fields without causing any disruption. With another shiver she returned inside. If Dylan still wanted to go for a walk, it might be better if they went out that morning, just in case.

She'd finished her second cup of coffee and had managed a couple of slices of toast when Dylan walked into the lounge, his jacket under his arm. The first thing she noticed as he sat down opposite her were the dark-circles under his eyes. 'Everything okay?'

He nodded. 'Yes, fine, thanks. The kids are having a lie-in so if you wanted that walk now would be a good time for me.'

'I'm ready when you are. I was only thinking earlier that we should go out while we can as the forecast for later isn't great. I brought my coat down with me.'

'Let's make a move, then.' They stood and he helped her with her coat before pulling his own jacket on.

As they entered the main entrance hall, Sadie pointed down the corridor that led past the ballroom and eventually towards the orangery. 'If you want to stick nearby in case the children need you for anything, I haven't had a chance to explore the gardens yet.'

Dylan's smile lifted some of the shadows from around his eyes. 'You're always so thoughtful – did I have that on my compliments list?'

'Don't start that again,' she warned him with a laugh as she started along the corridor.

He caught up with her in a couple of strides, and she didn't miss the way he adjusted his naturally longer stride to match hers. 'I still owe you a few. Give me a minute to remember where I left off on my list.'

It was definitely time to change the subject. 'I can't believe the long-weekenders are leaving us today,' she said as they walked into the orangery. The last of the craft projects were still out on display, waiting for the tree's final assembly, which would take place on Christmas Eve. 'I wonder if we'll get any new arrivals?'

Dylan opened the door leading out onto the patio and the gardens beyond, standing aside to let her go through first. 'I'm not interested in making any more new friends. I'd rather concentrate on the ones I've already made.'

She felt her cheeks heating, the cold air making them tingle, or perhaps that was the way he was looking at her. 'You really have to stop flirting with me.'

His expression grew serious. 'Is that what you want? Because the last thing I want to do is make you uncomfortable. I like you a lot, Sadie, but I'm more than happy if we just get to hang out with each other.'

She raised a hand to her cheek, which she was sure must be the most unflattering shade of crimson by now. 'It's not that I want you to stop, it's just, oh God, it's been so long since anyone showed even a flicker of interest in me that I'm afraid I'm hopelessly out of practice.'

With a smile he held out his hand. 'I don't want you to think I'm any kind of an expert when it comes to these matters either. Why don't we start slow and see what happens?'

She hesitated. Getting involved with him would be foolish in the extreme, because it couldn't go anywhere. Come the 28th they'd be going their separate ways. Then again, knowing they had a definite deadline reduced the risk of either of them getting hurt. And hadn't she promised herself she was going to start saying yes to things? Right now she couldn't think of anything she wanted to say yes to more than this lovely man before her. Reaching out, she placed her hand in his. 'Yes, I'd like that very much.'

They strolled in silence along the path and down the steps between the neatly clipped hedges that marked the start of the gardens. Sadie tried to focus on the precise geometry of the gravel paths separating the neat flower beds cut in diamonds and rectangles but it was hard to think beyond the sensation of Dylan's hand holding hers.

She couldn't remember the last time she'd held a hand that wasn't tiny, and usually sticky for that matter. Like many other small intimacies she'd once shared with Pete, it had slipped away over the years. It was another sad acknowledgement of how long they'd been drifting apart even before their split. Pete had always held hers palm to palm but Dylan had laced their fingers together and she liked that it was different.

Dylan tugged her hand gently to steer them onto the path that went off to the left. 'The old ice house used to be down here somewhere. I wonder if it's still there. Shall we go and see if my memory's any good?'

'I'm happy to go wherever you want,' she answered, truthfully.

'Is it strange for you, being back here when so much has changed?'

'It's better than I expected. The hall was getting so run-down before I left, so it's wonderful to see it back to full glory.' He gestured to the perfect lines of the garden. 'Most of this was taken over with weeds by the end. My grandmother did what she could, but she was suffering with arthritis and once the gardening staff were cut back to the bone she had to let some things go. I'm sure she'd love to know everything's being taken care of once more.'

'It sounds like the two of you were close.'

'Yes and no. She was such a different generation and had very strict rules for how she expected us to behave. Children were to be seen but not heard, that kind of thing. She was never unkind, just a little distant. My father was their only child and he wasn't interested in taking on the estate so my grandfather's focus switched to Ziggy when he was still very young.'

'Goodness, that can't have been easy.' She had no experience of such things, having inherited not much more than a few old photos and the contents of her mother's jewellery box. 'How many generations does your family go back here?'

'I don't know the exact count, but all those ghastly portraits we walked past earlier are my direct ancestors. I think the barony was established in the mid to late sixteenth century.' He laughed. 'Somewhere in the crypt my grandfather is turning in his grave at my lack of knowledge of our family history.'

'So your father is a baron? Should I start curtseying to you?' she teased.

Dylan laughed. 'You can if you like, but it's definitely not a requirement. And yes, technically, Monty holds the title but he's not interested in that any more than he is anything else to do with this place. If it was up to him, he'd get rid of the estate altogether.' A scowl marred his brow.

'I'm sorry. I'll stop asking you so many questions because it's obviously an uncomfortable topic for you.'

Dylan squeezed her hand. 'It's okay, it's just that Monty's not exactly my favourite person right now. Not that he ever was, really, but we had a massive row last night.'

Sadie stopped to face him. No wonder he looked tired this morning. 'Not at the reunion dinner?'

He shook his head. 'Not in front of everyone, thankfully, but outside. He's decided to pull one of his disappearing tricks again so Ziggy, Zap, Stevie and I told him he should go for good this time. It doesn't matter to me, but it's clear that he's tearing the others apart. They've invested everything in the estate and it means so much to them.'

'But not to you?'

'No. It'll never be my home, not really, not the way it is for them. But that's not the point. He's hurting everyone with his actions and I can't stand by and let it keep happening. Not now I know it's still going on.' He sighed. 'I never imagined he'd still be pulling the same old tricks as when we were kids.'

It was her turn to squeeze his hand. 'Parents. Who'd have 'em?'

'What a pair we are.' He straightened his shoulders, a determined look on his face. 'Right, enough of that. I'm not going to let him spoil a moment more of today. Let's go exploring.'

The formal gardens gave way to wilder, more natural planting, though a clear path still lay between the bushes and trees. They found the ice house, a large man-made hill in the landscape. The entrance had been sealed off with iron bars and a rusty padlock that looked as if it hadn't been opened for years. They pressed their faces up against the bars, peering into the inky blackness. A breath of cold, stale air kissed her cheek and Sadie stepped back with a shiver.

'I remember going down there once when I was a kid,' Dylan said as he turned away from the bars. 'There's a huge underground void and I remember my grandfather saying it had all been dug out by hand.' He pointed past the ice house towards where the land sloped sharply away. 'There was a lake here back in the day, where they kept fish in the summer and cut the ice in the winter. They dug that all out too, and diverted the river that runs through the estate to create it. Once they converted to electricity, the lake and the ice house weren't needed any more and they could use the land for arable crops instead.'

Sadie nudged him gently. 'I thought you didn't know much about the history of the place.'

He smiled down at her. 'Turns out I know more than I thought. Come on, let's head back. I don't know about you, but I could do with a cup of coffee.'

Sadie glanced up at the heavy grey sky. 'It feels like it's getting colder by the minute.'

Dylan put his arms around her and rubbed his hands up and down her back. 'How's that?'

'Much better.' His hands had stopped moving but he didn't seem in any hurry to let her go. 'Did you do that as an excuse to hold me?' she asked in a light, teasing voice.

'Guilty as charged.' Dylan grinned down at her. 'Do you mind?'

She curled her arms around his waist and leaned against his chest. 'No. I don't mind at all.'

He hugged her tight for a few moments before easing back. 'Now all I have to do is find an excuse to kiss you.'

Sadie laughed and stepped out of reach, though she extended her hand for him to take. 'You work on that and let me know when you've come up with something worth considering.'

'Challenge accepted.'

20

After Dylan had left her with a promise they'd see each other later, Sadie returned to her room. Though the walk had helped her fuzzy head, the cold and her late night seemed to tire her out and she decided to lie on the bed for ten minutes.

When she woke up, it was already growing dark outside her window and when she checked her phone she was surprised to find it was nearly 4 p.m. and she'd slept right through lunch. Deciding a skipped meal wouldn't do her any harm, she settled on the sofa with her Kindle to read for a bit before it was time to go down to dinner. It was a murder-mystery her son Jake had been raving about and she'd downloaded it on a whim. She couldn't deny the writing was good, but her mind wandered too much to grasp the intricacies of the plot. Setting it aside, she picked up her crochet and began to work, but that didn't hold her attention either. She looked around the room. As beautiful as it was and as comfortable as the sofa was, if she'd wanted to sit around on her own she could be doing that at home. It was only casual for dinner that night so she decided to change early and relocate to the lounge.

The cold had kept a lot of people inside, it seemed. Jon and Tara were seated in matching armchairs in front of one of the large windows, coffee cups and empty side plates scattered on the table between them. Jon had his nose in a huge hardback that made Sadie's wrists ache just looking at it and Tara was wearing headphones, her gaze fixed on the rapidly darkening skies outside. A group of other guests, including Marcus, were involved in what looked like a very competitive game of Scrabble. 'Hey, Sadie, want to join us?' Marcus offered, indicating a space next to him.

She shook her head with a smile. 'My spelling isn't up to scratch, I'm afraid, but thanks for the offer. I'm going to find a quiet corner and read for a bit.'

He nodded, his attention already drifting back to the board. 'Well, if you change your mind you know where we are.'

Sadie claimed one of the smaller tables, placing her bag onto a chair before fetching herself a cup of coffee. She helped herself to a miniature mince pie – true, she'd already decided that skipping a meal wasn't a bad idea, but wasn't there a rule that anything you could eat with one bite didn't technically contain any calories? She settled into her chair, opened her Kindle and scrunched her nose at the thought of dipping back into a world of murder and psychological turmoil. Flicking onto her library, she chose a book at random from her to-be-read list, attracted to the sunshiny yellow of the cover as much as anything else.

She lost track of time, the chatter and noise in the room fading as she explored a pretty seaside town along with the heroine in the story. A commotion from outside the room drew her back into the present and a voice she recognised as Dylan's shouted, 'Avery! Wait, you need to put your coat on before going outside.'

A grinning Theo appeared in the doorway of the lounge. 'It's snowing!' he declared before vanishing again.

Sadie wasn't the only one who glanced towards the windows. From the angle she was sitting at they were black mirrors reflecting the lights of the room back at her.

Tara, who had the perfect vantage point, sat up and leaned closer to the glass. 'He's right, and it's proper big flakes, not that horrid wet stuff we normally get.'

Sadie rose to take a closer look. In the external lights, huge fluffy flakes of snow danced and whirled. She didn't know how long it had been snowing, but a thin layer had already settled on the ground. Avery appeared in front of the window, her bright red coat hanging open, her dark hair spotted with white. Arms out, she raised her face to the sky and Sadie imagined she could hear the girl's laughter. Theo ran over to grab his sister by the hand and spin her around before the pair of them ran off, frolicking like a pair of exuberant puppies. Leaning closer to the window, Sadie looked to the left and spotted Dylan standing on the top of the stairs, his smile bright as he watched the kids enjoying themselves. Something tugged at her deep inside and, before she knew what she was doing, Sadie left the lounge, pausing only to retrieve her coat from the cloakroom.

Dylan turned as she pushed open the heavy front door. 'Hey,' he said with a smile. 'I was coming down to find you but we got a little distracted.'

Sadie came to stand next to him. 'I imagine it's something of a novelty for them, what with you living in Florida.'

'They've been skiing with their mom and Eric a couple of times, but, yeah, it's still enough of a rarity for them to get excited.'

'It's lovely to see them so free and happy.' She buttoned up her coat against the bitter chill and watched as the kids chased each other around the fountain. In the distance, colours glowed and shifted and for a moment she struggled to place them before realising they must be part of the illuminated walk. 'I wonder if it's snowing at home.' It would be the first white Christmas for Isla, Robbie and Zac if it was. She folded her arms around herself, soothing the sudden ache to be with her grandchildren. There would be plenty of other times. Robbie, the eldest, was barely four. Give it another couple of years and they'd be the perfect ages to really enjoy the magic of somewhere like Juniper Meadows and all the wonders it had to offer.

'What's put that look on your face?'

Startled, Sadie glanced up to find Dylan watching her, a frown of concern drawing down his dark brows. She shook her head to dispel the touch of melancholy. 'I was thinking about my grandchildren and wondering if they've got snow at home.'

'You don't look old enough to have grandchildren.'

Sadie laughed. 'I was a child bride. I met Pete when I was eighteen and he was twenty-three. We got married when I was twenty, much to my mother's disapproval.'

'I get the impression she disapproves of a lot of things.'

'You have no idea.' Sadie shrugged. 'I was probably a little too young to get married and the chance to get away from home was probably part of the attraction.' She shook her head. 'That sounds a lot more calculating than it was. I loved Pete very much and I always wanted a family of my own. We had Jake when I was twenty-three and Katie a couple of years after that. If it was only up to me I might have waited a little longer but Pete was always ready to do things a bit earlier because of the difference in our ages. When he decided he wanted to retire at sixty, I supported his choice, although I wish he'd decided to leave me before he persuaded me to retire too.'

'I thought he was a bastard before for leaving you, but

persuading you to give up your job and then walking out? That's really low.' Dylan sounded as indignant as she'd felt at the time.

'It was awful,' she agreed. 'I could've asked for my job back, but then I would've had to tell everybody what happened and face all their pitying looks and whispers behind my back. A clean break felt like the best thing under the circumstances. I've moved closer to the kids, and, even though my house is a lot smaller than what we had before, it's my own space. I've found a part-time job nearby that gets me out of the house a few days a week.'

'It must've taken a lot of courage to start again.' Dylan's voice was low, the flash of anger gone.

She nodded. 'I've learned a lot about myself these past few months and I feel a lot more resilient. Coming here feels like a moment of transition and, when I go home, I'm going to make some more changes. I've been content to follow along with what other people want, but that ends now. I'm not saying I regret the past, but the old me was too much of a bystander in her own life.' She held her arms out to her sides. 'You are witnessing the all-new Sadie Bingham.'

Dylan gave her a soft round of applause, his eyes bright with admiration. 'I'm a big fan of the all-new Sadie.'

A warm glow spread through her as she stepped towards him until they were almost touching. 'Good, because I think she's here to stay.'

Avery came running up, hair damp from the still falling snow and her cheeks pink from the cold. Sadie sprang away, but from the avid way Avery was watching them, she hadn't missed the moment of almost-intimacy.

'Everything okay?' Dylan asked, his voice casual as he closed the distance Sadie had made between them. Sadie wasn't sure if that was a good idea, but Dylan knew his kids better than anyone and she was glad he wasn't treating whatever was happening between them as some kind of dirty secret.

The smile on Avery's face wouldn't have looked out of place on the Cheshire Cat. 'It sure looks that way.'

Sadie bit her lip and refused to look away. She was too damn old to let a teenager make her blush. If her cheeks felt at all warm it was only because the air was so cold.

'Did you come over here because you wanted something? Because I've gotta say, your timing sucks,' Dylan said in a wry voice.

Avery giggled, then clapped her hand against her forehead. 'Oh, I nearly forgot! Someone's coming. Theo and I saw lights.' Turning, Avery pointed towards a yellow-golden glow in the distance. 'Theo went to investigate.'

Dylan put a hand on Sadie's back to urge her down the steps with him. 'I hope it's not a car or something, Theo hasn't got a torch.'

'It's probably something to do with the illuminated walk,' Sadie said, trying to reassure him, but she quickened her pace nonetheless.

They'd just about made it to the bottom of the long drive that led towards the main gates when Theo appeared, his breath coming in white clouds. 'Lanterns. The lights are lanterns. It's carol-singers. Shh, listen.'

For a moment the only thing Sadie could hear was Theo panting for breath but then she caught it, the faintest hint of sound. As they watched, the glow resolved itself into four separate patches of light and Sadie found herself smiling as she recognised the tune of 'Silent Night'. 'These must be our four calling birds,' she said. 'We should let the others know as they won't want to miss it.'

'We'll do it, won't we, Avie?' Without waiting for a reply, the kids dashed off towards the hall.

'Put your hats and gloves on before you come back out!' Dylan called after them. Taking his own advice, he pulled a simple black knitted hat out of his pocket and put it on.

The snow was falling heavier and Sadie raised a hand to her hair, surprised at how wet it was. Fishing in her pocket, she retrieved her own hat and tugged it down over her hair. Dylan glanced over at her, a smile spreading across his face. 'Not a word.' She pointed a finger at him in warning.

'It suits you,' Dylan protested.

'Did I mention how unattractive lying is?'

Laughing, Dylan grabbed the finger she was still pointing at him, entwining their fingers together before she could pull away. 'I mean it!'

They arrived at the base of the steps as the first guests pushed their way out of the door, still pulling on their coats. Sadie tugged and Dylan released her hand without protest as they climbed back up to the wide top step and took up position to the right of the door. Jon and Tara came to join them. 'The kids said something about carol-singers?' Jon asked.

'They're coming down the drive.' Sadie pointed towards the four golden lights.

The steps began to fill with people as Avery and Theo came to join them. 'Here, let me make room,' Sadie said, shuffling to one side to make a space.

'Oh, we're fine here,' Avery said, moving to stand in front of Dylan on the step below. 'Aren't we, Theo?'

'We sure are,' her brother agreed, coming to stand next to her. 'Don't stand over there on your own, Sadie, you'll get cold.' He was trying not very successfully to hide a laugh as he said it.

Left with no choice, Sadie shifted back until she was shoulder to shoulder with Dylan. 'Your children have got too much sass for their own good,' she mock whispered to him, sending the kids both into a fit of the giggles. When Dylan reached for her hand, she let him take it.

21

Right in that moment, Dylan didn't think it was possible to be happier, but then his sister went and proved him wrong by pushing open the front door and ushering out a team of staff carrying trays of steaming mugs. They weaved between the guests offering them a choice of mulled wine or a spiced apple warmer, which they assured him was alcohol free. Not being a huge fan of mulled wine, he took a mug of the apple warmer along with the kids. In what proved to be perfect timing, the guests quietened as they sipped their drinks just as the carol-singers moved into the arc of lights cast from the front of the hall. As well as carrying lanterns, the four singers were dressed in period costume, thick overcoats and top hats for the two men, long dresses and hooded capes for the two women.

As they sang the opening lines of 'The Holly and the Ivy' Sadie squeezed his hand and leaned closer to murmur, 'Oh, my favourite.' When the singers reached the chorus, she wasn't the only one who gasped as many more than four voices joined in. More golden lanterns flickered into life as around two dozen other carollers processed across the circular driveway to join the original four in a large circle around the fountain. When the carol ended, Dylan wasn't the only person who bent to place his mug down on the steps in order to give them a round of applause.

The carollers worked their way through a range of familiar tunes: 'Hark! The Herald Angels Sing', 'God Rest Ye Merry, Gentlemen', 'Once in Royal David's City'. They finished with a rendition of 'O Holy Night' that had Sadie sniffing and rooting in her pocket for a tissue. Dylan pulled out his clean handkerchief and handed it to her, earning a glistening smile as she dabbed at her eyes. The staff reappeared from inside the hall, bearing refill jugs as well as trays of fresh mugs, which they distributed amongst the carollers as they came to mingle with the guests.

'If I can have your attention, folks,' the ruddy-cheeked man who had been one of the original four singers called out. 'We hope you enjoyed the show—' A ripple of applause interrupted him and he held up a hand with a smile. 'You're very kind, thank you. Now, before we head off, we've got one more song we'd like to perform and we are going to need your help for this one, so my colleagues are going to help divide you up into groups, so please follow whoever approaches you.'

A plump, cheerful blonde lady in a bottle-green cape turned and smiled at Dylan. 'Do you want to come with me?'

Dylan exchanged a look with Sadie, who had been approached by another woman. The kids were already laughing and joking with a younger man as they went with him and a couple of other guests. 'Lead on, I guess,' Dylan said. He wasn't a huge fan of audience participation, but he supposed if everyone was involved then it wouldn't be too bad. The woman took him and a few others to stand at a point somewhere to the left of the fountain.

One of the male singers joined them with a couple of other guests. 'Right, folks, my name's Jim and this is my wife, Grace.' The blonde woman grinned and gave them a little wave. 'And all you need to know about us is that we are *very* competitive. We don't care about precision, it's all about the volume, okay?'

'Thank God for that,' one of the other guests muttered. Dylan laughed and felt his shoulders relax.

Jim grinned at the joker. 'Now, as soon as I tell you that we are seven swans a-swimming, I'm sure you'll get the idea. Our friends over there—' he pointed to where the original four singers had resumed their position at the front of the fountain '—they're going to lead the song. All we have to remember is to come in at the right time.' He looked around the small group. 'Everyone happy with what we're doing?' Dylan nodded along with the others. 'And what do we want?'

'Volume,' they replied.

Jim rolled his eyes. 'You'll have to do better than that. Don't let me down now.'

It was clear the other eleven groups had received a similar briefing because things grew ever more raucous as they worked their way through all twelve days of Christmas. A couple of the groups had added actions to their lines, which wasn't so bad for the leaping lords and the dancing ladies, but some of the gestures by the milking maids were downright obscene in Dylan's opinion. By the end of the last round he was hoarse from a combination of shouting the lyrics at the top of his voice and laughing at the antics of everyone else. The snow was still falling, his feet were blocks of ice and his fingers were numb even after he'd tucked them in his pockets. He didn't care a bit about the cold, not when the kids came running over to find him, their faces full of joy at the silliness of the past few minutes. 'Did you enjoy that?' he asked as Avery snuggled into his side.

'It was great! Can we go and do the illuminated walk next?'

Dylan wiggled his feet, trying to get feeling back into his toes. He hadn't anticipated them being outside this long and hadn't bothered with his boots. 'I think we should go inside and dry off.' When the kids protested, he held up a hand. 'Come on, guys, you're both freezing cold already and we haven't had anything to eat. Let's do it tomorrow when we've had a chance to plan things properly.'

Theo nodded. 'My feet are wet.' They all glanced down at the ends of his trainers, which had turned dark and soggy.

'And we don't want to risk getting sick and spoiling the rest of Christmas, right?' Dylan added, nudging a still pouting Avery. 'If you don't put your face straight, Santa won't come and visit.'

She burst out laughing. 'Santa isn't real, Dad.'

'He's not? I can't believe it!' They turned to see Sadie standing behind them, her face a mask of pretend shock, one hand pressed to her chest. 'So I've been a good girl for the whole year for no reason? How disappointing!' They all laughed.

'Come on, let's go in and at least change our shoes before dinner,' Dylan said, urging them all towards the beckoning warmth of the hall.

As they walked up the steps Avery linked her arm through Sadie's. 'We're going to do the illuminated walk tomorrow evening. Do you want to come with us?'

'If I'm invited, then yes, I'd love to join you.'

'Great, then it's a date!' With a grin, Avery unhooked her arm and skipped forward through the front door.

Theo groaned. 'Subtle, Avie, real subtle,' he grumbled as he followed her through the door.

Sadie's eyes met Dylan's as he reached out to hold the door open for her. 'Did you put her up to that?' she asked, eyes sparkling with mischief.

Dylan shook his head. 'Oh no, that was Little Miss Match-maker acting all on her own.'

She smiled. 'Well, I think it's sweet of her.' Sadie paused in the entrance hall and turned towards him, her face turning serious. 'She won't get her hopes up, will she?'

It was Dylan's turn to frown. 'About what?'

'About us.' Sadie placed a hand on his arm. 'I like you, Dylan, and your kids are fantastic and I am very happy to spend time with you over the coming days. But while we both know there's no future in this, I don't want the kids getting the wrong idea.'

Dylan stared at her for a long minute before nodding. 'I'll speak to them and make sure they understand.'

Her expression brightened. 'Great. Well, I'm going to hang my coat up and change my wet shoes. I'll see you back in the lounge?'

'Yeah, I'm going to do the same. The kids will probably want to have a quick chat with their mom so we might be a few minutes, but we'll find you in time for dinner.' He watched her disappear into the ladies cloakroom then turned in the opposite direction to go and hang his own coat up. It wasn't only the kids he'd need to have a word with because, if he wasn't careful, Dylan might find himself getting the wrong idea about what could happen between him and Sadie as well.

Dylan returned upstairs to find the kids already changed and on the iPad chatting to Jen. He left them to it to change his shoes and socks, leaving his wet shoes tucked behind the heated towel rail in his en suite to dry. He retrieved the kids' wet things and hung them up in the main bathroom. Once he'd started tidying up, he decided he might as well carry on and soon had a pile of washing ready to put into the hotel laundry. By the time he'd finished listing and bagging everything up, the kids were off the call to their mom and both nose-deep in their phones. Dylan dropped the bag outside their door before he returned to sit in a chair facing the kids on the sofa. 'Hey, guys, can we talk a minute?'

They both peered at him over the top of their screens. 'Are we in trouble?' Avery asked.

'No. Come on, phones down a minute. This is important.'

They both complied, Theo sitting up a little straighter, his brows drawn together in a frown. 'Is something wrong?'

Smiling to reassure them, Dylan shook his head. 'No, far from it, I just wanted to talk to you about the Sadie situation.'

'It's called a situationship,' Avery interrupted him.

'A what?'

'A situationship, like a relationship but you don't know where it's going or you haven't made an official commitment to each other.'

Dylan considered it for a moment. 'I guess that fits where we're at apart from one important thing – Sadie and I both know it isn't going anywhere. We're just hanging out with each for the next few days, okay? Once the holidays are over, we'll be heading back to Florida and Sadie will be going home to her family.'

'So more like a friends-with-benefits arrangement, then?'

Dylan closed his eyes for a long moment, as the two sides of his brain went to war with each other. The primal, protective bit of his brain was shrieking that Avery was still a baby who shouldn't even have the vaguest of understandings about this kind of thing. The sensible, rational part was reasoning that it was only natural for the kids to be curious and it was a good thing that they felt comfortable enough to joke about it. Wishing he'd tried harder at those meditation classes Jen had persuaded him to try back in the day, Dylan opened his eyes and forced something he hoped approximated a smile. 'No, not that either. Let's forget about trying to label it as anything other than a surprise friendship, okay?'

Avery nodded her head, her expression solemn. 'I was only messing around. Sadie seems really nice, is all, and I like that you smile more when you are around her.'

'I do?' Dylan considered that for a moment. He hadn't considered himself particularly in need of more smiles, but he couldn't deny that being around Sadie made him feel good in a way he hadn't in a long time. 'I don't want you to think I'm mad at you in any way, and I'm really glad you like Sadie too. I just want you both to understand that, while I don't mind you teasing me, please just be mindful of the way you speak to Sadie. She's had a really tough year and all I want to do is give her the best Christmas possible, okay?'

'Okay.' Avery came over to sit on the arm of his chair and Dylan put an arm around her waist as he looked over at Theo.

'You're very quiet, pal. Don't hold back if there's anything you want to say.'

'Avie's right, you do smile more when Sadie's around.'

Dylan laughed. 'You're going to make me paranoid. Was I such a grump before?'

Avery put her arms around his neck and kissed his cheek. 'Of course not. Well, apart from in the morning before you've had a coffee.'

Dylan scrunched his face up in a tight scowl, then immediately relaxed his features. 'Yeah, I'm going to have to give you that one.' He gently scooted her off the arm of the chair and stood. 'There's one more thing I need to say before we go down to dinner.'

Theo and Avery looked at each other, and Dylan didn't miss the way they rolled their eyes. He grabbed a scarf Avery had left draped over the sofa and flicked it at them, making sure the end had no chance of touching them. 'I was going to say that the two of you are still my priority above all else, but you can forget it.'

'Aw, Daddy, that's sweet.' Avery came over and hugged him.

Theo joined them, sliding an arm around Dylan's waist and resting his head briefly against his shoulder. 'You're our priority too, Dad.'

22

When Dylan woke the next morning there was something different about his room. He couldn't place it for a moment until he realised the light coming through the small gap in the curtains was much brighter than usual. Sliding out of bed, he shivered at the change in temperature and quickly grabbed the dressing gown he'd left draped over a chair, then pushed back the curtains. He couldn't hold in a gasp as he took in the view before him. It had stopped snowing at some point in the night, but not before several inches had fallen. The rolling vista of the estate grounds had been completely transformed into a winter wonderland. Snow covered the fields and roads in equal measure, flattening the landscape until the only thing that demarcated the road was a thick set of tyre tracks left by one of the family's big black Range Rovers that was parked outside the front of the hall.

From his vantage point he could see the collection of buildings that made up the farm, their roofs buried under a layer of white. Further to the left, the trees in the forest looked as if they'd been sprinkled in icing sugar. The sky was the pale blue of a Wedgwood vase with a few wisps of thin cloud dotted here and there. It looked so beautiful and he couldn't wait to wake the kids up and get downstairs for breakfast. They'd made arrangements to meet Sadie and he couldn't wait to show her more of the estate.

He was waiting for his shower to heat up when then the reality of what he'd just seen hit him and he checked his phone. It was just after 8 a.m. and the estate would be opening to the public in a couple of hours. Or perhaps not, given the state of the internal roads he could see. He opened his news app and a quick scan of the top story confirmed his fears: the snowstorm had affected a larger area than had been forecast and there were reports of blocked roads and drivers being stuck on several major roads overnight – including the M4 and the M5 just a few miles from the estate.

After the quickest shower possible, he dressed in jeans, a thermal long-sleeve T-shirt under a thick black jumper. He shoved his feet into his trainers, the thick socks he'd put on making them tight, but they were only a means to get him downstairs because if the snow was as deep as it looked he'd need to borrow a pair of wellies from the boot room. He went to Theo's room first and knocked on the door before walking in.

Theo cracked open one eye as he approached the bed and sat next to him. 'What time is it?'

'Just after eight. Look there's been a massive dump of snow overnight and I'm worried it's going to have a knock-on effect on the estate so I'm going to go and find Stevie and see what I can do to help.'

Theo bolted upright. 'I'll come with you.'

Dylan patted his leg and stood. 'No, it's fine. You and Avery can chill out. I just need you to keep an eye on things until I get back, okay?'

'There must be something we can do,' Theo argued, pushing

back his covers. 'Even if it's just shovelling a bit of snow off the steps or whatever.'

Pride bloomed inside Dylan. 'If you want to lend a hand, then I'm sure your aunt Stevie can find something for you to do. Look, I'm going to head downstairs. See to your sister and then come down when you're ready, okay?'

'Okay, Dad.'

Dylan's first stop was the lounge to grab himself a cup of coffee. Instead of the young girls he'd got used to seeing, his mother and Tasha were there handing out pastries to the few guests who had made it downstairs. All eyes were fixed on a wall-mounted TV Dylan hadn't noticed before. The sound was down but it was clear from the subtitles and the images on the screen that the weather overnight was the top story on breakfast news.

'Oh, Dylan, good morning,' his mother said, when she turned around and spotted him. 'Did you sleep well?'

'I slept fine, thanks, Mum.' Dylan bent to brush a kiss on her cheek, determined to keep pushing through that horrible distance that had always stood between them. He was rewarded for his efforts by a glowing smile and a pat on the arm. 'How are things after the other night? Are you okay?'

Alice gave him a sad smile. 'Your father went off in the van in a huff, but only as far as the pub car park.'

'He's still in the village?'

His mother nodded. 'If he's waiting for someone to offer him an olive branch, he'll have a long wait. Ziggy told me what happened when you all confronted him and you have my whole-hearted support. Monty knows what he needs to do to try and put things right. It's up to him now.'

Dylan had a feeling there was more than a touch of brave face to her attitude, but he wasn't going to mention it. Alice had chosen her side and stuck to it and he could only admire her. Not wanting to upset her, he decided to change the subject. 'What are you doing here?'

'Everything's topsy-turvy this morning because of the weather,' Alice replied. 'The staff who live outside the village are struggling to get in so Ziggy and Cam have taken a couple of the Range Rovers out to go and collect who they can. Poor Rhys has been out since before dawn trying to clear the drive with the tractor and plough and Zap is down at The Old Stable Yard assessing the conditions there. I couldn't just sit around and do nothing so I offered to come here with Tasha and help with breakfast.'

'I felt the same way as soon as I saw how much it had snowed. I want to help wherever I can.'

Alice patted his arm again. 'Of course you do, darling, it's what family does.'

Tasha came over to join them. 'Alice, can you take a couple of orders through to the kitchen for me?'

'Of course, dear.' Alice took the piece of paper from Tasha then glanced back at Dylan. 'You're not rushing off?'

He shook his head. 'I'm going to grab a coffee and a quick bite to eat. I'll still be here when you get back.' With a smile and a nod, Alice left the lounge. Dylan turned to Tasha. 'Where's Stevie? I want to know what I can do to help.'

'She's in the office trying to contact suppliers we are expecting deliveries from. Thankfully she persuaded the chef and a couple of his team to stay over once we realised the snow was setting in, but we might have to rearrange a few things. I've already had Lydia on the phone and we've agreed she shouldn't risk the journey.' Tasha sighed and glanced over her shoulder towards the window. 'We weren't supposed to catch any of it – so much for the forecast.'

'Do you think you'll be able to open at all today?'

She shrugged. 'It's too early to tell. Hope has already posted a notice on the website homepage that anyone with pre-booked tickets for the ice rink or the illuminated walk can transfer them to another day. We've said that we won't open before midday at the earliest and will provide regular updates. She's in the office to cover any calls and emails that come in and I'll go and back her up once breakfast is done.'

He should've known they'd have it all in hand, but still he couldn't just sit around. 'I want to help wherever you think I can be of most use.'

Tasha's cool professionalism slipped for a second as she grabbed his hand. 'Thank you, we need all the help we can get. Come in the hall with me a minute and we can speak to Rhys as he's in charge of the clear-up efforts.'

Dylan followed her out, passing Alice on the way. 'Oh, are you going already?' There was no missing the disappointment in her words.

He shook his head. 'We're just going to call Rhys and see where I can best help.'

Alice brightened. 'I'll sort out your coffee and something to eat while you do that.'

Dylan followed Tasha over to one of the sofas in the entrance hall and sat beside her while she made a FaceTime call to Rhys. 'I hope you're calling to say you're bringing me a vat of coffee,' he said by way of greeting. 'I'm freezing my bloody balls off.'

Tasha laughed. 'We can't have that. Yes, I'll get some coffee sent out to you, but I'm calling because Dylan is with me and he wants to know what he can do to help.'

'I've cleared most of the drive from the main gate to the junction, and I'm about to start on the road down to the stable yard. I reckon he'll be most use down there if he has a vehicle he can use.'

'I can drop him down there and bring you some coffee at the

same time,' Tasha said. 'I can nip into the office and see how Hope is getting on while I'm there as well. It's pretty quiet here so I'm sure Alice can hold the fort until I get back.'

The sound of footsteps on the stairs drew Dylan's attention and he waved as he spotted Theo and Avery. 'The kids have just come down and I know they're keen to help out. I trust them enough to run orders to the kitchen and fetch coffees or whatever.'

'That's sorted, then,' Tasha said. 'Do you need anything else, darling?' she asked Rhys.

'If you can rustle me up a bacon buttie, I'll love you forever.'

Tasha laughed. 'I'll see what I can do.'

Dylan had just finished making the kids promise they would listen to their grandmother for the third time, when Sadie walked into the lounge. 'Good morning. Can you believe how much snow fell overnight?'

'It's pretty bad. Have you seen the news?'

She shook her head. 'I haven't even switched on the TV in my room. What's happening.'

'Carnage on the roads. There's a big clean-up operation going on. We've got our own smaller version happening to try and get the estate ready to open so I'm just heading out to pitch in.'

Sadie's face fell. 'Oh, I didn't even think of that. I just opened my curtains and thought how beautiful everything looked.' She glanced around. 'What can I do?'

'It's all in hand, although I'd appreciate you keeping an eye on the kids while I'm gone. They're going to give their grandmother a hand with breakfast service.' He sighed. 'I'll have to take a rain check on our walk.'

Sadie reached out and placed a hand on his chest. 'That'll keep. You have more important things to worry about. Focus on doing what you can to help and I'll make sure everything's okay here.'

He immediately felt better. As much as he trusted them both, things might get hectic if there was a sudden influx of guests for breakfast. Sadie's capable calmness would make sure everything ran smoothly until Tasha got back. 'You're the best.' On impulse, Dylan leaned in and pecked a quick kiss on her cheek. Their eyes met and everything faded away for a moment.

'Ready when you are, Dylan,' Tasha called from the doorway, holding up a flask of coffee and an insulated bag.

'Damn.'

'You have terrible timing, Dylan Travers.' Sadie's laugh was a touch breathless.

He groaned. 'Tell me about it. We'll pick this up later, okay?'

'Is that a promise?'

He grinned. Damn right it was.

They found Rhys still working to clear the last of the snow from the junction. He switched off the tractor and jumped down with a smile, gathering Tasha into a bear hug as they got out of the Range Rover to greet him. 'You are a lifesaver,' he said as Tasha untangled herself and quickly poured a cup of steaming coffee into the lid of the flask.

'How's it going? Looks like you're making great progress.' Dylan glanced up the drive towards the main gate, which was now almost completely clear of snow.

'Not bad, eh? As soon as Denny and Jos are finished feeding and checking the animals they're meeting up with Graham, who runs the gardens and maintenance team. They're going to load some salt onto one of the flatbeds and go over what I've cleared. Ziggy's on his way back so hopefully we'll have a few more helping hands in the next half-hour or so.'

'Umm, I think we might have more than a few,' Tasha said in a voice full of wonder. She wasn't looking at Rhys, she was staring past him, pointing towards the drive.

'What the hell?' Where there'd been only an empty stretch of road a moment ago, there were people, lots and lots of people.

'Oh my God.' Tasha's voice was full of tears. 'That's Joe and Martha and Iain's with them too.' She turned to Dylan with a beaming smile. 'They run the shop and the pub.'

'They've got half the village with them by the looks of it,' Rhys said, with a grin.

Dylan gazed at the group of people marching down the drive. They were carrying an assortment of spades, brushes and buckets. It looked as though they'd grabbed whatever they could get their hands on they thought would be of use. In the middle of the group he spotted the familiar multicoloured splash of his father's patchwork jacket. 'Monty's with them.'

Rhys stiffened, his smile vanishing in an instant. 'We don't need anything from him.'

Tasha placed a hand on his shoulder. 'We need all the help we can get.'

He glowered for a moment, then nodded. 'Fine, but keep him away from me.'

Dylan surprised himself by volunteering. 'He can come to the stable yard with me. I'll keep an eye on him.' He was the least affected by Monty and wouldn't hesitate to say something if there was any chance of him causing trouble.

23

They got through breakfast without Sadie having to do much. Alice Travers had everything in hand and the kids were as good as gold, following her instructions. Sadie appointed herself unofficial liaison with the other guests and kept them in the loop about the wider situation on the estate. Several people volunteered their services and Sadie promised to have a word with Stevie and see if there was anything practical they could do. In the meantime, they were happy to keep themselves amused in and around the vicinity of the hall.

About half an hour after Dylan and Tasha had left, the two girls who normally served in the lounge came rushing in, their cheeks flushed from the cold. Stevie was right behind them, a woman Sadie estimated as being of a similar age to her by her side. The two of them were deep in conversation. When they finished, Stevie reached out to hug the other woman, who blushed and then ducked back out of the room. Sadie intercepted Stevie. 'I know you're busy, but I just wanted to let you know that if there's anything we can do there are a number of us who are willing to pitch in as needed.'

Smiling, Stevie touched her arm. 'That's so very generous of you. I might have taken you up on the offer but our head cleaner, Mrs Davies, has brought her entire team to our aid.' Her eyes drifted briefly to where the other woman had recently departed and then she met Sadie's gaze once more. 'Lunch and dinner might be a bit make-do but Chef is on the case and I have faith in his creative abilities. The only issue I have outstanding is this afternoon's entertainment. I was hoping Tasha would be able to step into Lydia's shoes but the phones are going crazy so she can't leave Hope on her own.'

'I'm sure no one will mind giving it a miss under the circumstances. Do you know what they had planned?'

'It was a board game Olympics. I have the winner's trophy in my office, but I don't know what events they'd come up with.' Stevie rubbed her forehead and Sadie couldn't help notice how tired she looked. 'Hopefully Tasha will be back in time to sort things out.'

Sadie looked around the room at the other guests. Some were still gathered beneath the TV, but most were eating breakfast or had settled with books or to chat over a second cup of coffee. She spotted Marcus sitting with a small group she recognised as part of the competitive Scrabble players from last night. 'I think I have an idea...' As she'd suspected, they were only too happy to take on the challenge and they soon had a list of both indoor and outdoor events.

They decided to make a start on the outdoor events while the weather was good, starting with a Christmas pudding shot-put event aided by a donation from the kitchen. The pudding survived longer than it had any right to and Sadie wasn't the only one who was glad she had opted out of the event when Jon, the winner, found out that his special prize was to eat what was left of the pudding after dinner. The next event was a three-legged race with added jeopardy as all contestants were required to wear wellies. Again Sadie demurred, preferring to stay on the sidelines and cheer Theo and Avery on to a well-deserved gold medal – a bag of chocolate coins liberated from one of the trees decorating the hall.

Up next was a snowman-building competition and this time Sadie allowed the kids to rope her in. There were a number of subcategories that would contribute towards the overall score including size, imaginative design and decoration. Theo and Avery opted for size over style points and had rolled an enormous ball for the lower part of the body. The only problem was that in order to balance it out, the upper part they rolled proved difficult for all three of them to lift. 'Need a hand with that?'

They looked up to find Dylan standing there. He looked tired and his jeans and the front of his coat were streaked with salt stains, but he was smiling. Sadie straightened up. 'How's everything going?'

'It's gone pretty well, all things considered, thanks to all the volunteers who helped out.'

'Volunteers? Stevie mentioned the cleaning team had all pitched up to help out at the hall, but I didn't realise you'd had help as well.'

Dylan nodded. 'The village turned out in force. When they realised the seriousness of the situation, Joe and Martha from the village store posted on the local Facebook group asking for help. The schools have broken up for Christmas so lots of people are already on leave. They opened up the village hall as a makeshift crèche for the younger children and everyone else who could spare a couple of hours showed up with shovels and buckets. It was the most amazing sight watching them march down the drive and a testament to how much the locals appreciate everything the family has done for the area over the years.'

Sadie found herself a little choked as she pictured it in her mind's eye. 'That's so lovely.'

'It really was. Penny and Sandra opened up the café and kept everyone working at the stable yard supplied with hot drinks and snacks.'

'Did you get everything sorted in time for things to open?' Sadie had got so invested in the morning's games she'd lost track of everything else.

Dylan shook his head. 'It was just too much to do in order for Ziggy to be confident about safety. But thanks to everyone's hard work, the estate will be able to open in full tomorrow so they've only lost a portion of today's revenue. Most people who had tickets for things today have chosen to defer rather than get a refund, thankfully, but the stallholders at the Christmas market have taken a bit of a hit.'

'Oh, that's a shame, but better safe than sorry.'

'Absolutely, and when I left Hope and Tasha were busy working out a compensation payment and discussing a preferential pitch fee for anyone who wants to take a stall at any of the seasonal events planned for next year.'

'So no walk tonight?' Avery asked in a sad voice. 'I was really looking forward to seeing the lights.'

Dylan hooked an arm around her shoulders. 'That's where I have some good news. Ben and Amelia took a group over to the illuminated walk and they've managed to clear enough of the walkways that, even though Hope and Ziggy decided to pull the plug on everything else, we'll be able to open that this evening.' It didn't escape Sadie's notice that he referred to 'we' rather than 'they'. Whatever distance had existed between him and the rest of the family seemed to have been overcome and it was clear he was fully invested in their success. She was pleased for him and what it would hopefully mean for the future for him and the kids.

'Well, that's definitely a silver lining, and it should look pretty spectacular against a snowy backdrop.'

'Yes, and as a thank you to everyone for their efforts, they've invited the whole village to enjoy the walk for free this evening. With so many tickets likely to be deferred it'll help to create a good atmosphere for those who do decide to make the trip.' Dylan nodded at the big heap of snow they'd gathered. 'Right, let me help you get this lifted up and then I'm going to get showered and changed.'

By the time he returned, they'd rolled and fitted the smallest snowball for the head and Sadie was busy packing and smoothing the joins between the three balls to help hold the snowman together and turn it into a cohesive piece. The kitchen had come through again, supplying the obligatory carrot noses, and Dylan and the kids went off to forage for sticks and stones to act as arms, buttons and eyes. The boot room was raided for hats, scarves and other accoutrements and soon a row of completed snowmen stood ready for judging. As she studied the efforts, Sadie decided that some people had taken things just a touch too seriously. Though she might be guilty of a preference bias, she thought theirs was the most traditional-looking and therefore the most appealing. When the judges declared them the winners, Sadie was thrilled – especially for the children.

Unfortunately, not everyone was a good sport about it. 'Oh, come on! You have to be kidding me! There's no way they deserved to win.'

Avery's face fell. 'What does he mean? Does he think we cheated?'

Theo put a protective arm around her shoulders. 'He's just a sore loser, Avie, ignore him.'

Sadie wasn't the only one who turned to glare at the red-faced man who was standing, hands on hips, next to a life-sized figure that was anatomically accurate enough that it wouldn't have looked out of place in an Antony Gormley art installation. He was one of the Scrabble players and one of the ones who had put Sadie off from the thought of joining in when Marcus had invited her.

'It's just a bit of fun, and the judges' decision is final,' Marcus said, walking over to clap him on the shoulder. 'Come on, it's time for lunch.' When the man made to shake him off, Marcus tightened his grip, his friendly smile turning a touched strained. Sadie wasn't sure what he said next as he'd lowered his voice to little more than a whisper, but the complainer looked chastened enough that he hurried up the stairs of the hall.

His smile returning to full beam, Marcus strolled over to congratulate them and Sadie was pleased at the way he focused on the kids, pointing out things he particularly admired, and soon they were basking in the glow of his praise. Stevie came over to join them, hugging each of the kids in turn. 'Congratulations on a well-deserved win. Now come on in out of the cold and get some lunch.'

Dylan ushered the kids ahead and Sadie noticed with a smile the way Stevie touched Marcus's hand briefly before she moved on to the next group to urge them inside. 'Thanks for stepping in,' she murmured to him as they followed the others up the steps.

Marcus gave her a toothy grin. 'It was my pleasure.' He leaned closer. 'I'll let you into a secret – we'd already decided that, after the way they stepped up this morning and helped with breakfast service, the kids were going to win at least one event. The fact we got to take Barry down a peg or two was just an added bonus.' Sadie was still chuckling over that when they entered the lounge to find a huge buffet had been set up on tables on either side of the bar.

The indoor games started after lunch and each round

inspired a number of inventive efforts to manipulate the results. A 'one wrong and you're out' game of Trivial Pursuit saw most teams drop by the wayside before a prize wedge had even been collected. As it progressed into a grudge match between two teams headed by Marcus and Barry, Sadie decided to retreat to one of the sofas with her crochet and let them get on with it. Avery flopped down beside her and rested her head on Sadie's shoulder. 'Why do people take things so seriously?'

'I have no idea, sweetheart, but I'd much rather be like us than be like that, wouldn't you?'

Avery grinned. 'For sure. Can I make something?'

'Of course.' Sadie rummaged in the bag beside her and produced a fresh ball and a hook. 'Do you want to learn how to make a spiral?'

It didn't take long for both Theo and Dylan to grow bored and join them. Dylan came to sit on the other side of Sadie while Theo sprawled himself sideways across an armchair nearby, his long legs dangling over one side. His earbuds went in and he was miles away in a moment, absorbed with whatever he was watching on his screen. Dylan seemed content to watch Avery's painstaking efforts but his head was soon nodding on his chest.

'Why don't you go and take a nap?' Sadie asked him. 'The kids will be fine here with me.'

Dylan cracked one eye and gave her a sleepy grin. 'I'm too comfortable to get up.' He slid down a little, extending his legs in front of him. His head lolled against her shoulder and in seconds he was fast asleep. Deciding to let him rest, Sadie abandoned her own efforts at crochet and focused on encouraging Avery. It shouldn't have been possible to create such an intimate moment in a room so busy with people, yet the four of them felt like a separate entity, a little haven of peace and calm in amongst the noise and laughter.

'This is nice,' Avery said, nestling against her other side, and Sadie could only silently agree with the sentiment.

24

Dylan woke to a soft hand stroking his hair. When he blinked open his eyes it was to find Sadie staring down at him, a wry grin on her face. 'You were snoring,' she said.

'Oh, sorry.' Dylan struggled up to a sitting position, wondering when in the hell he'd managed to end up with his head in Sadie's lap. He vaguely remembered abandoning Trivial Pursuit when one of the team members had started asking questions in Polish and it had descended into a friendly argument about the rules. He rubbed a hand over his face to chase away the groggy feeling in his brain. 'How long was I asleep?' He noticed then how quiet it was and looked over to find the lounge mostly empty. 'Where'd everybody go?'

'About two hours. The game players decamped to the ballroom for the Twister competition because they needed more floorspace.'

'Rather them than me.'

Sadie grinned. 'I was very disappointed to have to turn down an invitation to join in.' She sounded anything but. 'That finished about twenty minutes ago and most people were ready to call it a day and have gone upstairs to freshen up before the walk. The kids went upstairs to call their mum.'

Dylan glanced around the room once more, feeling guilty at using Sadie as a pillow. 'You should've woken me up earlier.'

'I was happy to let you sleep. You were out like a light so I figured you needed it.'

He rubbed a hand over his face, still feeling a bit jaded. 'I could do with a coffee.'

Sadie rose. 'I'll get you one.'

He jumped up. 'Hey, it's enough that you let me use you as a pillow, you don't need to start fetching and carrying for me.'

She followed him over towards the machine. 'I might get one myself and take it up with me. I want to freshen up before we go out.'

They parted on the first-floor landing with a promise to meet back downstairs in a few minutes. He let himself into the suite just in time to hear the kids saying goodbye to Jen. 'Hey, I'm sorry I crashed out on you like that.'

'That's okay, Dad,' Theo said. 'We were happy hanging out with Sadie.'

It was good to know they felt so relaxed around her. 'How was the Twister?'

Avery rolled her eyes. 'That grumpy man got knocked out in the first round and then started accusing other people of cheating. He really needs to get over himself.'

'He's an ass—' Dylan raised a warning eyebrow at Theo '—inine idiot,' his son hastily corrected himself.

Dylan grinned. 'He sure sounds like it. I hope he didn't spoil things for you?'

The kids exchanged a grin. 'Aunt Stevie told him he was clearly overexcited by the day and suggested he go and lie down.'

Dylan laughed. 'Good for her. Right, I said we'd meet Sadie

downstairs in a few minutes so I'm just going to wash my face and sort myself out.'

'Clean your teeth too,' Avery called after him as he headed towards his bedroom. 'You don't want to have coffee breath if you want to kiss Sadie later.'

Dylan kept walking, deciding it was easier to pretend he hadn't heard her rather than get into another conversation about appropriate boundaries around his relationship with Sadie. He did brush his teeth, though. And use plenty of mouthwash.

When they got downstairs, there was quite a group assembled ready for the walk up to the beginning of the lights. Sadie was waiting near the door, her coat already on and her hat and gloves in one hand. She was chatting to Stevie and Rowena, who were both also bundled up for the cold weather. 'Are you coming with us?' Avery asked, face wreathed in smiles at the idea of getting to spend time with her aunts.

'Yes, darling,' Rowena answered her. 'And we're going to meet the rest of the family on the way. We haven't had a chance to see the lights since they went up and we thought everyone deserved a little treat after all the hard work today.' She turned to Dylan. 'Is that all right with you?'

He nodded. 'The more the merrier.'

As they made their way along the drive in a large, loose group, Dylan took Sadie's hand. 'Hey, I forgot to mention earlier that my father was in amongst everyone when the villagers turned up.'

He felt more than saw Sadie glance up at him. 'I thought he'd left the estate.'

'I thought so too, but apparently he didn't get any further than the pub car park. He didn't say much, only that he hadn't come to fight with anyone, he just wanted to help out. I had intended to keep an eye on him, but there was no need.'

'At least he showed up. I suppose that has to count for something.'

'I guess so, but it'll take more than a morning shovelling snow to make up for what he's done.' Dylan sighed. 'I wonder if he'll show up again tonight.'

'What will you do if he does?'

Dylan shook his head. 'I don't know. I guess we'll have to wait and see what happens.'

The rest of the family were waiting for them at the top of the junction that led from the main drive towards the farmhouse. There was no sign of Monty and Dylan wasn't sure whether he felt relieved or disappointed. There was no time to dwell on it as they got caught up in a whirlwind of hugs and introductions for those members of the family who hadn't yet met Sadie. No one batted an eyelid about the two of them being together and he wondered which little bird had prebriefed them all – Rowena, he guessed from the approving way she was watching the two of them. He decided not to think about how the conversation might have gone. What were family for, after all, if not for gentle interfering? As they continued their walk towards the start of the trail, the kids moved off ahead. Avery was hand in hand with her grandmother and Theo was laughing with Ben and Amelia over something he was showing them on his phone. Ziggy and Daisy matched pace with him and Sadie and the two women soon fell into conversation.

'Thanks for helping out earlier,' Ziggy said, coming to stroll on his other side.

'You don't need to thank me.'

'Well, I'm going to anyway, and while I'm on the subject I'm going to thank you for making such an effort with Mum. I've been a bit worried about her because of this impasse with Monty so it's been great for her to have something positive to think about.

She's absolutely smitten with the kids, hasn't stopped talking about them since she came back from helping out at the hotel earlier.'

'I think it's an entirely mutual thing,' Dylan said, watching Avery cling to her grandmother's hand as she chattered away like a little bird. 'I hadn't thought about how much being separated from you all might have been affecting them.'

'Well, that's not something you have to worry about any longer.'

'True.' They walked along a bit further. 'What are we going to do about Monty?'

His brother sighed. 'Is it too much to hope that what we said the other night had enough of an impact on him for him to change his ways?'

'Probably.'

Ziggy half laughed, half groaned. 'Parents, who'd bloody have them?'

The answer as to whether Monty really was determined to change was answered when they reached the brilliant-white tunnel of fairy lights that marked the entrance to the illuminated walk. Monty was standing there, clutching a bunch of yellow roses. He'd made some effort with his appearance – the familiar patchwork coat was still in evidence but he was wearing a collared shirt and a nice jumper beneath it and his face looked freshly shaved. Dylan even caught a whiff of aftershave as his father stepped forward and offered the bouquet to Alice. She looked at it for a long moment. 'They're the same as when we got married,' Monty prompted.

'I'm surprised you remembered.'

Monty looked genuinely wounded. 'I'll never forget what was one of the happiest days of my life.'

'It's going to take more than flowers, Monty,' Dylan's mother said, sounding tired.

'I know, and I'm not asking for anything other than the chance to escort you around the walk.' Monty shuffled his feet. 'I miss you.'

Dylan felt Sadie's hand grip his tighter as there was another drawn-out pause and he squeezed back, feeling helpless to do anything other than stand witness. This had to be Alice's decision. She looked at Monty for a long moment before nodding once. 'A walk.' Monty's smile was brighter than the lights overhead as he offered Alice his arm and the pair strolled forward together, Monty still clutching the bouquet she'd refused to accept.

There were several sighs of relief around the family as they watched them go. 'Does this mean I'm going to have to forgive the old bastard?' Dylan heard Rhys grumble as he took Tasha's hand and they stepped into the tunnel of lights.

'I wouldn't go that far, son,' Zap said over their laughter. 'He's still got plenty of time to muck things up.'

Rowena hooked her arm through his. 'What will be, will be. Right now we have a chance to make some good memories so let's focus on that.'

'Wise words, my love.' Zap kissed her briefly and they walked beneath the tunnel, the rest of the family following in their wake.

'Is everything okay with Grandma and Grandpa?' Avery asked Dylan, looking pensive.

Dylan tucked an arm around her shoulders. 'I don't know, but it's not something you need to worry about, Avie, okay?'

She nodded, but didn't look convinced so Dylan turned her to face him. He'd always done his best to be honest with both the kids, but Avery had a tendency to want to fix things. He knew it came from him and Jen breaking up. As hard as they'd tried not to hurt them in the process, some things left a scar.

'Grandma loves Monty very much but he's caused a lot of hurt to everyone because of things that happened to him before you were born, before I was born even. Hopefully he's going to try and come to terms with that and move forward as part of the family instead of always standing against us, but people can't always find it in themselves to change, even when they want to. Your aunt, uncles and I have got Grandma's back and we'll support her however she needs, but that's our job, not yours. All you have to do is keep being your sweet self, okay?'

Avery nodded. 'I like Grandma a lot. Do you think she might like to come and visit us some time?'

Dylan pressed a kiss to the top of her head. 'We can definitely ask her, but not tonight, okay?'

'Okay.'

Dylan gave her another quick hug then released her. 'Come on, let's catch up with everyone.'

It didn't take long for the lights to distract Avery and she soon had her phone out, filming little clips and taking photos to share with her friends. Dylan was content to let her explore on her own, though he made sure to keep her in sight. Sadie linked their arms together and leaned against him. 'For what it's worth, I think you handled that very well.'

'Thanks. Sometimes it's hard to know the best line to take with her. She's growing up so fast, but she's still my little girl and I want to protect her. She's too old to be told not to worry about things though, so I have to give her enough information without dumping everything on her shoulders.'

'Well, it's clear she feels comfortable coming to you when something is troubling her so that's more than half the battle right there.'

Dylan glanced down at her. 'I get the impression you're close to your kids as well?'

She nodded. 'Yes, I'm very lucky that way. I did feel a bit guilty when they completely sided with me against their father, but they are old enough to make their own choice when it comes to him. If they decide in time to give him another chance, then I won't interfere. He was always great with the grandchildren and I'm sure he misses them terribly.'

Once again Dylan was struck by what a fool her husband must be to have thrown everything away so easily. 'Choices have consequences.'

Sadie smiled. 'They certainly do. And now I am choosing to forget about everything else and simply enjoy myself for the rest of the evening.'

'Now that's a plan I can get behind.'

Hand in hand they wandered along the trail. The volunteers had done an amazing job, and the temporary walkways felt secure underfoot. They moved with the ebb and flow of the crowd, delighting in the reactions of the little ones around them as much as the lights themselves. Avery was like a butterfly, flitting backwards and forwards between them and other members of the family. As each lighted tunnel ended, the view opened up to reveal a new display. A field of multicoloured circular lights that pulsed in time to the music; a sparkling herd of deer grazing. The snow enhanced everything, reflecting and amplifying the lights until everything seemed to shimmer. The walkway and tunnels led them on a meandering loop through the grounds and eventually on to one of the walking trails in the woods. Spotlights turned the branches overhead green and red and purple and Christmas carols played from hidden speakers. As they turned a corner, the music changed to 'The Twelve Days of Christmas'.

'Oh, look!' Sadie pointed to a clearing where an illuminated tree shone brightly. Golden pears sparkled against the green background and a silvery partridge nestled in the heart of the tree. The song led them along the path, each verse represented by a beautiful tableau set back in amongst the trees. Two turtle doves cooed at each other from opposite tree branches on either side of the trail. The three French hens pulsed from blue to white to red in the colours of the *Tricolore*. The four calling birds made them laugh as they shouted greetings to the people walking underneath.

Five golden rings spun like Catherine wheels, drawing gasps of wonder, while the six geese rested on woven nests. The swans swam across a circle of blue lights, two proud parents followed by a little tail of five tiny cygnets. There were more sound effects from some very disgruntled cows that clearly objected to being milked, by the amount of mooing. Nine ladies danced in a circle around the base of a huge ancient oak while the ten lords leapt and pranced around in the branches overhead. The display ended with an illuminated guard of honour, first from the pipers who filled the air with the rousing squirl of their bagpipes and lastly by the twelve drummers, their arms moving up and down in time to a rat-a-tat beat.

'That was spectacular,' Sadie said as they weaved their way through the people who'd stopped to admire the drummers and into a quieter part of the woods. Dylan could see the end of the trail up ahead and he glanced around, not ready to let the moment end. He spied an illuminated decoration hanging from the branches of a tree and tugged Sadie off the path until they were standing beneath it. 'What are you doing?' Sadie asked as he gently backed her towards the trunk of the tree.

Dylan grinned as he clasped her waist in his hands. 'Look up.'

She tilted her head and he watched as her eyes widened when she realised what she was looking at: a sparkling ball of mistletoe. Raising a hand, he cupped her cheek, drawing her attention back to him. 'You know it's the law that you have to kiss the person you stand under the mistletoe with, right?'

Sadie's laugh was low and sultry and it tugged at things deep inside him. 'I'm not sure it's actually the law.'

Dylan grinned as he leaned closer. 'Maybe not, but it's the excuse I've been looking for.' He touched his lips to hers, the softest of brushes to test the water. His other hand rested just over her hip, a gentle embrace she could break instantly free from if he'd misjudged the moment. He needn't have worried because Sadie raised her arms to circle his neck, pressing into him as she returned the kiss. It was hard to feel anything with the thick layers of their clothing between them, but her enthusiasm was enough to light a fire in his veins. Her hands shifted from his nape to his shoulders, a gentle pressure but one to which he responded immediately. He pulled back to look at her. 'Everything all right?'

She nodded, a rosy glow on her cheeks he was sure was from more than the cold. 'Not here, not in front of everyone.'

'Of course.' He stepped back to give her room, holding out a hand, which she instantly took, and they quickly rejoined the happy flow of people wending their way towards the end of the trail.

25

There were many times over the next couple of days when Sadie found herself questioning her sanity. She felt giddy as a school-girl, unable to resist whenever Dylan persuaded her into a quiet corner so he could kiss her and hold her against the firm strong length of his body. Sensations long dormant shifted and stirred inside her until she didn't know what to do with herself. Not that she was a passive partner in what was developing between them, not at all. Whenever they were together, Sadie found an excuse to touch him and more than once she caught herself scanning for a nook they could duck into and steal a private moment together. She knew she needed to be careful, to simply enjoy the moment and not let herself get carried away with fantastical thoughts of the future, but, oh, it was hard. Harder still to send him on his way when he walked her to her bedroom door every night.

As strong as the urge to be with him was, Sadie was also conscious of not monopolising all of his time with the kids. When they invited her on the treasure hunt to find the six golden goose eggs hidden around the hall, she demurred, saying she wanted to visit the Christmas market instead. It wasn't an excuse and she spent a lovely couple of hours wandering the stalls and picking up little gifts for Dylan and the kids. At the workshops she found some beautiful jewellery for Katie and Rachel handmade by Carrie-Ann the silversmith, a new wallet for Liam at the leather workshop next door and a selection of flavoured gin miniatures, which she knew would be well appreciated by Jake.

The entertainment the following evening was an ice-skating show on the temporary rink with a *Swan Lake*-inspired theme. Sadie allowed herself to be persuaded to join Dylan and the kids and she enjoyed both their company and the show, though she drew the line at joining in when the rink opened back up for casual skating. Theo refused as well, opting to fetch hot chocolate for both himself and Sadie. Which left poor Dylan to accompany Avery onto the ice. Even with the penguin-shaped skating aids that were supposed to help with balance, they both took more than one tumble, and by the time Dylan had wobbled his way around half a dozen times with zero signs of improvement, it was clear he'd had enough. 'I'll be black and blue for a week,' he grumbled as Sadie helped him over to the bench where he could remove his skates.

'Well, at least Avery is enjoying herself,' Sadie said, glancing over his shoulder to keep an eye on her, and she was rewarded with a cheery wave as the teen swooped past as if she'd been skating all her life, not less than half an hour. Oh, for the fearlessness of youth! 'Here, Theo's got something that will make you feel better.' She'd despatched him back to the drinks stall to collect the cup of spiced apple warmer she'd already paid for. There was a hot chocolate waiting for Avery when she'd finished too.

By the time they'd walked back to the hall they were all cold and tired and ready for an early night. Dylan was limping noticeably as they ascended the stairs, but he insisted it was fine as he escorted Sadie along the corridor to her room. 'I can find my own way,' she protested. 'You should go and have a hot shower.'

'There's a shower in your room,' Dylan said with a wicked grin as they reached her door. 'You could help me massage the stiffness away.'

'Dylan Travers!'

'What?' The look he gave her was all wide-eyed innocence apart from a telltale gleam in his eye. 'I was talking about my sore leg.'

'Of course you were.' She put a hand on his chest and gave him a gentle push. 'It's time for bed.'

'No massage?'

She laughed. "Fraid not. You'll have to settle for a kiss instead.' In the end he settled for a dozen kisses, leaving her breathless and more than a little weak at the knees. 'Will you be all right for tomorrow?' There would be more than eight maids a-milking as the family had arranged a visit to the estate farm for those who were interested. Sadie could've taken or left it, but the kids had begged her to come with them and she was finding it harder to stick to her resolution of not intruding on their family time. It wasn't just the chance to be with Dylan, either – she was growing increasingly fond of Theo and Avery and she would miss them as much as she missed their father.

The time had flown past so quickly and there was less than a week before they'd all be going their separate ways. While it had done her the world of good to get out of her sad little bubble and into the world again, the extravagant décor and warm welcome she'd received at the hall were going to make her little house seem even more pokey and depressing. She pushed the thought away. Her time at Juniper Meadows was all about living in the moment. No need to spoil what was left of it by worrying about what would happen once she was back home again.

The visit to the farm was much more fun than she'd anticipated. Tara and Jon had spoken to Stevie and arranged permission for their son-in-law, daughter and grandchildren to join them on the visit and the little ones had a whale of a time. Rhys was a fountain of knowledge. His passion for his project to use the farm to preserve rare breeds shone through, as did his dedication to his animals. Theo had a go at milking a cow, while Avery preferred to spend time helping Hope groom her horses.

The younger ones helped where they could, putting out fresh straw for bedding and helping to fill water troughs with little buckets. 'This takes me back years to when I used to take my children to a local farm park when they were this age. They used to spend hours petting the rabbits and guinea pigs,' Sadie said to Rhys as they watched the children spill more water than they managed to get in the troughs.

'We try to discourage rabbits on the farm, not give them homes,' Rhys said, wryly.

'Oh, not that kind of rabbits, these were specialist breeds with big lop-ears. There was a whole barn dedicated to child-friendly animals.' A memory came back to her and she laughed. 'Well, the miniature goat that butted my ex-husband in the bottom wasn't that friendly.'

'An animal with good instincts,' Dylan said with a laugh as he came to join them. 'Can I borrow you a minute? There's something I wanted to show you.'

Sadie excused herself from Rhys, who barely acknowledged their departure, his attention on the children and a deep frown creasing his brow. Dylan led her by the hand into a stall in the far corner of the barn and closed the half-door behind them. 'What did you want to show—?' The rest of her question was cut off by his mouth. With a sigh, Sadie sank into the now familiar warmth of him. How was it possible she'd grown so used to this in just a few short days? They emerged some time later to find the visit almost over. As they hurried to join the others out in the yard, Sadie reached out and hastily brushed away some straw that had stuck to the back of Dylan's fleecy jacket.

They found the kids standing with Alice, who was looking festive in a bright red jumper over a pair of jeans. 'We were just coming to look for you,' Avery said. 'Grandma has invited us to stay for lunch. Can we?'

'Of course,' Dylan agreed.

'You're very welcome to join us, Sadie,' Alice offered with a smile.

Sadie shook her head. 'I have things to do this afternoon, but thank you.' Spending time with Dylan and the kids was one thing, but she knew how fragile this burgeoning relationship he had with his mother was and it was important for them to strengthen those bonds.

'Another time, then,' Alice said with a smile as she reached up and pulled something from Sadie's hair.

She stared at the long stalk of straw for a moment, feeling the heat rise on her cheeks. 'Yes, another time.'

Dylan reached for her hand and gave it a quick squeeze. 'I'll catch up with you later.'

In the end they didn't get the chance to catch up. Lunch with his mother rolled on into dinner with the rest of the family. Dylan sent her a text to apologise but she assured him there was no need. Sadie spent a quiet afternoon catching up on her much-neglected reading and enjoyed a lovely FaceTime chat with Robbie and Zac, who had reached a level of excitement about Father Christmas coming to visit that Sadie was quietly thankful her kids had sent her to Juniper Meadows. Robbie in particular was worried about how Santa would know where to find her because she wasn't going to be at home and she had to reassure him that she'd sent her Christmas letter off with the correct address in time for the elves to update their database. Reassured, he ended the call blowing her so many kisses she felt almost tearful by the time they ended the call. After a good talking-to, Sadie joined Tara, Jon and Marcus for a light supper before returning to her room for a long, indulgent soak in the roll-topped bath. She fell asleep that night with a smile on her face as her mind replayed a montage of Dylan's kisses from earlier.

26

Saturday morning dawned clear and dry. After a busy couple of days, neither of the kids were in the mood to be sociable so Dylan agreed they could have a chill-out day in their rooms. He'd hoped that would give him a free day to spend with Sadie but they were just finishing a late breakfast when he got a text from Ziggy asking him whether he was free to lend a hand for a couple of hours. A combination of the clear, sunny weather and the estate being closed for three days between Christmas Eve and Boxing Day had brought the crowds out in force and there was already a queue of cars snaking through the village and threatening to cause chaos in the area.

'Of course you must go,' Sadie urged him.

'I know, but I was looking forward to a bit of time just the two of us,' Dylan said regretfully even as he was getting to his feet.

'You can be my date at the dance tonight,' Sadie said with a smile as she reached for the last slice of toast and spread butter and marmalade on it, then offered it to him. 'You'll need to keep your energy up,' she added, her smile warming to something that promised him all sorts of things he intended to make good on.

'It's a deal.' He bent forward to claim a quick kiss. 'The kids are having a lazy day so I don't expect you'll see much of them.'

'I'll probably stretch my legs around the gardens in a bit, but I'm not going far so let them know they can text me if they need anything.'

'Great. I'll see you later.'

By the time he'd been upstairs to let the kids know about his change of plans and got back down again, Ben was waiting outside for him in one of the Range Rovers. 'Ziggy and Rhys are sorting out the traffic, so we're on parking duties if that's okay?'

'I'm happy to pitch in wherever I'm needed,' Dylan assured him as he pulled on his belt and his nephew drove away. They reached the car park by the stable yard to find Hope waiting for them with a couple of fluorescent yellow vests with the word STEWARD printed in bold black print on the back.

Once they'd pulled on the vests, she handed them each a walkie-talkie. 'Brace yourselves because Rhys has just opened the gates. We decided it was better to let everyone in early before the queue backed up beyond the village and started to affect the bypass. I need to go and let the vendors know, if you two can handle this?'

'We've got it, sis,' Ben assured her.

With Ben positioned near the gate and Dylan at the other end of the car park they managed to control the flow of early arrivals. Thankfully most people were happy to follow directions, but there were inevitably a couple of jokers who decided their need to park as close to the entrance as possible was more important than not disrupting anyone else. Deciding it was not worth wasting time arguing the toss with them, Dylan focused on guiding the car nearest him into the next space. 'There's always one,' the driver said as he passed Dylan.

'Always. It just makes me extra appreciative of everyone else. Have a great day.'

Their ranks were soon swelled by a couple of local teenagers who were part of the roving support crew the family had employed, so Dylan released Ben to go and open his pottery workshop. Within an hour everything was running smoothly and Hope dropped by to say she was happy for the rest of the expected visitors to self-park. She deployed the teens to the Christmas market area to litter pick while Dylan popped into the café for a coffee to thaw out. Spotting a handful of tables waiting to be cleared, he gathered the dirty plates and cups on his way past. Penny thanked him profusely and he was soon on his way again with a complimentary cappuccino.

The workshops were busy but managing, so Dylan checked in at the distillery to find Zap dealing with a long queue. And so the morning passed with Dylan moving in rotation around the stable yard, pitching in for ten minutes here and half an hour there to ease any bottlenecks that had built up. He was just leaving the distillery when he bumped into Hope coming the other way. 'Oh, hey, you're still here,' she said, sounding surprised.

Dylan shrugged. 'No one told me I wasn't needed any longer so I've just been knocking around making myself useful.'

His niece smiled. 'Well, you've done a brilliant job, but I think we've got everything in hand now. I can drop you back off at the hall if you'd like? My car's just round the back.'

'If you're sure?'

'Absolutely. You're supposed to be on holiday after all.'

'I should go and check on the kids at least.' He'd texted them about an hour ago and got a thumbs up from Theo and an eye-rolling emoji from Avery. The reply he'd received from Sadie was more responsive. She'd been for a stroll around the gardens with

Tara and had been heading to her room for a nap before the party that evening.

Dylan followed Hope to her car, unclipped the radio from his belt and handed it to her as he climbed into the passenger seat. The short drive to the hall was uneventful and she was soon pulling up at the bottom of the steps. Hope leaned across the centre console and gave him a one-armed hug. 'Give the kids my love and I can't thank you enough for stepping in at such short notice this morning.'

'I was happy to do it.' He smiled, feeling a little bashful. 'It was nice to feel like I was doing something to help the family, even if it was only for a couple of hours.'

'You've helped us all more than you can ever know just by coming back. Even with Monty acting up, Mum is happier than I can remember her being since Ben came home last year.'

Dylan couldn't hide a grin. 'I'm not sure your mum's good mood has all that much to do with me.'

Hope narrowed her eyes at him for a moment and then a slow smile spread across her face. 'Tell me more.'

Dylan opened his door and backed out of the car. 'I know nothing.'

'Hmm.' Hope was leaning across the seat staring at him as though she wished she had mind-reading skills.

Laughing, Dylan closed the door and jogged up the steps.

* * *

The ballroom had once again been transformed for the evening's entertainment. The walls had been covered in black backdrops covered in tiny sparkling lights and a DJ booth had been mounted on the stage, flanked by large arrays of disco lights that flashed pink and gold and green. Disco balls hung from the base of each of the elaborate chandeliers, their crystal magnificence hidden under more carefully draped black cloth. Headphones covered a table on the right of the door and everyone was instructed to help themselves to a set and gather on the dance floor. Dylan took a pair and handed them to Sadie. She was looking particularly lovely tonight in a silvery top covered in crystal beads that shone with the colours of the aurora borealis when they caught the light at the right angle. She was wearing a pair of black jeans that clung to her hips and thighs and flared out at the ankles. On her feet she had a pair of pretty trainers, black with a floral design on the toes and heels. He'd also opted for jeans and a blue and white checked shirt with the sleeves folded back to his elbows. Sadie accepted the headphones with a smile, the collection of silver bracelets jangling on her wrist as she raised her hand. Dylan took two more pairs for the kids and a final one for himself. Together the four of them moved to join the other guests on the dance floor.

'Evening, folks!' the DJ said, moving to the front of the stage. 'It's great to see I'm going to have more than nine ladies dancing tonight. Now, quick show of hands, who's been to a silent disco before?' A couple of hands were raised, but not many. 'Okay, well, it's pretty straightforward. If you look on the side of your left headphone you'll see a set of control buttons. Top is on and off, the volume buttons are left and right and the bottom one is your channel selector. We'll have three channels in total. The first one is modern hits for the younger guests.' He smiled and nodded at Avery and Theo. 'The second is dedicated to everything eighties.' Dylan and Sadie shared a grin – that was much more like it. 'And the last one is for the rock and rollers with the best of the fifties and sixties. You can switch between the channels as you please and we'll change them up later in the evening for something a bit more mellow. Channel one will be chill-out instrumentals,

channel two will be a slow-dance mix for all you lovers out there.'
Dylan tried to ignore Avery's sudden poke in the ribs. 'And the
last channel will be smooth classics. Any questions about how
the headsets work?' Dylan looked at Sadie, who shrugged and
shook her head. It sounded simple enough.

The DJ moved back behind the mixing desk and Lydia took
his place at the front of the stage. 'The most important thing to
remember is to dance like no one is watching. Don't think about
anyone else, just focus on the music and enjoying yourselves. It
might seem a little strange at first because you'll be moving in
time to different songs.'

'Wouldn't matter if we were all listening to the same thing if
you've got two left feet like me,' Jon said in a wry voice, which
earned him a number of sympathetic chuckles.

Lydia smiled down at him. 'That's the joy of the silent disco –
everyone looks like they're getting the steps wrong. We'll turn the
lights down lower once we get started so that'll help the
atmosphere as well. There'll be plenty of refreshments
throughout the evening so don't forget to stay *hydrated*.' More
laughter greeted her emphasis of the word. 'Right, that's more
than enough from me. Let's get this party started, shall we?'

The moment she stepped back the crowd on the dance floor
dispersed and people made a beeline for the tables and chairs
scattered around the outside of the room. Dylan claimed a table
near the back, holding out a chair for Sadie while the kids helped
themselves to their own. The lights dimmed and the disco lights
began to pulse and flash, casting beams across the empty dance
floor. Dylan fiddled with his headset, adjusting it until it sat
comfortably and testing out the channels and the volume. Taylor
Swift urged him to shake it off on the first channel, while Duran
Duran were singing about Rio dancing on the sand on the
second. He flipped briefly to the third where The Beatles were

twisting and shouting, then clicked through until he was back on the eighties mix. The DJ was bobbing around behind his desk, waving his hands in the air like he just didn't care, but the dance floor remained resolutely empty.

'Why's nobody dancing?' Avery asked, her voice loud because she was wearing her headphones.

Dylan tapped his ear to indicate she should take them off and when she did so, he said, 'I suppose no one wants to be up first. Why don't you start things off?'

She shook her head. 'I'm not going up there on my own.'

Theo glanced up from where he was fiddling with his phone. 'Don't look at me.'

It was Sadie who came to the rescue. Standing, she held out her hand to Avery. 'Come on, let's show them how to party.'

Avery still looked a little uncertain but she took Sadie's hand and let her lead her towards the front. Sadie paused at a table nearby and collected Tara and Jon, the latter looking much less enthusiastic than his wife but still game to give it a go.

Bold as brass, her gleaming cap of golden hair shining in the disco lights, Sadie strode to the middle of the floor, released Avery's hand and began to sway from side to side. Avery moved next to her, clearly listening to something different from the difference in their pace. Off to the side, Tara and Jon faced each other, Jon moving with more grace that Dylan had expected given his earlier self-deprecating comment. The four of them were enough to spur a few others on and slowly the dance floor began to fill in dribs and drabs.

Sadie raised her arms over her head, spinning in a circle, her face lit up by a beautiful smile. She was lost in another world, uncaring about anyone or anything other than the music only she could hear. Dylan caught his breath, mesmerised at the sight. She'd transformed in just a matter of days and confidence seemed to radiate from her. She paused in her spin and looked towards where he was sitting. He doubted she could see much of him across the darkened room but when she stretched out her hands towards him, Dylan didn't hesitate.

They danced for what felt like hours and every time Dylan thought they might take a break another absolute banger of a song filled his ears and the urge to dance took him over again. The years fell away, the music taking him back to those sweaty, booze-filled nights wired into the collective energy of a nightclub packed with heaving, shifting bodies. But his body reminded him he wasn't eighteen any more and eventually he had to admit defeat and let Sadie lead him back to their table for a rest.

He tugged off his headphones, the sudden silence disorientating for a moment. Sadie handed him a bottle of water she'd snagged from the refreshment table, her own face shiny, her fringe damp and clinging to her forehead. 'Thank God I wore my trainers,' she said, collapsing with a grin into the chair next to him and taking a swig from her own bottle of water.

When he nudged Theo's leg, his son glanced up from his phone. 'What?'

'Are you not having a good time?'

Theo shrugged. 'It's all right but the music isn't really my thing.'

Dylan frowned. 'You don't have to stay down here if you're not enjoying yourself.'

Theo lounged back in his chair and propped his feet on an empty one opposite. 'I'm okay, Dad, really. You and Avie and Sadie are having a good time and I'm happy just hanging out. Aunt Stevie's already been and checked on me and she said there's a supper buffet coming out soon.'

Dylan leaned over and patted his leg. 'Okay, but I don't want you to feel like you have to stick around if you're bored.'

'I'll wait and see what the food's like and then I might go and game with my friends for a bit, if that's okay?'

Dylan checked his watch; it was not quite nine o'clock. The kids had had a lazy day and there was nothing on the agenda for tomorrow until a planned trip to the village church for Midnight Mass. 'Okay, you go up when you're ready, but lights out by eleven-thirty?' He doubted he'd be up that late himself but the time difference didn't make things easy for the kids to connect with their friends and he wanted Theo to have a chance to enjoy himself.

Avery wound her way towards them and plopped down on the chair next to Sadie. 'I'm boiling!'

'Let me get you a cold drink.' Before Dylan could move, Sadie was up and heading for the refreshment table. She returned with a bottle of water and a linen napkin. She handed the water to Avery, then dampened the napkin from her own bottle and folded it into a square. 'Here, see if that helps.'

Avery took the cloth and wiped her face with a happy sigh. 'Oh, that feels good.'

Dylan shuffled his chair closer to Sadie's and put his arm around the back of her chair, liking the way she shifted her body to lean slightly against him. 'You feeling okay, Avie?'

His daughter nodded. 'Yeah, I'm fine, it's just hot up there in the lights.'

'Well, we can chill out here for a bit. Theo says there's some food coming out in a minute if you want something to eat, and then he's going to go upstairs. You're welcome to stay with us or you can go upstairs and chat to your friends for a bit. It's up to you.'

In the end, the kids both headed upstairs, each with a plate loaded with sausage rolls, chicken goujons and all sorts of other goodies. 'You'd think they hadn't eaten for a month,' Dylan said, shaking his head as he returned to the table.

'Oh, for a youthful constitution that still burned calories that easily,' Sadie said, eyeing her much more modest plate.

With a grin, Dylan nudged it closer towards her. 'Eat up, you're going to need the energy because I intend to dance until we drop.'

27

Dancing with Dylan was a revelation. He gave himself over to the music in a way that spoke to the part of Sadie that loved to do the same. It wasn't that Pete never danced with her, he was always willing to get up at a wedding or a party, but he usually required a few beers and a big crowd he could hide in. And it had always felt as if he was going through the motions, as though he had a few safe steps that he'd learned looked okay and he stuck rigidly to those. He didn't feel the music, didn't get pulled into the rhythm, didn't dance because it was impossible not to move his body to the beat. The hair at her nape and temples grew damp with sweat and she was sure if she looked in a mirror her face would be shiny from the exertion. When she woke in the morning she'd probably regret it, but right now she didn't care about any of that. She just wanted to dance.

As the first insistent beats of 'Blue Monday' came through the headphones, Sadie glanced at Dylan and they exchanged identical grins. She couldn't remember the last time she'd heard the iconic track of her youth and yet it was as if it were yesterday. She knew every note, every transition before it happened, the lyrics coming unbidden to her lips. She wasn't a mother or a grand-mother, not a jilted wife, or a girl who'd been battered and bruised by a mother's indifference, not even a woman with the shimmering promise of love just over the horizon if she reached for it. They were all parts of her, but she was more than that. For the first time in forever all the separate bits of her – past, present and future – clicked into place and she felt whole.

The ricochet beats ended and Sadie opened her eyes to find a breathless, sweaty Dylan watching her. The heat in his eyes tugged at something deep inside her, asking a question that called an answering need so fierce it was almost frightening. Over the headset she vaguely heard the DJ burbling about slowing things down and then the opening bars of 'Love and Affection' filled her ears and there Joan Armatrading was, saying she wasn't in love but was open to persuasion.

You and me both, Joan.

And then she was in Dylan's arms, eyes closed tight, hands stroking the damp curls of his hair, the dip at the base of his spine, the rough denim of his jeans at his waist. She could feel him just as restless, just as needy, and when his hot lips scorched a line against the side of her jaw she jerked back. Their eyes met and then they were moving, cutting a line through the other couples on the dance floor, barely pausing to tug off their headphones and dump them on the table by the door. And then they were almost running in their haste to get upstairs. They got to her room and she was fumbling for her room key but her fingers were shaking and God why didn't women's jeans come with proper pockets and all the while Dylan's hot words were urging her to hurry, telling her how beautiful she was, how much he wanted her and she wanted to tell him to shut up and let her focus a second but then the slim plastic card was in her hand, in the slot, and they were through the door and kissing and kissing as if they needed each other to breathe.

There were too many buttons, too many zips and laces, and if anyone had invented a sexy way to take off a pair of socks then Sadie had never learned it, but somehow they made it to the bedroom and then there was no more time to think about anything other than how amazing it was that something so familiar could feel so very different, because it was Dylan who was touching her, Dylan who was asking what she liked, what she needed, and giving her all those things and so much more besides.

'Bloody hell,' Dylan gasped.

They were side by side, both staring up at the ceiling as they panted for breath. If Sadie could have got her brain to function enough to form words she would've agreed with him. She squinted, wondering why it was bright, and then a horrified realisation hit her. 'You put the big light on!'

Dylan laughed. 'It was that or break our necks trying to find the bed.'

'But the big light, really?' She scrabbled for the edge of the quilt, which was bunched up underneath her, trying to free enough of the material to tug it over her.

Dylan seized her hand in a grip that was both firm and gentle. 'Don't do that. I was enjoying the view.'

She rolled her head so she could mock glower at him. 'Can't you enjoy it in the far more flattering glow of a lamp?'

Chuckling, Dylan rolled off the bed and walked towards the light switch. There was a hint of softness at his waist and hips, but his shoulders were broad and his bottom as firm and muscular as she remembered it feeling under her hands. 'Maybe you should leave the big light on,' she found herself saying. When he paused to glance at her she shrugged. 'It'd be a shame to spoil the view...'

He left her in the early hours, apologies spilling from his lips between kisses as she nudged him towards the door with laughing assurances that it was okay. She completely understood why he didn't want the kids to wake up and him not be there. When he finally let her close the door on a promise they'd have breakfast together, Sadie leaned against the wall and closed her eyes with a sigh. How was it possible for something to be both the best and worst decision she'd made in her life? They were going home in a few days and right now she had no idea how she was going to be able to walk away from him.

28

Lovestruck. It was a word Dylan had often heard and dismissed as nonsense. Until now. He spent the first part of the morning in a daze, and even the protests of the kids as he got them up and dressed barely registered through the fog in his brain. They seemed oblivious to how late, or rather early, he'd got back. All he could think about was Sadie. How was she feeling? Had she woken up as full of hope as he had or was she regretting things in the cold light of day? He shouldn't have left her, but how could he have stayed? By the time he managed to calm the kids down and get the three of them downstairs for breakfast he was an absolute bag of nerves.

Sadie was waiting in the lounge, curled up in an armchair by the window. She looked as if she were miles away but, when they approached, she turned and the smile she gave him settled a lot of the butterflies in his stomach. Leaning down, he brushed a kiss on her cheek and managed to whisper, 'Everything okay?' low enough the kids didn't hear him.

She gave him the briefest of nods then turned her attention to Theo and Avery, who had tumbled onto the sofa nearby as though just the effort of coming downstairs had been too much. 'You'd think you two were the ones up dancing half the night, not us,' Sadie said to them with a grin. 'You look like you need to go back to bed.'

'This is not a civilised time for anyone to be up on a Sunday morning,' Theo grumbled.

'Why are we even awake?' Avery asked, yanking the hood of her sweatshirt over her head until it covered most of her face.

Dylan couldn't exactly tell them he'd dragged them downstairs because he'd been desperate to see Sadie, so he settled for pointing out that they didn't want to miss decorating the centrepiece for the entrance hall. 'You both worked really hard on the things you made – don't you want to see it all come together?'

A pair of grunts was their only response. With an apologetic shrug towards Sadie for their lack of manners, Dylan went to fetch himself a coffee. When he returned Sadie had pulled the empty chair closer to hers and he sank into it with a smile, taking it as a good sign that she wanted him to sit next to her. Her hand was resting on the arm of her chair and he couldn't resist reaching out to cover it with his own. The urge to touch her was too strong to ignore and when she turned her hand palm up so they could link their fingers, the last of his nerves melted away. Everything between them was going to be okay.

The children perked up a bit once they'd eaten and their bad mood dissipated as everyone gathered in the entrance hall to decorate the tree. Dylan was happy to sit back and watch – his contribution had been minimal and too many hands would just lead to a mess. Rowena clearly had the same idea and quickly took charge, appointing a small team who would actually hang the decorations while others prepped each piece and handed them over. Sadie worked with Avery, carefully attaching hooks to the loops stitched into the top of the crochet leaves and the half-a-dozen smiley-faced pears Sadie had made. They were an incongruous sight amongst the pottery and silver leaves but Dylan loved the sweet silliness of them.

When it was time to add the partridge centrepiece, Carrie-Ann invited Theo to step forward, his nimble fingers working quickly to help her wire the bird securely into place. When they moved back there was a round of applause and lots of congratulations and praise shared. A couple of the serving staff appeared with trays of Buck's fizz and straight orange juice and the party atmosphere that was never far from any of the events at the hall soon spread as everyone took turns to admire the tree.

Dylan was sitting with the children watching Sadie chat to one of the later guests who'd arrived after the long weekend and had missed the crafting sessions when Stevie approached them with a smile. 'I've got a favour to ask the three of you about our plans for Midnight Mass later...'

* * *

They assembled back in the hall just before eleven-fifteen that night, everyone bundled up ready for the long walk through the estate and into the village. The kids had been excited since talking to Stevie earlier and it had taken some persuasion to have a decent sleep in the afternoon. Dylan had snuck away to Sadie's room, and fallen fast asleep tangled in her arms. She was standing next to him now and he knew for certain he was completely smitten because he couldn't help thinking how beautiful she looked in her ridiculous bobble hat. Rowena caught his eye from over by the door and nodded. 'That's our cue, guys, come on.' He smiled at Sadie. 'I'll see you in a minute, okay?'

'So mysterious,' she said with a laugh.

'Stevie swore us to secrecy and I'm not brave enough to go up against my big sister!'

The three of them slipped past Rowena, who was guarding the door. As they stepped outside he heard her saying, 'Give us a couple of minutes, folks.'

Though Stevie had explained the plan, Dylan still found his breath catch as he saw it in the flesh. His family was lined up at the bottom of the steps in age order from Alice to Hope, each of them holding the illuminated figure of a leaping lord on a pole above their heads. Amelia, Tasha and Cam stood at the top of the steps, each holding a figure, which they handed over to Dylan, Theo and Avery before hurrying down to stand with Daisy. Pride filled Dylan to the depths of his soul as he led the kids down the steps to take their places in the line. This was where he belonged. No matter how many miles separated them, this was where his heart lived.

The doors opened and Rowena led everyone out. Gasps of delight greeted them and as the guests descended, Ziggy gave the instruction to turn and walk. Alice led the line around the fountain and across to the foot of the long drive, where they stopped and formed up across the width of it. 'Ready?' Ziggy asked and then they were moving again. As they walked along the drive, lights appeared off to the left, the glow of torches and mobile phones. It was the workers who lived on the estate and they joined the back of the group forming an unofficial escort to make sure none of the guests strayed from the path and got themselves lost. As they reached the top of the drive, the gates stood open ready for them to pass through and there were more lights beyond – villagers waiting to join the procession. A familiar figure in a patchwork cloak waited by the gate and Dylan felt a catch in his throat as their mother walked over to Monty and offered him the figure she was holding. He hesitated for a second before accepting it with a nod and taking her place in the line beside Ziggy. Alice slipped through between them to take her place in the second row with Daisy, Rowena, Cam and the others who were part of their family. Dylan's heart soared when he spotted Sadie in amongst them. *Where she belonged.*

He didn't have time to dwell on that because they were moving again, a slow steady walk towards the church. The road was lined with people and as they passed they moved to join the procession, swelling the numbers until it seemed like every member of their community was walking with them.

The vicar waited at the door of the church, the members of the choir lined up next to him. With a gesture from the choirmaster, the piercing clear notes of 'Once in Royal David's City' filled the air. The vicar turned and walked into the church, the choir following behind. There was a small delay as, under instruction of the churchwarden, they placed their illuminated lords against the wall of the church in a happy, leaping row before they mingled with everyone going inside. Dylan managed to catch up with Sadie in the jostle, taking her hand and leading her towards the front of the church where the family pews lined either side of the top of the aisle. When she realised where they were headed, she shook her head. 'Oh no, those are for family.'

Avery hooked an arm through hers and smiled. 'And you're part of the family, at least for the next few days.'

'Come and sit with us,' Theo urged, leaving her with the choice of giving in or making a scene.

'Did you put them up to that?' she whispered at Dylan through a fixed smile as she took the seat beside him.

'Nope, that was all their own work.' He glanced across the church to where Hope was leading a surprised but smiling Marcus to sit with her and Stevie. It looked as though his niece had done a bit of detective work since their little chat the other morning. He nudged Sadie and nodded at them with a grin. 'There's no point in fighting it. Once the Travers family get hold of you, they don't let go.'

Sadie laughed and took his hand. 'I'll play along for now, but come the 28th it's back to the real world.' Dylan squeezed her hand. He knew she was right, but he'd cross that bridge when they came to it.

The service was the traditional nine lessons and carols format. They were nearing the end and Ziggy was at the lectern, reading the final lesson. When he finished, Dylan waited for the organ to begin, but the vicar stepped forward and smiled. 'Ladies and gentlemen, it's been a very special year, not only for all the many times I've watched this community come together and support each other in both good times and bad, but because those long lost have found their way home.' Dylan shifted uncomfortably in his seat and watched his father do the same. Sadie's fingers closed around his and he held tight as he wondered where this was leading. Things were still very fragile between Monty and the rest of them; it was too soon for this. He caught Ziggy's eye and his eldest brother shook his head, the very briefest movement but Dylan felt himself relax.

'As many of you will know, Dr Cameron Ferguson has been leading an archaeological dig on the estate over the past eighteen months investigating the ruins uncovered there. As a part of their work a number of high-status graves were uncovered. We do not know who they are, but I have every faith that Cam and his team will get to the bottom of that mystery before too long.' He smiled over at Cam, who grinned and held up his crossed fingers. Hushed laughter rippled around the church.

'I find a prayer or two helps,' the vicar said with a wink, earning more laughter. He shrugged. 'Come on, it's literally in my job description. Anyway, I am pleased to say that, with the permission of the bishop and with the help of many members of our community, we at Saint Saviour's will be offering an appropriate shelter for our long-lost brethren until the research work has been completed and they can finally be laid to rest.'

He walked to the back of the church where a number of stone sarcophagi stood in front of the altar. It had been decades since Dylan had been in the church and he had assumed they'd always been there. The carved figures on the top were pitted and broken, but it was still possible to make out the shape of their heads and hands clasped in prayer. Six of the choir stood, each carrying a wreath of holly, which they placed gently at the foot of each stone coffin as the vicar moved amongst the tombs, placing a hand on each as he murmured a blessing. The members of the choir returned to their seats and the organ played the introductory notes for the final carol, 'O Come, All Ye Faithful'.

When they left the church, they collected the leaping lords and began the long walk back. They got only as far as the main pathway when Monty stopped and handed his figure to Alice. 'Thank you for letting me be part of tonight,' he said, tucking his hands in his pockets as he took a step back.

'It was good to have you with us, Dad,' Stevie said, always the kindest-hearted of them.

Ziggy nodded. 'We're having lunch tomorrow at the hall. I understand that might not be easy for you, but you'd be welcome to join us.'

'Drinks are from noon onwards,' Rowena added.

Monty was silent for long enough that Dylan clenched his fists. If he threw this back in their faces there'd be no going back. When the old man spoke, his voice was gravelly. 'It would be my pleasure.'

29

Sadie woke late the next morning. It seemed so strange that it was Christmas Day and she had nothing she needed to be doing. No last-minute push-around of the hoover, no double-checking the turkey was properly defrosted, no sprouts to peel and pare, no hunting in the fridge behind a mountain of cheese for that jar of horseradish she knew she'd bought but that had somehow disappeared. She lay there for a moment waiting for the feeling that she was somehow missing out to arrive. When it didn't show up, she smiled to herself, made a cup of tea and climbed back into bed to read. Dylan and the kids had invited her to join them but she'd turned them down. After last night at the church, it was important to re-establish some boundaries. She couldn't deny how special it had been to sit amongst the family and feel part of such a wonderful community, but deep down she'd known she didn't belong there. Couldn't belong there even if she wanted to because it was simply too impractical apart from anything else. It might have been different if he'd lived here at Juniper Meadows. If that were the case then she might have allowed herself to think about a future where they might explore the idea of a relationship over a series of long weekends, but Florida might as well be the moon.

Not wanting to dwell on what she couldn't change, Sadie finished her tea and treated herself to a long soak in the bath before making calls to first Jake and then Katie to wish them a merry Christmas. 'Look at what you're missing,' Katie said, wincing as another piercing scream filled the air.

A frazzled-looking Liam appeared in the shot, a red-faced and very unhappy Isla under one arm, a dolly with a missing arm in the other. 'Hi, Sadie,' he called out over his daughter's screams. 'Katie, love, any idea where the superglue is?'

Sadie covered her mouth to hide a smile. 'Oh dear. Look, my darlings, I am going to leave you to it. I'll see you in a couple of days. Lots of love and merry Christmas.'

'Merry Christmas, Mum, love you, sorry!' The screen turned black and Sadie set her phone aside with a smile and a shake of her head. No, she was absolutely not missing out on anything.

She'd just finished dressing and was fiddling with her hair in front of the mirror when there was a knock on her door. Pulling it open, she was confronted with a smiling Avery holding a little package wrapped in silver paper, Theo and Dylan standing just behind her. 'Happy Christmas!' Avery declared, thrusting the present at her.

Accepting the gift with a smile, Sadie stepped back. 'Thank you. Would you like to come in for a minute?'

Avery walked past her, eyes looking everywhere as she checked out the room. 'It's a lot different from ours.' She made a beeline for the window. 'Oh, you have a lovely view over the gardens!'

'Hey, Sadie,' Theo said as he passed her.

'Hello, darling, merry Christmas.' The endearment slipped out and she blamed it on the fact she'd been speaking to her own children earlier. He didn't seem to mind, giving her a shy smile before heading over to where his sister was still looking out of the window.

'Avery wanted to bring you something she picked up at the market the other day,' Dylan said by way of explanation after she rose up on tiptoe to accept a kiss from him.

'It's fine.' She closed the door and turned back to him. 'It's more than fine, it's lovely. I've got something for each of you,' she said, pointing towards the coffee table. 'I was going to bring them down later but this is probably a better idea.'

They settled on the sofa and chairs, Avery's eyes gleaming when Sadie offered her a flat parcel wrapped in shiny red paper. 'What is it?'

'Open it and find out,' Sadie said with a laugh. Avery ripped the paper open, letting out a squeal of delight at the set of liquid eyeliner pens. 'I texted Charlie for her advice and she said these are the same as the ones she used when she did your make-up for the murder-mystery night.'

'I love them, thank you!' Avery jumped out of her seat to throw her arms around Sadie's neck.

Sadie accepted the enthusiastic hug, her heart full of affection for this sweet, open-hearted girl. 'Your turn,' she said, handing a slightly larger package to Theo once Avery had abandoned her to go and play with the eyeliner in front of the mirror.

'Thank you, you didn't have to.' He was much more careful with the wrapping, peeling back the Sellotape from each end before folding the halves of the paper back. 'Oh, wow.'

'I hope it's the right size,' Sadie said as Theo lifted out a Peaky Blinders-style cap. 'I remembered you said you wanted to get one. The stall owner said you can exchange it if it's not right.'

Theo put it on, pulling the brim down on one side so it covered one eye. 'What do you reckon?'

'Looks good,' Dylan said. 'What do you say?'

'Thanks, Sadie!' Theo leaned across and pressed a quick kiss on her cheek. 'You're the best.'

'Is that for me?' Dylan pointed at the small box she was holding in her hands.

She stared down at it for a second. It had seemed like a good idea at the time, but now she was worried she might have overstepped. Well, it was too late to change her mind. 'There you go,' she said, thrusting it into his hands.

He turned the box around with a quizzical smile then slipped the ribbon off and opened the lid. 'Christ, Sadie.'

She closed her eyes for a second as heat blazed in her cheeks. She'd got it wrong, stuck her nose into business that wasn't hers. 'I'm sorry, it's too much, isn't it?' In a panic she tried to snatch the box back.

Dylan lifted it out of reach, shaking his head. 'No, no, don't you dare apologise.' He sounded choked and his eyes were glistening as he lifted out one of the delicate silver cufflinks she'd had Carrie-Ann engrave with the Travers family crest. 'How did you know?'

She shrugged, feeling a little tearful herself. 'I asked Tasha for a copy of the design. I just wanted you to have something to mark your visit home.'

'They're perfect.' Their eyes met. *You're perfect,* he mouthed silently.

Sadie pressed a hand over her galloping heart. Oh, goodness, what was the man doing to her? What were all of them doing to her?

Avery bounced over, two exaggerated wings of eyeliner stretching on either side of her lids. 'You look like an Egyptian goddess!' Sadie said with a laugh.

'That's coming off before we go downstairs for lunch,' Dylan said, making his daughter roll her eyes in disgust.

'You don't get it, Dad.'

'Oh, I get it all right and the answer's still no.'

Avery pouted and Sadie leaned towards her. 'We'll wash it off in a minute and I'll help you do it again.'

Avery brightened in an instant. 'Now it's your turn to open your present.' She snatched the package Sadie had set down and thrust it into her hands.

Sadie unfastened the paper and found herself staring at the back of a silver-edged photo frame. Turning it over with shaky hands, she gasped at the photo. It was of the four of them framed under a glittering arch of white fairy lights. Sadie was standing next to Dylan, his arm around her waist, his other arm around Theo's shoulders. Avery was on Sadie's other side, their arms linked together. Rowena had taken it the night they'd walked around the illuminated trail. 'We wanted to give you something to remember us by,' Avery said in a quiet voice.

'As if I could forget you,' Sadie replied, reaching out to cup the girl's cheek. 'Thank you, I'll treasure it always.'

'You should come back to Florida with us,' Avery burst out.

'Avie!' Dylan sounded as shocked as Sadie felt and she knew this was the first he'd heard anything about it.

Avery spun to face her father. 'What? I'm just saying that it's clear you two really like each other and Theo and I really like Sadie too. Why can't she come back and visit with us?'

'We'll talk about this later.' Dylan blew out a breath. 'Sadie, I'm sorry, that wasn't fair to put you on the spot like that.'

'I didn't mean to upset anyone.'

Avery's face had gone red and Sadie felt sorry for her. She held out a hand. 'It's okay, sweetheart, I'm not upset. You just took me by surprise, that's all. And if things were different then it would be lovely to spend more time with you all, but I've got my own family and I need to go back to them.'

'But you and Daddy really like each other—'

'Enough, Avery.' Dylan stood. 'Come on, let's go and wash your face and put our presents away.' He put an arm around Avery's slumped shoulders and steered her towards the door. 'We'll see you downstairs in a bit, okay?' he said to Sadie as he urged the kids out in front of him.

'Okay.' Sadie reached out and placed a hand on his chest. 'Don't give her a hard time. It's not her fault we've given her the wrong idea. We should've been more careful.'

Dylan stared at her for a long moment before he nodded once and turned away. Sadie closed the door and once again found herself needing the support of the wall to hold herself up. Oh God, how had they managed to make such a mess of things?

30

By the time he'd convinced Avery that she hadn't ruined everything, the thick black eyeliner was smeared around her eyes so much she looked like a sad little panda. Dylan took her into the bathroom, sitting her on the edge of the bath while he ran a flannel under the hot tap. Holding her chin, he wiped the mess from her face then pressed a tender kiss to her forehead. 'There you go, all better.'

'I'm really sorry, Dad.' Her voice gave a telltale wobble and Dylan crouched in front of her and took her hands, shaking them gently.

'Hey, no more tears, okay? I'm not mad at you and neither is Sadie. Remember how she said that if things were different it would be a lovely idea? I know it came from a place of kindness, darling, and Sadie understands that too.'

'But if you like each other then you should be able to spend more time together,' Avery protested.

'We do like each other, but it's simply not possible, darling.'

'Why not?'

Dylan didn't have it in him to argue the point any more, mainly because a large part of him agreed with her. 'Come on, let's try your eyeliner again and then we can go downstairs and see everyone. You don't want the rest of the family to know you've been crying, do you?' She shook her head. 'That's my girl.'

With Theo's help, they found some make-up tutorials on YouTube and soon the upset was forgotten as the three of them pulled faces in front of the mirror and practised putting on the eyeliner. 'You look great, Dad,' Avery said between giggles.

'A smoky eye really suits you,' Theo said, sounding exactly like one of the girls from the video.

Dylan tilted his head as though considering his reflection seriously. 'Do you know what? I think you're right. I'm keeping it on.'

'Daddy!' Avery burst out laughing again.

Dylan caught Theo's reflection and sent him a ghost of a wink. 'I think I'll keep mine on too,' Theo declared. 'And I'm wearing my hat.'

And so somehow the three of them ended up walking into the lounge with matching cat-eye liner. They earned themselves a few raised eyebrows, but when Dylan worked his way across the room to where Sadie was sipping champagne and chatting to Marcus, she didn't say anything, just gave him a knowing smile as Avery slipped between them to curl an arm around Sadie's waist. Sadie returned the hold and Dylan watched her hand move in slow circles over his daughter's back, soothing and reassuring her. When a server passed with a tray full of fizzing glasses, Dylan helped himself to one and asked the girl if she could fetch them a couple of Buck's fizzes. 'Heavy on the orange juice, though, yeah?'

She nodded. 'I'll be back in a minute.'

When she returned he handed them to Avery and Theo with

a warning look. 'Sip it slowly and it's back on juice or soda after this, okay?' They'd had a little bit of champagne at Jen and Eric's wedding reception and been fine. He was sure both he and Jen would have to deal with some foolish behaviour as the kids grew older, but they'd reasoned that allowing the children to try a little bit now and then under proper supervision would lessen their curiosity. Canapés were passed around next, in lieu of cold starters, one of the servers explained when Dylan shook his head. 'Oh, well, in that case.' He helped himself to a miniature toad-in-the-hole.

The rest of the family arrived for lunch, including Monty, who was looking very smart – for him – in clean jeans, a dress shirt and a bright red bow tie. Dylan didn't miss the way he clung to Alice's hand, as though afraid if he let go he'd lose her again. Silly old fool. He'd come so close to throwing everything away. As the clock ticked past one, the servers circulated once more, this time with empty trays, and began gathering up glasses. Dylan was happy to surrender his half-drunk champagne, which had grown warm in his hand. A high-pitched hum had heads turning towards the door, including his. Dressed in full Highland regalia, a piper stood there. Silence fell as he began to play, the gathered guests parting as he marched in slow time around the room and back towards the door.

Ziggy offered his arm to Daisy and the two of them followed the piper, leading everyone from the lounge and along the corridor to the ballroom. The tables had been set out in the same arrangement as for the murder-mystery night, although they looked even more impressive with decorated centrepieces and crackers laid across each plate. The family mixed and mingled in, sitting in couples at different tables so all the guests had a chance to talk to them. The piper had disappeared towards the kitchen, but the sound of his pipe could soon be heard coming back up the corridor and this time when he appeared he was followed by a line of staff, each person carrying a silver salver full of food. The chef and his assistant came in last, bearing a huge bronze turkey on a platter between them. They completed a circuit between the tables before quickly dispersing behind a long serving counter with heat lamps suspended over it to keep the food warm. The piper departed to a round of applause and they were led table by table to the counter to choose whatever they wanted from the selection on offer.

Much later they were lingering over coffee and mince pies, everyone too full to move even the few steps it would take to go back to the lounge. Avery's head lolled for a second and Dylan caught her around the shoulders before she managed to fall asleep. 'You okay?'

She nodded. 'I think I ate too much, though.'

'I think we all ate too much. Do you want to go and have a lie down?'

'That sounds like a good idea,' Sadie said, getting to her feet. 'I keep telling myself I should go for a walk, but it's getting dark already.' Dylan checked his watch. It was after four so they'd been sitting there for the best part of three hours.

'Come on, let's make a move.'

Stevie was waiting for them by the door. 'There'll be a light supper in the lounge between six and eight,' she said, earning herself a chorus of groans.

'I never want to eat again,' Theo said, hands clutching his belly.

Dylan steered them upstairs, Sadie just behind them. When they reached the landing he turned to her. 'Can I come to you later?'

'Of course.'

Once the kids were settled in their rooms, Dylan kicked off his shoes and lay back on his bed. He was tired after the late night and too much food but he felt too wired to sleep. Though he'd done his best to enjoy lunch, two words had been bouncing around his head – *why not?*

It was as if Avery had opened Pandora's box and now the idea had been spoken aloud he couldn't let it go. He understood that Sadie needed to get home and see her family, but that didn't mean that when she left they had to say goodbye forever. If it was down to money, then she didn't have to worry about that because he would cover the cost of an aeroplane ticket without thinking twice about it. It wouldn't be easy and it would mean going weeks, probably months, without seeing each other, but he was willing to try if she was. Even if things didn't work out in the long run, wouldn't it be worth the risk on the off chance it did?

He was still mulling over how to raise the subject when he knocked on Sadie's door later that evening. When she opened it wearing nothing but a bathrobe and a very welcoming smile, the well-rehearsed words vanished from his brain and they only came back to him much later as they lay tangled in the sheets. Sadie's fingers were tracing a slow, distracting path up and down the inside of his arm and Dylan was contemplating whether he had it in him to persuade her to stroke other bits of him when she spoke. 'Do you know what I keep wondering?' she mused.

Dylan rolled onto his side. 'What?'

'What do you think Millie the Minx did exactly with a shot glass, a golf ball and a peacock feather?'

He stared at her for a long moment then burst out laughing. 'I have no idea, but now I really want to know if we can work it out.' The logistics failed them, but they had a great time trying and Dylan didn't think he'd ever laughed so much in his life. 'God, Sadie, give me half a chance and I could fall in love with you.'

He'd been half joking but, instead of laughing, she turned and buried her face in his shoulder. 'Don't say that.'

Cupping her face, Dylan coaxed her to look at him. 'Why not if it's true?'

She shook her head. 'You know why. This can't be, Dylan, we both agreed that from the start.'

'I know it's a lot to think about and there's a million reasons for us to walk away, but none of them are as good as the one reason to try.'

Sadie swallowed hard enough he saw her throat bob. 'And what's that?'

'Because we both want to.'

She closed her eyes and dropped back against her pillow. 'We can't always get what we want, though.'

He propped himself up on his elbow to stare down at her. 'Why not? Look, if it's about the money, I can cover the travel costs.'

'It's not just the money, is it? We have too many responsibilities, family, jobs.' She ticked each item off with her fingers. 'And when would we see each other? Once or twice a year at best. What's the point in that?'

'But that wouldn't be forever. Once the kids are older, I'll have more time...'

'To do what? Give up the life you've built over the past thirty years to shack up with me in a pokey little two-up, two-down?' Tears glistened on the ends of her lashes as she reached up to stroke his cheek. 'If we were twenty I'd take your hand and run anywhere in the world you wanted to take me, but we're not, and I can't. I'm sorry. We can still be friends.'

'Can we? Is that honestly enough for you? Because it sure as hell isn't enough for me!' He didn't mean to snap at her, but how could she give up on this so easily?

Her fingers stilled against his cheek. 'I'm sorry you feel that way. I never meant to hurt you, I never meant for any of this to happen, we just got carried away in the moment.'

Dylan closed his eyes against the pain welling in his chest. 'You're not even willing to try.'

Her hand fell away. 'I think you should go now.'

His eyes snapped open. 'You're throwing me out?'

'No, I just can't give you what you're asking of me. It's too much, Dylan, I'm sorry. I don't want us to fall out over this though, that's why I think you should go.'

'Sadie...'

'Please, Dylan.'

Wishing he'd kept his mouth shut, he climbed out of bed and gathered his clothes. They didn't speak while he dressed, but Sadie pulled on her dressing gown and followed him to the door. 'I'm sorry,' she said, and when he glanced down at her, her face was streaked with tears.

Christ, now he'd made her cry. 'Come here.' He pulled her into his arms, kissing and stroking her hair as she sobbed against his chest. 'I'm sorry, I shouldn't have said anything,' he murmured over and over again.

After what seemed like forever, her tears subsided and she shifted in his arms. 'I'm sorry, I didn't mean to get upset.'

Dylan stroked her cheek. 'I hate to leave you like this.'

'I'll be okay.' She turned her face to press a kiss to his palm.

'At least we have a couple more days together. We can make the most of it,' he said, dragging a smile up from somewhere.

Sadie shook her head. 'No. I think it's best for both of us if we call it a day now. Spend these last two days with your family. You owe it to them and the kids.' She placed a hand over his heart. 'You owe it to yourself, too.'

He felt as though she were tearing him in two. 'This can't be goodbye, Sadie.'

She stretched up on tiptoe to brush a kiss over his mouth. 'It is, Dylan. It has to be. It's the best decision for both of us.'

He walked away, the salt taste of her tears on his lips. There was nothing else he could say because Sadie had clearly made up her mind.

31

What are you smiling at? Sadie cast a baleful glare at the Nutcracker drummer that had been her parting gift from the team at Juniper Meadows as their final nod to the twelve days of Christmas theme. She'd dumped it on her dressing table after getting home the night before and now it seemed to be mocking her with its toothy grin. She got out of bed and threw it face down in one of the drawers before slamming it shut. The temptation to slide back under the covers and sulk was huge, but everyone was expecting her and she'd already wasted the final part of her holiday hiding away to avoid Dylan. Another day in bed would only make her feel worse. If that was even possible. While her head knew she'd done the right thing, her heart was still not on board with her decision to end things the way she had. It might've been easier if she'd been able to come home earlier, but the trains hadn't been running due to essential maintenance works over the Christmas break.

Just a few hours and it would all be over. It was a depressing thought and not one her family deserved of her. Giving herself a mental kick in the bum, Sadie headed for the shower, blew-dry her hair and picked out a nice outfit from her wardrobe. The black velvet trousers were at least ten years old, but they never let her down and, paired with a silvery vest top and matching cardigan, they were dressy enough for the occasion. At least with Jake and Rachel having decided to have a lunch party everyone would get home before it was dark. Sadie hated driving in the dark, especially when it was raining.

She grabbed her silver sandals and the matching bag and tucked both away in the bag-for-life along with the little gifts she'd picked up for everyone at the Christmas market at Juniper Meadows. After tucking the ends of her trousers into the faux-fur-lined boots that would keep her feet warm until she arrived at Jake's, Sadie gave her reflection one final check in the hallway mirror. She was getting more confident at styling her new haircut, though she didn't think she'd ever capture the perfect sleekness the stylist had managed. Her face didn't look quite right, though, and she realised she'd grown used to wearing make-up again over the past week or so. She'd given up after Pete left her and it was only as she'd felt more like her old self again that she'd got back into the habit while at Juniper Meadows. She hadn't bothered with any today because getting dressed up had been enough of an effort and, besides, it was only her family going to be seeing her.

You didn't bother because Dylan won't be there. The realisation stopped her in her tracks. Taking more care with her appearance hadn't been about him, well, hadn't *only* been about him, it had been an act of self-care. An acknowledgement that she deserved to be the best version of herself both inside and out. Was she really going to backslide into her old mousy ways without so much as a fight?

Returning upstairs, Sadie whipped out her buffer brush, dusted on a coat of foundation, added a dash of blush to both cheeks and applied mascara to her lashes. By the time she'd run a rose-pink lipstick around her lips, she was smiling at herself in the mirror. Not the full works, but a happy medium.

To get herself in the mood, Sadie connected her phone to the car speakers and blasted an eighties playlist from Spotify all the way to her mother's house. Sitting at the traffic lights at a junction, Sadie bopped in her seat and drummed her fingers on the steering wheel in time to 'Ant Music'. Happening to glance across at the car beside her, she was briefly horrified to find it was packed full of young lads who were all grinning and laughing at her through their windows. The old Sadie would've cringed with embarrassment and switched off the radio, but she wasn't the old Sadie any more. Instead she raised her hand and gave them a cheery wave as the chorus kicked in again and the lyrics she hadn't heard in years came back to mind and she sang along. As the lights changed, the lads beep-beeped as they pulled away and she grinned at what they must have thought of her as she waited for the feeder light for her lane to change.

The last strains of the song faded as Sadie pulled up in one of the visitor parking spaces outside her mother's and she sighed in happy remembrance at her teenage crush on Adam Ant. He'd had such lovely dark hair, a bit like Dylan's. She wondered if Dylan had gone through a New Romantics phase and thought perhaps she'd ask him when he messaged her.

If he messaged her.

She'd not heard from him since his brief reply to her text to say she'd got home okay. Perhaps he was waiting to hear from her, or perhaps he'd decided that there was no point in keeping in touch. She had no one to blame for the situation other than herself. He'd told her he wasn't interested in being friends, that it would never be enough for him. She could've been on her way to the airport right now instead of sitting in the rain. Reaching out, she turned off the radio and let the teenage dreams fade in the silence. The reasons why she'd chosen to stay hadn't changed. Sadie took a deep breath, flipped up the hood on her coat and opened the door to dash the few metres to the covered porch entrance of the retirement complex. She hadn't finished pressing the code on the intercom to call her mother's apartment when the automatic door began to whirr open.

'You're late,' Margaret said by way of greeting.

'I said between half past and quarter to,' Sadie countered. 'Did you have a nice Christmas with Aunty Celia?'

'I made the best of it, though I'm glad to be away from her constant chattering.'

Had she really given up the chance of spending the winter in Florida for this? 'I'm parked over there,' she said, pointing to her car. 'Do you want to wait here and I'll move closer?'

'You can't move any closer, you'll be blocking the emergency vehicle bay. It's only a bit of rain, it's not like I'm going to melt.'

'Unfortunately,' Sadie muttered under her breath as she tried to adjust her hood before they turned back out into the rain.

'What was that?' her mother snapped, those radar ears of hers not missing a thing.

Old Sadie would've cringed and apologised, but new Sadie was having none of it. She thought about the way the Travers family had been around each other, so full of warmth and love, the only words shared ones of encouragement, and most of all the constant laughter. How different things could've been if Margaret had been able to give even one inch of the love she'd spent the past two weeks surrounded by. 'I said it's a shame that the rain won't melt you away, Mother. Now, shall we go?'

Without waiting for a reply, Sadie marched back to the car and held open the passenger door as she waited for Margaret to catch her up. 'I don't know what's got into you, Sadie,' her mother said once they were both seated and were fastening their belts.

'But there's no need for such rudeness. Are you having some sort of breakdown because Pete left you?'

It was tempting to say she was just following Margaret's own example, but now wasn't the right time to pick a fight. 'I'm just starting to see things in a new light, that's all. Right, let's get going, because Jake's expecting us.' Sadie placed her hand on the key, then hesitated. 'Look, Mum, can you try and make a bit of an effort today, for everyone's sake?'

'I don't know what you're talking about. I always make an effort.'

Sadie gritted her teeth and started the engine. Not wanting to drive in silence, she turned the radio back on, but selected Classic FM because if Margaret heard her eighties playlist she really would be convinced Sadie was having a breakdown. The 'Sussex Carol' filled the air and she was immediately transported back to when the carol-singers had entertained them all outside the hall. Safely cocooned in those happy memories, Sadie drove them in silence the ten minutes it took to reach Jake's house. She slowed down as they approached, eyes flicking left and right as she looked for a parking space on the busy road. When she pulled level, she recognised the two cars parked closest. Jake and Rachel must've moved their own cars earlier. As she reached their small drive, she saw Liam had parked his and Katie's mini SUV as far over to the right as possible, leaving enough room to tuck her car beside it.

'Here we are, then.' Sadie turned off the engine, took off her belt and climbed out. She opened the back passenger door to retrieve the bag full of gifts, stopping to frown at her mother, who had made no move to get out. 'What's the matter?'

'What on earth have you done to your hair?'

Oh, that. The rain had stopped so she'd pushed down her hood and she supposed it was the first Margaret had seen of it.

Trying to ignore the criticism implied by the question, Sadie turned her head left and right to show off her new cut. 'I had it done while I was away. It was in desperate need of sorting out and I decided to brighten things up with a few highlights while I was at it.'

'It's far too short,' her mother snapped. 'I've told you before that with an unfortunate chin like yours, you need to keep it longer.'

The last shred of Sadie's temper frayed. Timing be damned, she was not going to take a second more of Margaret's spiteful tongue. 'Well, I like it, Mother, and quite frankly I couldn't give a flying baboon's red arse what you think.'

'There's no need to be rude! I'm just trying to help you.' Her mother had the temerity to actually sound hurt!

Shutting the back door, Sadie climbed back into the driver's seat and turned to face her mother. 'How on earth can you think insulting the way I look is in any way beneficial to me? Seriously, Mother, tell me how, because I've put up with you bullying me and picking at me for more than fifty years and I have had enough.'

'Bullying you? All I wanted was the best for you, for you to want the best for yourself. I had to settle for the life I ended up with and I never wanted the same for you. I wanted you to have a bit of pride in yourself, a bit of ambition, rather than settling for less.' Her mother's voice hitched on those last words.

'Is that how you feel about your life, Mum? That you settled for less? Is that what's made you so bitter all these years?'

'You don't know what it was like!' Her mother almost snarled the words. 'To have more intelligence than anyone around you and be denied the chance to make the most of it. Your uncle wasn't half as smart as me. Do you know how he passed his eleven plus and got into the grammar school? Because I coached him, that's how! But did I get a chance to go? No! Because my father didn't want me getting ideas above my station. What was the point in wasting a good education on me and Celia when we would have to give it all up when we got married anyway? Not that Celia cared, she was too busy thinking about boys.' Margaret's snort of disdain said what she thought of that. 'So while we went out to work, your uncle got to go on to higher education.'

Why had her mother never told Sadie about this before? 'I'm sorry that happened to you, but that doesn't explain why you gave me such a hard time when I was growing up.'

'I wanted you to be more like me, but you were a carbon copy of your father. I thought he had potential too when I met him. Oh, he had a good brain on him but no ambition. His only aim in life was to be comfortable and make things as easy as possible.'

'So you thought that being horrible to me would make me fight harder for things?' Sadie couldn't get her head around the twisted logic.

'I was being cruel to be kind, Sadie. There's a reason that saying exists, you know. You were too soft, too easily hurt, and the odds are already stacked against us women. I wanted you to toughen up a bit, to understand that life isn't sweetness and roses, that you have to push for what you want.'

'But don't you see that what you did had the opposite effect? You crushed what bit of spirit I had in me. You didn't teach me how to fight for anything, you taught me that nothing I did was good enough, so in the end I gave up trying.' Sadie pressed her fingers into the corners of her eyes, forcing back the tears that were threatening to spill.

'That's your answer to everything, isn't it? Cry and make the world feel sorry for you.'

The laugh that escaped Sadie surprised them both. 'What a

waste. I'm sorry that your life didn't work out the way you hoped when you were younger, Mother, but the fact you're nearly eighty-five years old and still eaten up with bitterness is nobody else's fault but yours. You made my life hell when I was growing up, but you know what I did? I moved on the best I could and I vowed to never make the same mistakes with my children. I gave them every ounce of love I had inside me and I made sure they knew every day how special they were.'

'You don't understand what it was like. The pressure, the expectation to get married and have a family.'

'As I said, I am sorry that you felt like you had some of your choices taken away from you, but that's still no excuse to punish everyone around you, especially your *child*.'

'I was jealous of you, don't you understand?'

'Jealous? But just now you were saying you thought I'd wasted my life.'

'I hated being pregnant. It was like having an alien or a parasite growing inside me. My body didn't belong to me any more, and, God, I was so sick. Morning sickness they called it, but it was morning, noon and all bloody night. And it never stopped. I didn't blossom and bloom the way you did when you carried your two, I withered.' Her mother sounded as though she was crying, but Sadie couldn't move to comfort her, she was too stunned by what she was hearing. To know her mother had carried all this inside her all these years and never breathed a word of it – was it any wonder it had choked her up and poisoned everything?

'Everyone told me it would get better once you were born, but somehow it was worse. Physically I recovered, but I didn't know what to do with you. I couldn't even feed you because my milk never came through properly. Every time I held you, you cried, but as soon as your father picked you up you were good as gold. The world told me the only thing I was destined for was to be a mother and I was useless at it. I wanted to love you, to be easy with you the way your father always was, but I didn't know how.'

'Did you even try? I'm not trying to shame you for what sounds like a horrific experience, but, in all the years since, when did you ever try to make things different?'

Her mother stared at her for a long time and Sadie found she was holding her breath in anticipation. Could this be it? Could this be the moment when things finally changed between them? It would be hard to let go of the past, but she'd seen Dylan manage it with his parents. Wouldn't it be better to make the most of what little time they had left? A shuttered look fell over her mother's face, her eyes returning to a blank coldness that sent Sadie's hopes plummeting. 'I am who I am and there's no point crying over spilt milk.'

No, no, there wasn't. But she could stop keeping filling the bottle and expecting a different result. 'Then you'd better make the most of this evening, Mother, because if you're not willing to change things, then I'll have to.'

'What are you talking about?'

Sadie met her gaze and held it, ignoring the quaking child inside who was still so very afraid of the woman in front of her. 'Having access to me and my family is a privilege, not a right. You've done too much damage and it stops here and it stops now. I'll give you one last chance to spend time with your grandchildren and great-grandchildren, but this is the last you'll see of them or of me until you agree to change your ways.' Sadie got out, rounded to the passenger side, and offered a hand to her mother after opening her door. 'One wrong word out of you and you'll be back in this car and back to your flat before you know what's hit you. Have I made myself clear?'

* * *

'Nan's very quiet,' Katie said as she walked into the kitchen carrying her eighteen-month-old daughter, Isla, in her arms. Sadie straightened up from where she'd been loading a few dirty things into the dishwasher and held out her hands to take Isla.

'How's Grandma's gorgeous girl?' Sadie asked, nuzzling the little girl's cheek until she giggled. 'Come on, let's stand over here out of the way.' Sadie moved into the corner, Katie following her.

Jake and Rachel had both assured her they had everything in hand, but it wasn't in her nature to sit around and be waited on so Sadie was doing bits and pieces where she could while not getting under their feet.

'Shh,' Jake said from where he was frying sausages in a pan while Rachel mashed what looked like a mountain of potatoes on the counter next to him. 'Don't jinx it!'

Sadie smiled at their shared laughter, but didn't say anything. She didn't want to burden their afternoon with what had happened and there would be plenty of time to explain later. She was quite surprised her mother had even agreed to come inside, but she'd taken a seat in one of the armchairs and accepted everything she was offered with a polite word of thanks. Perhaps she'd taken things to heart and Sadie wouldn't have to follow through with her threat after all. Then again, the day was still young.

'Speaking of quiet, you've not said much, Mum. Is everything okay?' Katie asked.

'I'm fine, darling, just a bit tired after my trip, but it's so lovely to be back with you all,' Sadie reassured her.

'We've been dying to hear all about it,' Rachel said, putting a lid on the potatoes and setting them to one side. 'Did you have a good time?'

'I had a wonderful time, and I met so many lovely people.' One even lovelier than she'd ever dreamed it was possible to be.

She couldn't help glancing at the clock. It was nearly twelve. Dylan would be waiting to check in about now.

'Oh, I'm glad you made some friends,' Jake said. 'I was a bit worried we'd packed you off with a bunch of strangers.'

'It was the best thing for me. I'd got so used to it just being me and your dad that I was rather out of practice meeting new people. It was the push I needed to get out of my rut and I'm determined to be more sociable from now on.'

'That's lovely, Mum. I'm so proud of you.' Katie leaned over to kiss her cheek. 'And do you think you'll keep in touch with anyone you met while you were there?'

Sadie couldn't stop the heat from rising on her cheeks. 'I don't know, maybe.'

'Mum?' Katie was grinning at her like the Cheshire Cat. 'Did you meet someone *special*?'

'That's none of your business.'

'Oh my God!' Rachel exclaimed. 'You did!' Abandoning the potatoes, she hurried over. 'Come on, Sadie, don't hold out on us. Give us all the juicy details.'

There was no way she was giving them any of the juicy details! 'I met a very nice man called Dylan. His family own the estate, actually, but he lives with his children in Florida so he was only here for a short visit. They're due to fly back this afternoon, actually.'

'Oh, that's a shame he lives so far away. Still, maybe you can visit? A bit of Florida sunshine would do you the world of good.' The way Katie waggled her eyebrows, it was clear she wasn't thinking only about the sunshine.

Laughing, Sadie shook her head. 'He did invite me to go back with them, but I didn't see the point. Our lives are too different and I have too many responsibilities here. I'd prefer to keep things between us as a lovely chance encounter.'

'You should've gone with him!' Katie cried, shaking her head. 'Love doesn't come around often enough to walk away from it.'

'Who said anything about love?' Sadie protested with a laugh as she cuddled Isla close. 'I'm far too old to believe in fairy-tale happy endings. I'll leave that to our little princess here. My life is here and his life is there and that's all there is to it.'

'You care about him, though,' Katie insisted. 'I can tell by the look in your eyes that he meant something to you.'

'Well, yes, of course he meant something to me, and under different circumstances then perhaps there'd be the potential for it to grow into something more meaningful, but I can't drop everything and chase a man halfway around the world.'

'What if you asked him to stay?' Rachel asked.

Sadie rolled her eyes. 'I would never have said anything if I'd known it was going to turn into an interrogation.'

Katie hooked an arm around her waist. 'We don't mean to give you a hard time, Mum. We just want you to be happy.'

'I am happy. Being with all of you makes me happy.'

'But being with Dylan might make you happier. Look, answer me one thing and then I promise to drop it, okay?'

It was on the tip of her tongue to refuse, but it was sweet that they were so concerned about her. 'One thing.'

'If you weren't tied to your life here by us, would you have gone with him?'

'What's the point in speculating on hypotheticals? It's not going to change anything.'

'You promised me, now answer the question.'

Sadie sighed because she was pretty sure she hadn't promised anything. 'Well, yes, of course I would.'

'Then you have to go!' Katie burst out. She turned to Rachel. 'Back me up on this!'

Rachel held up her hands. 'I'm on your side, but at the end of the day it's up to your mum to decide what she wants to do. Give her a break, Katie. It can't have been easy to say goodbye.'

Katie shook her head. 'Has no one in this family got any romance in their soul? Every problem Mum has raised is logistical.' She turned back to Sadie. 'I'm not saying you should pack up and move to the States or anything, but I also don't think you should close the door on things either. Even if nothing further comes of it, he sounds like a nice person and the two of you could at least stay friends.'

'He doesn't want that.'

Katie raised her eyebrows. 'He said he didn't want to be friends? Maybe I've got the wrong end of the stick about him after all.'

'No, you haven't, you've just misunderstood. He said he couldn't be friends because it would never be enough for him.'

'Oh, hell, I would've definitely got on that plane,' Rachel said, raising a hand to fan her face.

'Hey!' Jake poked her arm in a playful gesture. 'Remember me?'

Laughing, she curled her arms around his neck and pressed a quick kiss to his lips. 'How could I forget you? You have to admit it's pretty romantic, though.'

Jake screwed up his nose. 'That's my mother we're talking about. There are things a man just doesn't need to think about when it comes to their mother.' He turned to Sadie. 'Now, if you weren't my mother, then my advice would be to call him.'

'And tell him what? That I'm sorry things didn't work out because of our circumstances?'

Jake shrugged. 'That'd be as good a place to start as any.'

Isla started to wriggle in her arms, so Sadie let her down and the little girl grabbed a handful of her trouser leg to keep herself upright. Resting a hand on Isla's head to steady her, Sadie glanced back up at her son, frustration rising that none of them would just let it go. She'd done the right thing – why couldn't they see that? 'And then what? Should I tell him that I wish things could be different, that I wish I were the kind of person who could just seize the day? That I wish I were braver and less scared that I might really fall in love with him and then if things didn't work out it'd be so much worse than not trying at all and that's why I walked away?' Sadie clamped her free hand over her mouth.

Katie's arm around her waist tightened. 'Yes, Mum. That's exactly what you should say.'

Sadie felt her eyes fill with tears. 'What if it's too late?'

'What if it's not?'

32

'If you guys are finished up, we should think about making a move to check in,' Dylan said, putting the lid back on his empty coffee cup and placing it on the tray next to the remains of the wrappers and boxes that were all that was left of the kids' fast-food meal. They'd arrived early to find everyone else had had the same idea and the check-in hall was packed to the rafters. Rather than stand around in a queue, they'd taken the opportunity to get something to eat. He would have been happy to wait until they got on the plane, but the food choices could be a bit hit and miss sometimes and this way at least he knew they'd had something.

The children had wanted a McDonald's, probably because they knew it was their last chance as their mother never let them eat it, and he wasn't sure there would be one airside. They still had over an hour before check-in closed, but things had quietened down a lot and he wanted to make the most of it in case there was another sudden influx of people.

'I'm almost done, five more minutes.' Avery raised the milk-shake cup that was almost taller than her head to show him the dark shadow of the remains in the bottom of it.

'Okay, but then we really need to go. Start sorting out your things while you finish up. Make sure you've got everything you want on the plane in your rucksacks and just double-check there's nothing that's going to cause a problem at security. Is all your make-up stuff and your wash kit in your case?'

'Yup.' She didn't even pause from her one-handed typing of whatever life-and-death message she was sending.

'You'll need to switch your phone off when we go through security so finish that up.'

'I can put it on silent,' Avery protested.

'Off-off. I mean it, Avie.' She pouted, but nodded and Dylan turned to Theo, who was already sorting through his stuff.

'Do you think this will be okay?' Theo held up his reusable water bottle and shook it.

Dylan shook his head when it made a sloshing sound. 'No, we'll have to empty them before we go through. There'll be water stations on the other side where we can fill up again.' He held out his hand. 'Here, give it to me and I'll sort it out. Avie, give me yours as well.'

Three bottles in hand, Dylan carried them to the restaurant's cleaning station and tipped them out over the liquid disposal point. There was only a dribble in the bottom of his, but better safe than sorry. Returning to the table, he tucked all three in his rucksack and checked his watch. 'We'd better use the bathroom while we're here as well.'

'Yes, Dad,' they both chorused, but they went to do as they were told while he cleared up the table and threw away their rubbish.

Check-in was running smoothly and they were almost at the front of the queue when Dylan's phone began to ring. 'Phones off for security,' Avery said in a sing-song voice as she wagged a finger at him.

'You have too much sass for your own good,' Dylan said with a laugh as he pulled his phone out of his pocket. His laughter died as he saw the name on the screen. 'It's Sadie.'

'Well, answer it, then!' Avery said, all but jumping with excitement. 'What if she's changed her mind?'

Dylan shook his head as he pressed the answer button and raised it to his ear. 'She's probably just calling to wish us happy new year before we board. Hey, Sadie.'

'I'm not calling to wish you happy new year,' she said. 'Well, I mean, of course I am, so happy new year, but that's not why I called.' She was talking so fast the words were tumbling out on top of each other.

Dylan frowned. 'Is everything okay?'

'Hey, buddy, get off the phone or get out the queue,' a loud American voice called out behind him. Dylan turned to find a red-faced man wearing a Miami Dolphins cap glowering as he gestured towards the desk. 'You're holding everything up, man!'

'Sorry!' Dylan grabbed his case by the handle and wheeled it to the side, the kids following suit. 'Sorry,' he said again, this time to Sadie. 'We're just about to check in. Is everything okay?' he repeated.

'Everything's fine. Look, you're obviously busy. I can call you back some time. It's nothing important.'

'Tell him, Mum!' He heard a faint voice in the background.

'Who's that?'

'It's my daughter and she really needs to mind her own business,' Sadie replied, sounding somewhat harassed. 'We're at Jake's for lunch and we got talking and—'

Dylan found himself chuckling softly. 'Sadie, whatever it is just get to the point, darling, because I'm about to get thumped by a very angry man for holding up the queue.'

'Oh! Well, the reason I'm calling is to say that I was wrong.

About us, I mean. And, well, yes, I was wrong and you were right and while I couldn't just jump on a plane with you, I mean you understand why that was impossible under the circumstances, so technically I wasn't wrong about that, but the other stuff about saying we shouldn't try and see if things might work out between us. That's the bit I was wrong about. So, um, yes, well, that's it really.'

Happiness coursed through him, filling every inch of him so intensely Dylan found himself looking down at the ground to check his feet were still touching the floor. 'We have the worst timing in the world, you know that, right?'

Her warm laughter echoed down the line. 'But we're working it out, right?'

Dylan pulled his bag even further away from the queue and smiled at the glowering man as he stomped past to take his place at the check-in counter. 'God, I hope so.'

'What's going on, Dad? Is she coming with us?' Avery's eyes were bright with expectation.

'No, sweetheart,' he said, shaking his head. 'It's too short notice, and there's too many security checks and things to do.' He spoke into the phone. 'Avery wants you to know she wishes you were coming home with us now.'

'Oh, I wish I were too, but maybe we can sort out a date and I could come out and visit? It won't be for a couple of months because I'll have to juggle a few things around, and save up a bit as well, but I just wanted you to know that I'm not ready to say goodbye.'

'I'm not ready to say goodbye, either. Look, I don't want to hang up but I need to get us checked-in. Let me sort that out and get through security and then I can call you back before we board, okay?'

Theo waved a hand frantically in front of his face, shaking his head when Dylan looked his way. 'Hold on, Sadie.' He tilted the phone away again. 'Give me a second to say goodbye, okay?'

'No, don't hang up, tell her you're going to stay,' Theo said.

Beside him, Avery was nodding as if she were a bobblehead and someone had flicked her spring. 'Yes, Dad, you should stay.'

'What are you talking about? Our flight leaves in a couple of hours.'

'*Our* flight leaves in a couple of hours, but you don't need to be on it,' Theo said. 'I'm old enough to be responsible for Avie.'

'I can look after myself,' his sister cut in, hotly. 'I'm not a baby.'

'I meant legally, Avie,' Theo sighed.

Dylan held up a hand before they could start bickering. 'Guys, guys, there's no point in arguing over something that's not going to happen. Hey, Theo, where are you going?'

'I'll be back in a minute,' Theo called over his shoulder.

Dylan turned back to where poor Sadie was still hanging on the phone and put her on speaker. 'I'm sorry, it's chaos here all of a sudden. The kids are trying to tell me they can fly home on their own and I should stay.'

Sadie laughed. 'Oh, bless them, they are the sweetest. It's a nice idea, but you've got the same problems I had about going back to work and taking care of them.'

'Technically I work from home most of the time so I can do that anywhere and once the kids are back they'll be with Jen and Eric...' It was a mad idea, he couldn't possibly consider it... 'Besides, how on earth would I get to your place anyway? I've handed in the hire car and a taxi would probably cost a fortune.'

'I could come and pick you up.'

She couldn't be serious. 'It'd take hours.' He frowned, realising he had no idea where she actually lived.

'Not really. Jake's place is about half an hour from the airport.'

She laughed. 'I can't believe we're even entertaining this. It's a lovely idea, but we can wait. Go get checked-in and call me back.'

'I asked the lady at the desk and she confirmed it,' Theo said as he returned. 'I'm sixteen so I can accompany Avie. All we need is a parental consent form and you can sign that now.' He said it as if it were a done deal.

'Your mom would kill me if I put you two on a plane alone.'

'I bet she wouldn't mind, not when we tell her why,' Avery countered, pulling her phone out of her pocket. 'I'm going to call her.'

'No! Just wait a minute and let me think, okay?' Dylan closed his eyes. *Was he really considering this?* Now the shoe was on the other foot he was starting to realise what an impossible position he'd put Sadie in by asking her to come home with them.

It must have taken a huge amount of courage for her to make this call. He needed to prove to her that it was worth it, that he was worth taking a chance on. If he got on the plane she might change her mind in the cold light of day. All those practical reasons why they shouldn't try and make things work weren't going anywhere. It might be months before she was able to sort things out and arrange a visit and anything could happen in the meantime. Taking the phone off speaker, he turned his back on his children and walked a few steps away. 'Are you sure about this?' he murmured into the phone. 'If I can square everything away at this end, are you sure you want me to stay?'

'More than anything in the world.' Sadie sounded as though she might be crying, and he had to admit the lump in his throat was getting hard to talk around. 'But it's okay if you can't stay because I'm not letting go, Dylan.'

'Let me call you back.'

33

'I can't believe I'm really doing this,' Sadie said for the hundredth time as the familiar sight of the model Airbus sitting in the middle of the roundabout at the entrance to Heathrow came into view. 'Do you think I'm crazy?'

'Maybe a little bit,' Katie said from the driver's seat. 'But it's the good kind of crazy. Now, which lane?'

'There, where it says short-stay parking, Dylan said he'd meet us at the McDonald's restaurant near the check-in desks.'

'Plane!' Isla piped from her chair on the back seat. She'd made such a fuss about them leaving without her that the only way to stop her crying had been to bundle her into the back of Katie and Liam's mini SUV.

Katie had insisted on driving, and honestly Sadie was grateful because her nerves were shredded and she didn't think she'd have been able to concentrate on the road. 'What if I'm making a terrible mistake?'

'You're not,' Katie reassured her in a no-nonsense tone. 'But, if you are, then Dylan can fly home in a few days' time. At least this way you'll both know rather than spending the rest of your lives wondering what if.'

They found a parking space and Sadie reached to open her door. 'I won't be long.'

'Hang on, I'm coming with you.'

Sadie shook her head. 'There's no need, I'll be fine.'

Katie laughed as she unbuckled her belt and opened her own door. 'I'm sure you will, but there's no way I'm missing out on this!' She got out and opened the back door to release Isla from her seat and pick her up. 'Come on, darling. We're going to meet Grandma's new boyfriend!'

'Oh God, don't call him that!'

Katie shot her an evil grin over the roof of the car as she clicked the central locking button on her keys. 'What should I call him, then, Mum? Your loverrrrrr?' She waggled her eyebrows as she dragged out the final consonant.

'Dylan! Just call him Dylan.' Sadie could hardly get the words out for laughing. She felt giddy and light-headed and wondered if she was making a fool of herself. *Oh, well, it was too late to start worrying about that.*

The departures area was mayhem and Sadie was grateful Dylan had chosen such a well-recognised symbol when she spotted the familiar golden arches floating high above the crowds. They weaved their way through an obstacle course of people, cases and trolleys and she couldn't help the little sigh that escaped her when she spotted him standing right beneath the sign. 'There he is.' She raised her hand and called his name. Dylan looked their way, his face breaking into a broad smile when he saw them.

'Jeez, Mum, you didn't tell us he was that good-looking,' Katie said, voice filled with admiration. 'No wonder you didn't want to let him go.'

There was no time to laugh because suddenly he was right there in front of her and for a moment Sadie didn't know what to say. It didn't matter, because he let go of the handle of his suitcase and then she was in his arms and everything felt *right* again. She buried her face in his neck and clung tight to the back of his jacket until there was a very deliberate throat-clearing sound next to them.

'Hi, I'm Katie. You must be Dylan.'

Sadie forced herself to let him go. She tried to step back, but before she could move too far, Dylan snagged her arm with his hand, sliding his fingers down in a deliberate caress until he could tangle their fingers together. He smiled at Katie. 'Hello, it's great to meet you.' His gaze focused on Isla, who was sitting on Katie's hip, and his smile broadened. 'And who is this?'

Katie grinned. 'This is Isla.' She looked down at her daughter. 'Isla, do you want to say hello to Dylan?'

Instead of speaking, Isla held her arms out and leaned forward. Quick as a flash, Dylan released his hold on Sadie's hand and caught Isla before Katie could drop her. 'Hey, steady there!' he said with a laugh, adjusting his grip so he had the little girl balanced in his arms.

Isla giggled as if it were no big deal while Sadie pressed a hand to her racing heart. 'Good catch!' She held out her hands. 'Do you want to come to Grandma?' Isla shook her head and leaned against Dylan's shoulder.

'She's fine,' Dylan said, resting a hand against Isla's back to hold her securely against him. 'If someone can bring my case?'

'I'll get it,' Katie said, grabbing the handle. 'We're over in the short-stay car park. It's not far.'

Sadie settled a hand on Dylan's back as they walked side by side, not quite able to believe he was really there. 'Did Theo and Avery get through security okay?'

Dylan nodded. 'Yes. I stood right by the gates and once I explained to the woman stationed there what I was doing, she let me stay until I could see they'd gone through the scanner without any problems. Theo's just texted me to say they've found the gate okay and they're expecting to board soon.'

'And you're sure about letting them travel on their own? It's okay if you've changed your mind.' As thrilled as she was at the prospect of them spending more time together, his children had to come first.

Dylan paused to smile over at her. 'I'm very sure. They're smart kids and Theo has a really good head on his shoulders. Jen and I talked it through and we decided the responsibility would be good for him. He's promised he'll tell one of the stewards when they board what the situation is, and Jen and Eric will be waiting at the other end to meet them.'

'I suppose they have to grow up some time. It's not easy, though. I still fuss about my two probably more than I should.'

'Definitely more than you should,' Katie said with a laugh from the other side of her. 'But don't stop, Mum, because we love it.' She grinned at Dylan. 'I still have to text when I'm home if she knows I'll be out late.'

'You don't *have* to text,' Sadie said, worried Dylan would think she was a bit neurotic.

'I know, but you like it when I do and I like it too, Mum. I'm only teasing.'

They arrived back at the car park, where Sadie and Dylan nearly had their first argument over who was going to pay the ticket charges. Sadie won in the end by pointing out he had only a US credit card and the currency conversion charges would probably be more than the cost of the ticket. She won again when she insisted he go in the front seat where there was more leg room while she sat in the back next to Isla's chair.

'We won't have to stay long at Jake's,' Sadie promised him as Katie pulled out of the car park and headed towards the main road. 'But everyone was excited at getting to meet you so I couldn't really say no.'

Dylan turned in his seat so he could look back at her. 'I'm looking forward to meeting them. After all, you've met my lot.'

He had a point there. 'And we'll have to drop my mother off on the way home once we leave.'

'Oh, we can do that,' Katie protested.

Sadie shook her head. 'It's in the opposite direction for you and she's only five minutes from my house.'

When Katie risked a meaningful glance at her through the rear-view mirror, Sadie smiled back at her. 'I appreciate it, darling, but Dylan already knows Mum can be a bit difficult and you'll want to get Isla home in time for bed.'

'No one can be worse than Monty, that's for sure,' Dylan said with a laugh.

'He wasn't too bad in the end,' Sadie reminded him.

'Yeah, we shall see. I'm sure most of that was simply a ploy to get back in Mum's good books. Leopards and spots and all that.'

Sadie sighed. 'It'd be nice to think it's not too late for anyone to make a change.' And she wasn't thinking only about Monty as she said it. 'Perhaps it's not too late for a Christmas miracle.'

Their very late lunch at Jake's tasted better than it had any right to, considering they'd had to keep everything warm for the hour and a bit it took for the airport dash. Jake had fetched a spare chair down from one of the bedrooms and, with a bit of goodwill and shuffling around, they all just about managed to squeeze around his and Rachel's dining room table. There was a sticky moment when Robbie, Jake and Rachel's four-year-old, left his seat to try and climb onto Sadie's lap and Margaret opened her mouth ready to tell him off.

Sadie raised her eyebrows and her mother clamped her lips tight and stared back down at her plate. Turning to Robbie, Sadie smiled down at him. 'It's not like you to forget your manners, darling. What's the matter?'

'I'm not hungry.' Robbie pulled a face.

'You've hardly eaten anything,' Rachel protested. 'Come and sit back down.'

To everyone's surprise Margaret set her knife and fork together. 'I'm not hungry either, Robbie. Why don't we go next door and finish watching our film?' Without waiting for an answer, Margaret came around the table and held out her hand to her great-grandson. 'Come on.'

Sadie wasn't the only one who watched the pair trot out of the room. 'I'll go and make sure they find the right channel,' said Liam, who was seated nearest the door. He returned a few moments later and sat back down.

'Everything okay?' Rachel asked, sounding nervous.

Liam shrugged a shoulder. 'Everything's fine. The pair of them are sat on the sofa together. I didn't know Margaret was a secret Pixar fan.'

Katie looked over at Sadie. 'What exactly happened between the two of you earlier?'

It was Sadie's turn to shrug. 'It must be that Christmas miracle I was talking about.'

* * *

Not wanting to test her mother's new-found patience too far, Sadie gave her the option of staying for coffee or heading back home. When Margaret chose to leave, Sadie couldn't say she was sorry. It had been lovely to see everyone, but she wanted to be alone with Dylan. Robbie was very unhappy at his new friendship with his great-grandmother being interrupted and he clung to Margaret's leg until she patted him on the head and promised she would see him soon. She glanced over his head at Jake. 'Perhaps you might come over and visit when the weather's better. There's a very nice park not far from my apartment.'

Jake tucked his hands in his pockets. 'We'll see.'

Margaret nodded once as if accepting that was the best she was going to get. Sadie didn't blame Jake for being cautious, it was going to take a lot more than a couple of hours to fix everything, but she was grateful that her mother seemed at least willing to make the effort. 'I'll wait by the car. Thank you for lunch and happy new year to you all.'

Sadie and Dylan made quick work of their goodbyes and, when they went out to the car, Dylan stood deliberately by the back passenger door before Sadie could even think of suggesting he go in the front. She was grateful because, although her mother was still pretty nimble for her age, it wouldn't have been comfortable for her. They might have driven in silence had it not been for Dylan. He asked Margaret all about her flat and how she liked living in the complex. She had a few grumbles about people not following the rules, but she managed to be positive about a few things, including a card-playing group she'd apparently joined. They had a lively chat about cribbage and bridge, both games Dylan said his grandmother had taught him to play.

'It's been a long time since I've played either, so I'm probably rubbish,' he said with a laugh.

'Yes, you more than likely will be.'

Sadie cringed at her mother's signature bluntness but Dylan simply roared with laughter. 'Bloody hell, Margaret, you don't pull your punches, do you?'

When they pulled up outside her mother's complex, Dylan was out of the back seat before Sadie had even put the handbrake on and opened Margaret's door for her. 'Trying to impress me?' her mother said somewhat archly as she let him help her out.

Dylan shook his head. 'Nope. The only woman I'm interested in impressing is your daughter.'

Margaret looked him up and down and then, to Sadie's utter surprise, a small smile twitched her lips. 'Well, that's me told.' She turned to look at Sadie. 'You'll be busy for the next few weeks, I suppose.'

Sadie nodded. 'I will, but I'll call you in a few days, okay?'

Her mother nodded. 'Not on Wednesday, that's coffee morning.'

'And your card club is Thursday afternoon. Perhaps Saturday morning?'

'That will work. Well, it's too cold to stand here chatting. Happy new year to you both.' And with that, she walked off.

Dylan raised his eyes at Sadie over the top of the car. 'Maybe that Christmas miracle will extend into the new year,' he said, softly.

'We'll see.' Sadie wasn't counting a single chicken when it came to her mother. 'Come on, let's go home.'

'Sounds good to me.'

EPILOGUE

They were walking home from the station a few days later, having spent the day in London. Charlie had met them for lunch, after which they'd gone for a wander around the sights. The heavens had opened and they'd run giggling into one of the cinemas on Leicester Square and spent a very happy couple of hours sitting in the back row. They hadn't seen much of the movie and, by the time they'd emerged out into the late afternoon gloom, they'd only wanted to get home.

'Shall we get a takeaway tonight?' Sadie suggested as she dropped Dylan's hand to fumble in her bag for her front-door key.

'Can we eat it in bed?' Dylan asked, waggling his brows at her.

'You have a one-track mind, mister,' she scolded him as they turned off the road and onto the little path that led to her front door.

'And you love it.' Dylan grabbed her waist from behind and yanked her back against him, making her shriek.

'Stop it, I almost dropped my keys!'

'Hello, Sadie.'

The laughter froze on her lips as she turned towards the horribly familiar voice. 'What are you doing here?'

Pete rose from his perch on top of a large suitcase. He hadn't been wearing a hat, she thought, taking in the red and peeling skin on the tip of his nose. 'I didn't have anywhere else to go.'

Behind her Dylan barked out a laugh. 'And whose fault is that?' He took the keys that were hanging limply in Sadie's fingers. 'I'll leave you to deal with Pete the Perv here and ring for that takeaway.' He strode up the path and stood right in front of Pete. 'You're in my way.'

Sadie didn't think she'd ever seen Pete scramble before, but he almost tripped over his case in his haste to step aside. He stared after Dylan as he let himself into the house then turned back to shoot Sadie an incredulous look. 'Who's that?'

'That's Dylan.'

'I'm her lover!' Dylan shouted from inside.

Sadie covered her mouth to stifle a laugh, then grew serious. 'What are you doing here, Pete?'

'Gemma left me. Shacked up with some greasy waiter. I couldn't stand being in the villa on my own, so I came back.' He gave her a look that he no doubt expected would make her feel sorry for him, and in a way she supposed she did. He looked ridiculous, his jeans some sort of narrow cut that she guessed was in fashion but made his legs look like pipe cleaners. His tight T-shirt under a leather jacket only served to outline the little paunch of his belly. Beneath the tan he looked ten years older than when she'd last seen him.

'And how is that my problem?'

Pete shrugged. 'I don't know, it's just I got back to Gemma's house and there was nothing in the freezer, there's no sheets on the bed and I couldn't even find any clean ones in the airing cupboard. On top of everything else, the heating's packed up. I've made a terrible mistake, I see that now.' He stepped forward, holding out a hand towards her. 'Life's not the same without you, Sadie.'

Because she was the one who'd always done everything for him. 'I've got the number of our old plumber somewhere. I can let you have that if you like.'

Pete shook his head, giving her another one of those hangdog looks. 'After all these years, that's all you've got to say to me?'

Oh, there was plenty she could say, starting with piss and ending in off, but she couldn't be bothered. It had been a long day and all she wanted to do was curl up with Dylan in front of the telly. 'If you're really stuck, there's a Premier Inn next to the station.'

'Can't I at least sleep on your sofa tonight until I can get myself sorted out?'

Sadie couldn't help laugh at the absolutely bloody cheek of it. 'No, Pete, you can't sleep on the sofa,' she said, pushing past him and inside the house. Her house. It might be small and the curtains might be ugly and too short for the windows, but it was hers. She gripped the edge of the door. 'I've got plans for the sofa. Exciting, filthy plans with my lover and I'm afraid you sitting there looking sad would rather put a dampener on things.' And with that she swung the door shut.

She slumped against the wall, her eyes meeting Dylan's; he was standing in the entrance to the lounge, grinning from ear to ear. 'Can you believe he had the nerve to show up here like that?'

Shaking his head, Dylan closed the distance between them to slide his hands around her waist. 'Forget about him and tell me more about these exciting, filthy plans you've got in mind.'

Laughing, she linked her hands around his neck. 'Well, I was thinking more along the lines of us eating that takeaway, maybe watching a bit of TV.'

'Oh, I think we can do better than that,' he murmured, ducking to press a hot kiss to the spot on her neck that always turned her weak at the knees. 'We still haven't figured out the trick with the shot glass, the golf ball and the peacock—' She cut him off with a laughing kiss.

ACKNOWLEDGEMENTS

And so we bid farewell to Juniper Meadows!

It's always sad to say goodbye at the end of a series and I shall miss the lovely Travers family very much. I am excited to let you know that I have signed a new contract and I cannot wait to take you all back to the seaside as I build a brand new community for us to explore together in beautiful Halfmoon Quay.

Huge thanks to Sue Smith (Copy Editor) and Paul Martin (Proof Reader) for keeping me on track.

Special thanks to my wonderful editor, Sarah Ritherdon. I wouldn't want to work with anyone else. xx

A massive shout out to everyone at Boldwood Books. I love being with such a supportive publisher and I am looking forward to growing Older and Bolder with you all!

Alice Moore has pulled off another beautiful cover – she really has captured the essence of Juniper Meadows throughout the series.

I ran a competition in my newsletter to name Dylan's children. Congratulations and thanks to the winners, Lynda Dyer (Theo) and Grace Power (Avery).

I am blessed to have some of the most wonderful writer friends. Phillipa Ashley, Jules Wake, Bella Osborne and Rachel Griffiths, Donna Ashcroft, Rachel Burton, Jessica Redland and Portia MacIntosh to name but a few. I couldn't do it without them.

And, as ever, the biggest thanks of all go to my husband. xxx

ABOUT THE AUTHOR

Sarah Bennett is the bestselling author of several romantic fiction trilogies. Born and raised in a military family she is happily married to her own Officer and when not reading or writing enjoys sailing the high seas.

Sign up to Sarah Bennett's mailing list here for news, competitions and updates on future books.

Visit Sarah's website: https://sarahbennettauthor.wordpress.com/

Follow Sarah on social media:

facebook.com/SarahBennettAuthor

x.com/Sarahlou_writes

bookbub.com/authors/sarah-bennett-b4a48ebb-a5c3-4c39-b59a-09aa91dc7cfa

instagram.com/sarah_bennettauthor

ALSO BY SARAH BENNETT

Mermaids Point

Summer Kisses at Mermaids Point

Second Chances at Mermaids Point

Christmas Surprises at Mermaids Point

Love Blooms at Mermaids Point

Happy Endings at Mermaids Point

Juniper Meadows

Where We Belong

In From the Cold

Come Rain or Shine

Snow is Falling

LOVE NOTES

LOVE IN EVERY CHAPTER

WHERE ALL YOUR ROMANCE
DREAMS COME TRUE!

THE HOME OF BESTSELLING
ROMANCE AND WOMEN'S
FICTION

 WARNING:
MAY CONTAIN SPICE

SIGN UP TO OUR
NEWSLETTER

https://bit.ly/Lovenotesnews

Boldwood

Boldwood Books is an award-winning fiction publishing company seeking out the best stories from around the world.

Find out more at www.boldwoodbooks.com

Join our reader community for brilliant books, competitions and offers!

Follow us
@BoldwoodBooks
@TheBoldBookClub

Sign up to our weekly
deals newsletter

https://bit.ly/BoldwoodBNewsletter